George Colman, William Powell

A True State of the Differences Subsisting Between the Proprietors of Covent-Garden Theatre

in answer to a false, scandalous, and malicious manuscript libel, exhibited on Saturday, Jan. 23, and the two following days

George Colman, William Powell

A True State of the Differences Subsisting Between the Proprietors of Covent-Garden Theatre
in answer to a false, scandalous, and malicious manuscript libel, exhibited on Saturday, Jan. 23, and the two following days

ISBN/EAN: 9783337409913

Printed in Europe, USA, Canada, Australia, Japan

Cover: Foto ©Andreas Hilbeck / pixelio.de

More available books at **www.hansebooks.com**

T. HARRIS

DISSECTED.

BY

G. COLMAN.

LONDON:

Printed for T. BECKET, near SURRY-STREET, in the STRAND.

MDCCLXVIII.

T. HARRIS

DISSECTED.

AFTER having, in February laſt, publiſhed a moſt clear and ample refutation of the many falſhoods circulated about that time in the printed and manuſcript libels of Meſſ. Rutherford and Harris, I determined never more to trouble the world on the ſubject of the ridiculous ſquabbles wherein I had unfortunately involved myſelf, by a connection with two of the moſt impracticable men that ever diſturbed the peace of civil ſociety. My friends unanimouſly applauded this reſolution, thinking, that as I had ſo plainly proved Mr. Powell and myſelf to have been the only parties injured, the Publick would pay no attention to the future complaints of men, who already ſtood convicted of ſo much falſhood and diſingenuity. Mr. Harris, however, has lately dreſſed up another tale, in which, as well as in the firſt Narrative publiſhed by him and Mr. Rutherford, he has, in many inſtances, not told the truth; in many others he has not told the *whole* truth; and in moſt he has, by additions and miſrepreſentations, *diſguiſed* the truth: a ſpecies of *ſtory-telling* more dangerous than peremptory falſhood, as it lies leſs open to detection, and is conſequently more likely to deceive. My friends, therefore, thoſe very friends who firſt diſſuaded me from publication, knowing how fully I could juſtify my conduct, now think ſuch a juſtification a debt due to my own character, as well as to the Publick, who have been pleaſed to honour our diſputes with more notice than they deſerve. Something has indeed been occaſionally thrown out in my behalf in the publick papers; but their circulation, however extenſive, is but tranſient; and it was imagined that a ſummary of the real facts would more effectually detect the impoſi-

B tions

tions of T. Harris, than occasional comments on particular parts of his publication. In giving this *true ſtate* of the circumſtances referred to by him, I ſhall neceſſarily be drawn into an examination of his pamphlet, which, with ſome other occurrences, will ſerve as a diſſection of the heart and mind of the man. Paſſion (as I told him before) is a human frailty, and therefore in ſome degree excuſable; but rancour and malice, ſupported by falſhood, are diabolical.

The prefixed Addreſs to the Publick (which is a compound of ſervility and inſolence, at once appealing to their tribunal, owning their authority, and refuſing to ſubmit to it) contains only *one* charge which is not repeated in the body of the pamphlet. The charge is that of my having *inſulted ſeveral ingenious writers*. Among the many brilliant exploits of Meſſ. Rutherford and Harris, after the forcible entry of the ſeventeenth of June, Mr. Harris has not told the world, that beſides breaking open the prompter's office, and carrying off the prompt-books, he alſo rifled a cabinet in that office, containing *my private letters*, all which he examined, and left in a condition that teſtified what *civil* perſons had been there. He there read ſeveral letters that had paſſed between me and gentlemen who had offered pieces for the ſtage. Some of theſe letters to and from me are, I believe, now in Mr. Harris's poſſeſſion; but with all this evidence in his hands, thus *delicately* obtained, I defy him to produce one proof of my having *inſulted* any writer whatever.

Mr. Harris opens his Letter with a charge of my writing all the news-papers, the St. James's Chronicle in particular. The few things which I have lately inſerted in the laſt-mentioned paper, are written in a manner that ſhews I did not wiſh or mean to be concealed. Many other letters, &c. in the publication of which I had not, directly or indirectly, the moſt diſtant concern, have appeared in that and other publick papers: but it ill becomes Mr. Harris to throw out theſe inſinuations, while he is himſelf continually running to all the news-printers in town with his own ſcurrilous letters and paragraphs, and his friend Mr. Kenrick's dirty epigrams in his pocket; having abſolutely opened an account current with the publiſhers, and undertaken to pay a round price for their ſuffering their papers to become the regiſters of his falſehood, and journals of his malignity.

Mr. Harris then recurs to the firſt tranſactions that paſt between us. Here, relying on the unmindfulneſs of the reader, who might have long ago thrown by my publication, he ſtruggles hard to overturn the credibility of my Narrative; exerting all his ſophiſtry to prove me the contriver of Mr. Powell's precluſion, and that I had originally formed a latent deſign to ſtrip my aſſociates both of their power and their property.

Fiction is various, and assumes a thousand different shapes and colours, according to the present purpose. Truth is simple and constant. In speaking therefore of these transactions, I can only repeat what I have said before, leaving it to the reader to compare our several relations of the same facts, and submitting to him two or three observations tending to establish the credibility of what I formerly laid before him as *A True State* of the Case.

On the thirtieth of March, all the four parties met at Mr. Powell's. Mr. Colman being asked by Mess. Rutherford and Harris, whether he had considered of the affair which Mr. Powell had at their desire communicated to him, replied, that he thought himself much obliged to Mr. Powell for his good opinion, but could not think of availing himself of such a partiality, unless they concurred in Mr. Powell's sentiments; and that if they were not of opinion that Mr. Colman's advice and assistance were essential to the welfare of the undertaking, he would by no means think of becoming a party concerned merely from the nomination of Mr. Powell. Their reply to this declaration was conceived in the most handsome terms; and, to convince Mr. Colman that the many civil things they said on this occasion were not words of course, they afterwards recurred to this subject, and repeatedly assured him of the great value they set upon his accession to their scheme, independent of every other consideration than their thorough persuasion of the advantage that would result from it in the success of the Theatre. Being late, it was agreed, after a short conversation on the intended purchase, that *the four* should have a second meeting the very next night, in order to come to a final determination; and to enter into articles of agreement among themselves concerning the purchase. Just before their parting, Mr. Colman, addressing Mess. Harris and Rutherford, observed, that managing a Theatre was like stirring a fire, which every man thought he could do better than any body else. "Now, gentlemen, said he, I think I stir a fire better than any man in "England." To this they replied, "Do you manage; let Mr. Powell act; all "we want is to have good interest for our money." March 30. 1767.

The next evening we met again; and, at the desire of Mess. Rutherford and Harris, Mr. Hutchinson, a gentleman whom they particularly recommended for his abilities and integrity in his profession, attended with an instrument prepared for us to sign. By this agreement, Mess. Rutherford and Harris were empowered to treat for the purchase of the Theatre, &c. at any sum not exceeding 60,000 l. forty thousand to be raised by themselves, and twenty by Colman and Powell, whom they were to assist with a loan of 5000 l. each, to make up their proportions of the purchase-money. On Mr. Hutchinson's reading over this instrument, when he came to that part of it wherein it was recited, that the four parties *should be jointly and equally concerned in the management of the Theatre*, Mr. Colman begged leave to interrupt him, and told him it was a settled point that he (Mr. Colman) was to be invested with the direction of the Theatre; whereupon, to his very great surprise, Mess. Harris and Rutherford declared, that they never had the least intention of forming such an article; that, as they had the turn of the scale in the purchase-money, they could not think of lowering their consequence in the purchase, &c. Mr. Colman said, that he took it for granted (as he most certainly did) that this matter had been previously understood March 31.

 on

on all ſides; and that he had plainly declared to Mr. Powell, on his firſt application, that he would never be concerned in the purchaſe, unleſs he ſhould be inveſted with the theatrical direction. Mr. Powell allowed the truth of this aſſertion, but *ſaid nothing in approbation of Mr. Colman's claim of the management*; and Meſſ. Rutherford and Harris ſeeming ſenſible of his ſuperior utility in this province, but unwilling to acknowledge that ſuperiority under their hands, the agreement was at laſt ſigned by each of the four parties, in the form in which it had been originally prepared.

This tranſaction paſſed on the thirty-firſt of March, though the manuſcript paper exhibited at Slaughter's, as well as the printed Narrative, for the ſame purpoſe of fallacy that will appear through the whole, place it much later.

April 1. The next morning I ſet out for Bath, where I remained till the third or fourth of May. In the mean time, Meſſ. Harris and Rutherford contracted for the purchaſe, depoſited 10,000 l. and agreed for the payment of the remainder on the enſuing firſt of July.

I have been extremely particular in the above relation, becauſe I am reſolved not to ſuppreſs or diſguiſe the moſt minute fact, that may ſeem in the leaſt favourable to Meſſ. Rutherford and Harris. For a like reaſon I ſhall ſuppreſs all my reflections and reſolutions declared to particular friends, till I had the pleaſure of ſeeing thoſe gentlemen again, which was not till ſome days after my return to town; the ſame melancholy occaſion that ſummoned me from Bath ſooner than I propoſed, having alſo ſecluded me from company. In the mean time, Meſſ. Rutherford and Harris expreſſed the greateſt impatience for an interview with me, *apart from Mr. Powell.* On the very firſt conference, they teſtified, in the warmeſt terms, their earneſt deſire that I ſhould be inveſted with the theatrical direction, complaining at the ſame time of the indiſcretion of Mr. Powell, to whom they aſcribed the notoriety of our intended purchaſe, which was now become the common talk of the town, and our names inſerted in every news-paper.

May, 1767.

It is but juſtice to Mr. Powell to declare, that it afterwards appeared that, from the peculiar circumſtances of Mr. Rich's will, his widow thought herſelf bound in honour to declare to ſome other candidates for the purchaſe, that ſhe had given notice to the truſtees of her having contracted for the ſale. This circumſtance, as well as the neceſſary applications by each of the parties to their friends for the requiſite ſum, tended to make the treaty publick. One part of Mr. Powell's conduct on this occaſion, though it certainly contributed to betray our operations, is very much to his honour, though the written Narrative, with the ſame ſpirit of candour that animates the whole, endeavours to interpret it to his diſadvantage, and to tax him with a ſcandalous breach of faith to the Patentees of Drury-Lane Theatre. The truth is, that the very day after Meſſ. Rutherford and Harris had applied to Mr. Powell, he communicated the matter to Mr. Lacey, who very kindly aſſured him of his beſt wiſhes, and a continuance of the ſame friendſhip which he had ſhewn to Mr. Powell on every former occaſion. Mr. Garrick was then at Bath.

May, 1767. In a word, Meſſ. Harris and Rutherford now inſiſted on the expediency of inveſting Mr. Colman with the direction of the Theatre, and were extremely ſolicitous to ſettle this point before Mr. Powell's ſummer-engagements ſhould call him out of town. To this end it was propoſed, that we ſhould each of us conſider of that and ſome other neceſſary articles, and

throw

throw our thoughts concerning them upon paper. I did ſo; and Mr. Harris, in a few days, took occaſion to call upon me one morning *alone*. I then ſubmitted to him a paper containing a ſketch of ſome articles, and among the reſt, one relative to the management, which was as follows:

"That George Colman ſhall be inveſted with the theatrical direction, that is
" to ſay, the power of engaging and diſmiſſing actors, actreſſes, ſingers, dancers,
" muſicians, &c. &c. of receiving or rejecting ſuch new pieces as ſhall be offered
" to the Theatre; of caſting the plays; of appointing what plays, farces, &c. ſhall
" be performed; together with the ſole conduct of all ſuch things as are generally
" underſtood to be comprehended under the dramatick and theatrical province:
" *Provided always that the ſaid George Colman ſhall not do any act contrary to the opinion*
" *of* ANY TWO *of the other partners in writing expreſſed: and that if the four part-*
" *ners ſhall be equally divided in opinion, that the matter in diſpute ſhall be referred to*
" *two arbitrators, one for each party*; *and if the ſaid two arbitrators cannot agree, that*
" *they ſhall join in appointing one other arbitrator, whoſe opinion ſhall be deciſive and final.*"

On peruſing the above rough draught of an article, Mr. Harris did me the honour to obſerve, that the footing on which I was willing to reſt my management was extremely generous, and agreeable to the candour which I had ſhown in my whole tranſaction with them; but that he thought it neceſſary that I ſhould have *more power* than ſuch an article would give me; that he had the greateſt eſteem and regard for his friend Mr. Rutherford, whom he thought a very honeſt, good-natured man, but that there were no two perſons in the world more likely to differ in opinion than himſelf and Mr. Rutherford; ſo that if Mr. Rutherford and Mr. Powell ſhould happen to join in oppoſition to any of my meaſures, an obſtruction in the management muſt neceſſarily enſue; that his brother-in-law, Mr. Longman, had told him, that he and Mr. Rutherford *might* differ, but that he and Mr. Colman *never could*; he could wiſh, therefore, that I would agree to put Mr. Powell entirely out of the queſtion, and to place the whole *negative power* in himſelf and Mr. Rutherford, and then (added he) "*You will always be ſure of* ONE *of us.*"

Although this ſcene paſt entirely between Mr. Harris and me, yet the truth of it does not reſt on my bare aſſertion; for I recapitulated all theſe circumſtances to Mr. Harris ſome weeks ago at the Theatre, in the preſence of Meſſrs. Rutherford, Powell, and Hutchinſon. He allowed the facts, but added, that he had been miſtaken in me. I returned him the compliment.

I fell into the ſnare, and ſaid, that if Mr. Powell could be prevailed on to aſſent to ſuch an article, I had no objection to it. Mr. Rutherford, in this inſtance, as in every other, implicitly ſubmitted to the opinion of Mr. Harris. Mr. Powell, however, ſhewed *great repugnance* to giving me the direction. On my expoſtulating with him alone on this ſubject, and reminding him of his firſt application to me, and my declared reſolutions at that period, he frankly confeſſed that *he had been adviſed to the contrary*; but that, on reflection, he returned to his original intentions, and was content to put his fame and fortune into my hands.

This is the *real* hiſtory of the article reſpecting the management, which was accordingly ſigned by all parties on the 14th of May, and is as follows: May 14th.

"WHEREAS Thomas Harris, John Rutherford, George Colman, and William Powell, by certain articles of agreement, dated the 31ſt Day of March laſt, did agree

agree to purchase of the Representatives of John Rich, Esq. deceased, two patents for exhibiting theatrical performances, and the several leases of Covent-garden theatre, and the rooms, buildings, conveniences, furniture, cloaths, scenes, decorations, music, entertainments, and all things belonging to the said Theatre; and the said Thomas Harris and John Rutherford were thereby authorised to treat for, and purchase the same, at a sum not exceeding 60.000 l. and the purchase-money was to be advanced by the said parties equally, and they were to become jointly possessed of, and interested in, the premisses so to be purchased, and were to be jointly and equally concerned in the management of the said Theatre, and were to execute proper deeds and instruments for that purpose, when the said purchase should be completed. And whereas the said Thomas Harris and John Rutherford have accordingly contracted and agreed with the representatives of the said John Rich, for the purchasing of the said patents, leases, premisses, and things, at and for the sum of 60,000 l. and such purchase is to be completed on the first of July next: Now the said several parties, having perused and fully understanding the purport and contents of the said contract, do approve of, and confirm the same. And having also, in consequence thereof, taken into their consideration the Management of the said Theatre, they have, for the better and more easy conducting of the business thereof, as well as for their joint and equal benefit and advantage, agreed, and do hereby mutually declare and agree, that, notwithstanding any thing contained in the said agreement already made between the said parties, the said George Colman shall be invested with the Direction of the said Theatre in the particulars following, viz. that he shall have the power of engaging and dismissing performers of all kinds; of receiving or rejecting such new pieces as shall be offered to the said theatre, or the proprietors thereof; of casting the plays; of appointing what plays, farces, entertainments, and other exhibitions, shall be performed; and of conducting all such things as are generally understood to be comprehended in the dramatic and theatrical province. And that the said Thomas Harris and John Rutherford shall be desired to attend to the comptrolment of the Accounts and Treasury, relative to the said theatre. *Provided always, and in as much as the said Thomas Harris and John Rutherford will have leisure to attend to the affairs of the said theatre, and the said William Powell is to be engaged as an Actor or Performer upon the Stage (for which purpose separate articles are intended to be entered into between him and the other parties), in which his time and attention will be chiefly employed and taken up, so that he will not be able to apply himself in managing the business of the theatre; it is therefore hereby further agreed, that the said George Colman shall, from time to time, and at all times hereafter, communicate and submit his conduct, and the measures he shall intend to pursue, unto them the said Thomas Harris and John Rutherford; and in case they shall, at any time, signify their disapprobation thereof, in writing, unto the said George Colman, then and in that case the measures, so disapproved of, shall not be carried into execution, any thing before contained to the contrary thereof notwithstanding. Yet, nevertheless, with respect to the said William Powell, it is intended and agreed, that he shall, at all times, give his advice and assistance relative to any part of the business of the said theatre, when thereunto desired by the other parties.* Witness the hands of the said parties, this 14th day of May, 1767.

Witness,
JA. HUTCHINSON.

T. HARRIS,
JNO. RUTHERFORD,
G. COLMAN,
WILL. POWELL."

My

My own ſketch of the article here inſerted, relative to the management, *providing that I ſhould not do any act contrary to the opinion of* ANY TWO *of the other partners in writing expreſſed*, inconteſtibly proves the falſhood of T. Harris's aſſertion, *that it appears evident from the* Harris's Let. *very firſt*, *that Colman uſed every means* TO ENGROSS THE WHOLE p. 9. POWER TO HIMSELF. That the *negative power* ſhould be transferred from ANY TWO, and the controul afterwards veſted *ſolely* in Rutherford and Harris, could be the contrivance of none but thoſe who were to engroſs the power reſigned by Mr. Powell. Mr. Harris himſelf ſays, *We thought it prudent to give a particular charge and precaution to Mr.* Harris's Let. *Hutchinſon*, OUR ATTORNEY, *to take a ſpecial care to guard* p. 8. *and ſecure our rights and authority in this new inſtrument relative to the management*. Here it appears that the gentleman who drew the article was at that time ſolely *their* attorney, and that Powell and Colman repoſed ſuch an entire confidence in their good faith, as to employ on this occaſion no attorney at all. Mr. Hutchinſon, however, unfortunately for Meſſ. Rutherford and Harris, was a plain man, and did not underſtand what was meant to be *conveyed* by their *ſecret* inſtructions *to guard and ſecure* THEIR *rights and authority in this new inſtrument*; ſo that he incautiouſly left certain *openings*, as T. Harris calls them, into which the rights and authority of the other partners have inſinuated themſelves. For this, and other offences equally heinous, Mr. Hutchinſon long ago received his diſmiſſion, as attorney to the Theatre, from Meſſ. Rutherford and Harris; together with a letter from the laſt of thoſe gentlemen, more impudent and inſolent, if poſſible, than any which they have ſent to their partners. Mr. Hutchinſon was too dull to conceive the meaning of dark hints about *guarding and ſecuring their rights and authority*: it behoved them therefore, in the formation of this new inſtrument, to have employed ſome able dexterous attorney, to whom they might have *ſpoken out*, and have told him in expreſs terms, "Powell has agreed to reſign his power to Colman: take care, Mr. "Attorney, that Colman ſhall have no power at all!"

As to the anecdote relative to a tranſaction in November, the *real fact* is as follows: The four proprietors, attended by Mr. Hutchinſon, met to ſettle a body of articles of partnerſhip. On this occaſion Mr. Colman remonſtrated, that Mr. Powell's precluſion having been made ſo notorious by their publickly reading the article on the ſtage on the ſecond of November, Mr. Powell was degraded in the eyes of the whole Theatre. It was propoſed therefore to recur to my original plan of an article, which left him, as well as them, an equitable controul in the direction. This Meſſ. Rutherford and Harris flatly refuſed, but offered, as they have often done ſince, *to burn all articles*. As it is impoſſible

ble not to ſee the drift of this propoſal, it is no wonder that it has on our part been conſtantly rejected.----I ſhall now (in the words of T.
Harris's Let. Harris) *leave the impartial reader to determine which of us is*
p. 11. *guilty of* ſuggeſting, *of* accompliſhing, *and of* continuing
the excluſion of Mr. Powell.

Harris's Let. *The ſeaſon at length arrived for opening the Theatre*, and Meſſ.
p. 14. Harris and Rutherford *entered the Theatre with all the chearfulneſs of young men, fond of a new, promiſing, and agreeable purchaſe.* Pretty maſters! what an idea, I warrant, had they formed of a Theatre! A play-houſe, like a play-thing, as it was *new*, was *agreeable*. But how were theſe *young men* received by that ſour *old fellow* Colman? He never introduced them to the performers. The truth is, Colman himſelf had no perſonal acquaintance with the majority of them, and had introduced himſelf by taking the men by the hand, and ſaluting the women. Meſſ. Harris and Rutherford might have done the ſame; or if any thing further was neceſſary, the late manager, if deſired, would no doubt have been ſo obliging as to attend, in order to introduce the
Harris's Let. new proprietors to the performers. That *I ſtopped them ſhort,*
p. 15. *and bade them go off the ſtage*, is a moſt notorious falſhood. They were there ſome minutes, at the end of which the performers, as is uſual, betraying ſome impatience at ſo long an interruption, I ſaid, neither rudely nor uncivilly, *Come, let us go on with our buſineſs!*—I ſhould be aſhamed of twice refuting this ſilly charge, if the malice was not equal to the folly of it.

Harris's Let. *On the fourteenth of September the Theatre* opened, and which
p. 15. party betrayed *inſolence*, will appear from a ſhort recapitulation of the facts already before the Publick. *In two days* Mr. Harris's ill humour broke out on the ſubject of Mrs. Leſſingham's dreſſing-room; immediately after ſucceeded that lady's inſolent epiſtle (probably dictated by T. Harris) to the prompter; and immediately after that an open act of hoſtility from Meſſ. Harris and Rutherford, attended with *the moſt flagrant violation of our articles*, by their altering the caſt-book, and ſigning a liſt of parts allotted to Mrs. Leſſingham; a proceeding the more inſulting and offenſive, as it meant to expoſe my ſuppoſed ſubjection to them to a principal officer of the theatre. Theſe tranſactions and thoſe which followed relative to Cymbeline, and the engagement of Mr. and Mrs Yates, are ſo familiar to the town, that I agree with Mr.
Harris's Let. Harris *the time would be miſpent in agitating an obſolete queſtion:*
p. 15. but the truth of my repreſentation of thoſe matters being chiefly founded on the evidence of his own letters, muſt ſurely be allowed to be incontrovertible.

Their

Their enquiries into the wardrobe were merely an act of ſpleen, in conſequence of the repreſentation of Cymbeline. Why will Mr. Harris ſay then, WE WERE TOLD BY THE WARDROBE-KEEPERS, *that great part of the property was in the poſſeſſion of Mrs. Powell, at her houſe in Ruſſel-Street, Covent-Garden?* Why will he oblige me to tire the Publick by repeating, in the words of the *True State*, that "They had, by the "advice of Mrs. Rich, approved of keeping *the unappropriated cloaths* "out of the wardrobe; and had not only joined with me in deſiring Mrs. "Powell to take the care of them, but agreed to purchaſe Mrs. Rich's "dwelling-houſe, adjoining to the theatre, for the reſidence of Mr. and "Mrs. Powell, allowing a very large abatement of the rent, in conſi-"deration of their reſerving a room for the occaſional meetings of the "managers, and other apartments for the purpoſe of lodging therein "*the unappropriated cloaths.*" It is true, indeed, Meſſ. Rutherford and Harris afterwards thought proper to recede from this agreement, which Powell and Colman thought themſelves bound in honour and juſtice to fulfil.

As to my Management of the Theatre, whatever reflections T. Harris may endeavour to throw on it, however he may prevaricate by talking of the ſmall *profits* that have reſulted from it, the *ſucceſs* of it is inconteſtible; and the extraordinary *receipts* of the laſt ſeaſon are an irrefragable proof that Covent Garden Theatre has attracted the particular notice and favour of the Publick under my direction. If the *diſburſements* have been very large, great part of thoſe ſums muſt be conſidered as the firſt expence of *ſetting up in buſineſs*, having been employed in what may be called *ſtock in trade*, which is at this inſtant of great intrinſick value, and will prevent future expence; and, large as thoſe diſburſements have been, I was not the promoter of them, except in the ſingle inſtance of engaging Mr. and Mrs. Yates, more than Mr. Harris; and that ſingle inſtance was honoured with Mr. Rutherford's approbation, till *his colleague* exerted his undue influence over him, and taught him to object to it.

Now I am on the article of *expence*, it may not be amiſs to lay before the Publick a ſhort anecdote. When Mr. Powell, at a meeting of all the proprietors, propoſed ſome additional illuminations, I objected to them, at leaſt for the preſent, ſaying that they would have a happier effect at the commencement of a ſeaſon. Mr. Harris ſaid, the meaſure being adviſeable, the ſooner it was carried into execution the better. Mr. Powell accordingly gave the neceſſary orders; but when the bills came in, Mr. Harris and *his colleague* forbad the payment of the ſum charged for two luſtres to their Majeſties box, ſaying it was *a meaſure that had not been ſubmitted to them.*

The pitiful charge concerning *orders* ſent into the Theatre, as far as it is imputed to me as an artifice to ſupport my reputation, Mr. Harris knows to be falſe. Mr. Rutherford and himſelf have told me more than once, that I ſent in *fewer orders* than any of the proprietors. The little piece at which his malice points was, with all its faults, extremely ſucceſsful, and of great advantage to our Theatre laſt ſeaſon. The people ſent to the houſe *on one night in particular*, did not go at my deſire in ſupport of my piece, but at the inſtance of all the proprietors in ſupport of the houſe, which was threatened to be pulled down; and it was thought a very cheap expedient to ſacrifice a hundred pounds, to prevent a tumult which might perhaps have occaſioned a loſs of one or two thouſand. As to the piece, good or bad, being very well acted, it brought great houſes, and was received with much applauſe; ſo that however Mr. Harris may prove the ſoundneſs of his taſte and judgement, he certainly does not manifeſt his *gratitude* by a publick diſapprobation of it.

I am now arrived at that period, where I ſhould think any preſent appeal to the Publick, if any were neceſſary, ought to have begun: but as T. Harris choſe to go over the old ground again, I was obliged to follow him, and to trace him through all his doublings of cunning and ſophiſtry. What follows is entirely new matter, which has ariſen ſince the tenth of February, the date of my laſt publication.

Feb. 14. 1768. The firſt new act of hoſtility on the ſide of the *negative managers* was intended, like their late proceedings, as a *negative general*, being calculated to deprive us of the very ſinews of war. On the fourteenth of February they ſent, without our knowledge, the following letter to the bankers where our money was depoſited.

Meſſ. Freame, Smith, and Co.

"Gentlemen,

"We deſire you will *not pay any money*, or deliver any property in your hands belonging to the proprietors of Covent Garden Theatre *to any perſon whatſoever*, until further notice from us. And we deſire you in like manner, *to retain any further ſums of money* belonging to the ſaid proprietors that may be ſent to you. We are, &c.

London, 14th Feb. 1768.

T. Harris.
J. Rutherford."

At the beginning of the ſeaſon the Bankers had received an order, ſigned by all the Proprietors, *to pay all draughts of Mr. Garton, our Treaſurer*. It is a queſtion therefore whether *any two* of the Proprietors had a legal right to revoke the joint order of *the four*, and to deſire the Bankers *not to pay any money to any perſon whatſoever*. However that may

may prove, a ſtep of ſuch importance could not have been too early communicated to Mr. Powell and me. It was a meaſure that ſtruck at the very being of our Theatre; yet certain it is, that the Bankers, who were recommended by Mr. Rutherford, kept this order *to pay no money, and in like manner to retain all further ſums*, and even ſuffered the Treaſurer to pay in two ſuch *further ſums* to a very conſiderable amount, without ſaying one word of their having received ſuch an order to us or to the Treaſurer, who accidentally came to the knowledge of it at the end of three weeks, by happening to give directions for the purchaſe of India bonds.

A few days after the following letter was ſent to the Treaſurer:

To Mr. JONATHAN GARTON.

" SIR,

" We deſire you will, with all poſſible diſpatch, ſend to each performer, officer, and ſervant of Covent Garden Theatre, *whoſe articles expire this ſeaſon, or who are not under articles*, a copy of the incloſed letter: and that you will take down the names of thoſe to whom ſuch copy is ſent, and return us a liſt thereof ſigned by yourſelf.

" We alſo deſire you will have your accounts ready for our examination, *and your balance for inſpection*, on Monday morning next at eleven o'clock, as we ſhall then be at the office for that purpoſe. We are, Sir, your moſt humble ſervants,

Thurſday 25,
Feb. 1768.

T. HARRIS.
J. RUTHERFORD."

Letter incloſed.

" I AM directed by Meſſ. Harris and Rutherford, to give you notice that *you cannot be conſidered as belonging to Covent Garden Theatre, after the expiration of this ſeaſon*, unleſs the engagement you may enter into for the *next* be confirmed in writing by one, or both of them. Your's, &c.

Feb. 28, 1768.

J. GARTON."

The determined reſolution of Meſſ. Rutherford and Harris *to reſcind the article reſpecting the management*, appears in the above notice, wherein they aſſume, contrary to the letter, ſpirit, and common ſenſe of that article, the power of *diſmiſſion*, the diſmiſſion of almoſt the whole Theatre, as well as the power of *ſigning the articles of agreement*; to which alſo they have not any right. The ordering the Treaſurer to tranſcribe and circulate theſe notices was undoubtedly intended as a new inſult to me; and perhaps the Treaſurer, who was now growing obnoxious to them, becauſe he would not further their attempts to ſtop the buſineſs of the Theatre, was purpoſely diſtreſſed with this order, that they might take offence at his denial to comply with it. I had not the moſt diſtant intention of ſettling the future ſtate of the company with[illegible] communicating the plan of it to them. This, whatever they might [illegible] learnt from their *informers*, my ſubſequent conduct teſtified. I ſuff[illegible]

how[illegible]

however, the poor young men to continue to expose themselves. The notices were actually served on the persons they required, and I passed over this new instance of their insolence and irregularity with the most silent contempt.

The performers indeed, some of whom had remained in the Theatre, under verbal agreements and a confidence in the good faith of the managers, upwards of twenty years, were extremely mortified, and burnt with indignation at these billets of dismission. The very inferior part of the Company, and servants of the Theatre, trembled for their

Harris's Let. p. 19. subsistence. If the emotion of *one gentleman in particular* broke out too violently, it was not at my instigation; and

Ibid. I am very sorry that any *military man* of my acquaintance should ever have threatened violence to him and his col-

Ibid. league, or have talked (*before great part of the company*) of *thrusting them into the fire.*

Towards the end of March I transmitted to Mess. Rutherford and Harris a plan of the arrangements which I proposed in the future settlement of the Company; and at the interposition of a gentleman, who, though employed as a solicitor on their part, wished to appear and act as a friend to all parties, an interview was appointed not only to adjust that matter, but to bring all our unhappy differences (if possible) to an amicable conclusion: yet even after the appointment made for that purpose, they were indelicate enough to send me comments on my proposals, apparently dictated by that hostile spirit, which had influenced their actions during the preceding three months. The interview, notwithstanding, took place; and I appeal to the above-mentioned gentleman, whether we or they shewed the most conciliating spirit. By his friendly mediation some objections on their part, which plainly betrayed an unmanly remembrance of past differences, were surmounted; and my plan seemed to be ratified with their approbation: but at length, to my very great surprise, they began to talk of interfering in the agreements. The gentleman told them, that, *according to the article respecting the management, when an agreement was once approved, the care of entering into that agreement rested wholly upon me.* Mr. Rutherford was then willing enough to saddle me with that trouble; but he, as *his colleague* T. Harris has done ever since, insisted that I should insert certain clauses in the articles, which gave *them* an immediate controul over the performers, &c. and put *the positive management* of the Theatre into *their* hands. They required also, that Mess. Younger, Garton, and Sarjant, the Prompter, Treasurer, and House-keeper, should each be engaged under a *particular* article. This *particular* article, and those *clauses*, were all manifestly intended to annul and subvert the original

2 article,

article, by which I was invefted with the direction of the Theatre. An article however was, at their inftance, drawn up in the form they defired. In this form an alternative of *two new claufes to be inferted in the articles with performers* was propofed. Their intended operation, to render Meff. Rutherford and Harris pofitive managers of the Theatre, and to leave me no power at all, was obvious. The firft claufe abfolutely *reverfed* the article of the management; and the fecond their own counfel, at one of our interviews, (though openly defired by Meff. Rutherford and Harris to make no conceffions on their part) fairly confeffed to be *a variation* of that article. It is no wonder, therefore, that I objected to thefe flagrant attempts to infringe the original compact between us. They then defired a perufal of the form of the article under which I meant to engage performers. My counfel immediately prepared fuch a form, and perfonally affured Meff. Rutherford and Harris that it was drawn up *in ftrict conformity to the articles between the proprietors*, as well as agreeable to the form heretofore ufed for that purpofe: notwithftanding which, Meff. Rutherford and Harris ftill infifted on the form propofed by themfelves; declaring, that they would *put a negative* on *all* engagements till I agreed to adopt *the claufes in queftion*; after which, having, by a *negative general*, difabled me from engaging the performers, they would take upon themfelves to engage them. It alfo was thrown out, that *there would be two companies*; after which, and fome other expreffions of ill humour, they departed.

Thefe fruitlefs interviews, intended to bring about an accommodation, were three; at the laft of which arofe one occurrence which T. Harris, after his ufual manner, has grofly mifreprefented. I had, at our former meetings on this occafion, expreft my forrow for paft heats and animofities, and given them the moft folemn affurances that if they were really difpofed to proceed amicably for the future, I would do every thing in my power to convince them of the fincereft cordiality on my fide. Finding, however, by their obftinate adherence to thefe new *claims*, that nothing would fatisfy them but, *directly* or *indirectly*, to refcind the article which invefted me with the Theatrical Direction, I propofed, at this laft interview, to leave the theatre to themfelves for three years, provided they would infure the *receipts* for that term to be equal to thofe of the prefent feafon, the *balance* never to be lefs; and if greater, that I fhould have the advantage of it. They would only infure the *balance* not to be lefs; which, notwithftanding the great fuccefs of the feafon, they thought they might fafely venture to do, on account of the great expences of the wardrobe, illuminations, &c. They alfo offered me a bank note of 100 l. if I would name a give-and-take price. I called the offering me money a paltry propofal; exclufive of which, it

was

was unfair to throw the naming that price upon me, though I will now treat with them on that footing whenever they will please to name such a price themselves.

April. The situation of our affairs now began to grow very critical. The last of these fruitless interviews, for the purpose of an accommodation, was on the 16th of April. On the 18th they served me with a formal prohibition, containing a recital of the article of the 14th of May, 1767; but this, it seems, being intended to be soon afterwards made *publick* and distributed among the performers, concluded with a declaration, that they did not mean to put any *unreasonable* negative; and that in case of any breach of articles they would pursue all *legal* remedies to procure redress. The next day, however, notwithstanding so candid a declaration, they sent me a private letter, revoking their consent to every arrangement that had lately been adjusted between us, and prohibiting me to enter into any articles of agreement without inserting *the new clauses* in question.

It now became an open contest, and certainly a most ruinous one in such a kind of property, whether Mess. Rutherford and Harris or I should engage the performers. Mr. Powell kept strictly within the limits prescribed by our articles; and though he approved of my proposed agreements, made no efforts to engage the performers himself. Mr. Harris, in his late publication, at the same time that he has wilfully misrepresented my conduct, has most shamefully slubbered over the part which he and *his colleague* took in this transaction. It is notorious, however, to the whole Theatre, that, on this occasion, they attempted, *in open violation of their compact with me and Mr. Powell, to take the management into their own hands, and to enter into articles of agreement with the performers, without our knowledge or consent.* No borough was more industriously canvassed at the late general election, than the Theatre last April by Mess. Harris and Rutherford. Some of the performers they parleyed with at the Theatre, others they visited at their houses, and others they summoned to attend them in Surry-Street: on all which occasions they used every soothing and menacing expedient to cajole or frighten the performers into agreements; offering them indemnification if they would break any contract formed with me, and private security for the payment of their salaries, provided they would enter into theatrical engagements with themselves. At the same time they issued printed edicts, and hung up tremendous manifestos in the Green-Rooms; construing their *negative power*, in contradiction to the obvious sense and direct import of words, into a *positive power*, and denying Mr. Powell and me to have any power at all; because, forsooth, he was a Player, and myself a Dramatick Writer. At this time

Mr. Macklin alone, after two fruitless negociations with me, I am well informed, declared publickly that he was *retained* by Mr. Harris. If by being *retained*, the having entered into a theatrical engagement was signified, no other performer could be prevailed on to follow his example. Their counsel indeed (for many of them applied to counsel) instructed them, that according to the article, as it stood in our several publications, no person could form an engagement, or receive a dismission, but through me, in whose power, as the Director, those acts of management were particularly specified.

The situation to which the cruelty, oppression, and irregularity of the *two controuling proprietors* had reduced me at that instant was exactly this: By submitting to their *negative general* on *all* engagements, I was to leave the Theatre destitute of performers: by suffering *them* to form such engagements, I was to submit to a gross violation of our articles, and, at the manifest risk of my property, to assign the theatrical direction to them: or, by engaging the performers myself, I was to enter into such agreements at my peril. Of all these difficulties I chose to encounter the last; but not in the manner represented by T. Harris. I engaged no part of the company *to myself only*, or *under pretence that our differences were amicably adjusted: I took nobody unawares: I deceived no person whatever*. Yet, says Mr. Harris, *one in particular of eminence in his profession assured us, he was so much concerned at being thus deceived, that he would go immediately to Mr. Colman, and endeavour to get his agreement cancelled*. The letter annexed, in order to corroborate this assertion, is itself a refutation of it; and the party concerned has since published the following testimony in my favour, whence the world is left to judge of the credit due to Mr. Harris.

Harris's Let. p. 21.

Ibid.

Liverpool, Aug. 1, 1768.

"Understanding that my name has been made use of to the prejudice of the character of Mr. Colman, in justice to that gentleman, and at his desire, I think it incumbent on me to declare, that I never said I had been deceived by him, and that I never formed any engagement with him, wherein he acted in an indirect or clandestine manner, or otherwise than became a man of honour and integrity.

The reason of my demanding a formal cancelling of my agreement, as appears by my letter to Mr. Harris, of the 28th of April was, that he said he could only consider me as a Colman, and of consequence, an enemy to Mr. Rutherford and himself, if I did not ask Mr. Colman for my engagement, which would satisfy them entirely.

GEORGE MATTOCKS."

Nothing indeed could be more open than the transactions on both sides, which were so notorious, that it betrays an uncommon contempt of all the parties concerned, as well as the most lofty disregard of truth

truth and the publick opinion, to have endeavoured to misrepresent them. Two days after the circulation of their printed paper of April 27, the following considerations were submitted to the performers in manuscript.

" Many performers and other persons belonging to Covent Garden Theatre having been made uneasy by the receipt of a letter some weeks ago signed Jonathan Garton, as well as by a printed paper lately distributed, signed Thomas Harris and John Rutherford, it may not be improper to consider the original article concerning the management, as it appears in the different publications of the several patentees. By that article it appears, that according to the agreement of the 31st of March 1767, the four gentlemen were to be jointly and equally concerned in the management of the theatre; but on the 14th of May following, having taken into consideration the management of the theatre, they for the better and more easy conducting the business, as for their joint and equal benefit and advantage agreed, that notwithstanding any thing contained in the first agreement, Mr. Colman should be invested with the direction of the theatre in the particulars following, viz. That he should have the power of engaging and dismissing performers of all kinds; of receiving and rejecting such new pieces as should be offered to the theatre; of casting the plays; of appointing what plays, farces, and other entertainments should be performed; and of conducting all the dramatic and theatrical province: but it was also further agreed, that Mr. Colman should communicate and submit his conduct and intended measures to Mess. Harris and Rutherford; and in case they should at any time signify their disapprobation in writing *unto the said George Colman*, then the measures so disapproved of should not be carried into execution.

" This is the substance of the article; from which it appears that Mr. Colman has the sole power of engaging and dismissing performers of all kinds; and that no performer, officer, or other servant of the theatre, *can form an engagement or receive his dismission* from any other of the proprietors. Mr. Colman is invested with the management, and the performers and other persons of the theatre are to receive their directions immediately from him. In case of any difference of opinion between the proprietors, Mess. Harris and Rutherford may signify their disapprobation in writing *unto the said George Colman*; not to any other person; and if Mr. Colman afterwards carries the measures into execution, it is at his own peril. The performers, &c. are justified in acting as Mr. Colman directs, because nobody else has any legal authority to give them any directions. They have nothing to do with any private differences among the proprietors, and it is very hard they should be involved in such disputes. Mess. Harris and Rutherford have no further right to act in the management than occasionally *to signify their disapprobation in writing unto the said George Colman.* Mr. Powell might with equal right take upon him to engage or dismiss performers, &c. as Mess. Harris and Rutherford, who cannot legally execute any act of management. It is certain from the original article, that no engagement can be binding on all the proprietors, except an engagement formed by Mr. Colman. If he forms any engagement of which Mess. Harris and Rutherford have signified their disapprobation *to him* in writing, *he* perhaps may suffer for it; but the performer is sure to receive the benefit of his contract; to which he can by no means be entitled under an engagement with any of the other proprietors.

29th April, 1768.

How

How far law or equity will warrant the part I thought myself bound to take for the preservation of my property on this occasion; what the Publick will judge, now the *true state* of the case is before them; I will not pretend to decide: nor will I, like Mr. Harris, hawk the names and opinions of my counsel in our idle pamphlets; but it is certain that I did not proceed *without advice*. The performers, as I observed before, took the like precaution; and not one to whom I applied refused, except Mrs. Bellamy, assigning for a reason that she had already refused Mess. Rutherford and Harris, and that she could not enter into any *written* agreement without the concurrence of *all* the proprietors. I do not mention this in order to cast any reflection on that lady's conduct. For my own part, let the fact be duly considered, and it will appear that the engagements I have entered into with the performers, &c. are but a continuation of the old retainers to the Theatre, the business of which could not possibly be carried on without their assistance. Mess. Rutherford and Harris, having not the shadow of claim to any *positive* or *executive* power, had certainly no right to *dismiss* the whole company of comedians, officers, and servants, at one stroke, under an article by which the power of *dismissing*, as well as *engaging*, is vested in me. Turn the tables for a moment, and suppose that *I*, on any pretence whatever, had proposed so bold a *dismission*, and as the *executive* king of Brentford had thus endeavoured to realize the Roman emperor's wish, by cutting off all my people with a single blow; with what propriety might the *two controuling monarchs* have then exercised their *negative power*, by signifying their disapprobation of such a *dismission!* They certainly might have *objected* to a *dismission*; but they certainly had no authority *to dismiss*. The step they now took was, in effect, (to the manifest injury of Mr. Powell, myself, and the whole Theatre, as well as themselves) an endeavour to restrain me from opening our doors; a resolution which they have since avowed, and which I too truly prophesied in my first publication. True State, p. 58.

At the beginning of May Mess. Rutherford and Harris, finding this *second* attempt *to take the theatrical management into their own hands* as vain as their *former* efforts of that kind on the second of November, at length inclined to capitulate; and not being able to rescind the *whole* article, they resolved at least to endeavour to get rid of *a part of it*. To this end they varied their mode of operation. Mr. Rutherford accosted me one evening at Ranelagh; but, so far from *being by accident pressed by the crowd close to me*, he most industriously sought me all over the room, and I was the last of my party that evening who knew that he wanted to speak with me. It is strange that Mr. Harris cannot deviate into truth about matters of so little importance. May 2. Harris's Let. p. 29.

On this occasion Mr. Rutherford declared that he was ashamed of what had past: that during the last fortnight, consumed on their part in fruitlesly tampering with the performers, he had sorely experienced the mortifications and difficulties incident to the management of a Theatre, and pitied my situation: that he had heard I had declared, that in case *they* formed any engagements advantageous to the Theatre I would confirm them, which he thought a *manly* proceeding: that neither he nor Mr. Harris wanted to be concerned in the direction; but that he thought it would be more to my credit to attach myself to *them* than to Mr. Powell: and that, in case of such a coalition, we might keep all the actors in order, *Mr. Powell as well as the rest.*

After this overture made on his part, he said he hoped that I would manifest a desire of a speedy accommodation on mine, and by a note or a message appoint the time and place of another interview. I could not think of such an interview without Mr. Powell's being of the party; to which Mr. Rutherford consenting, I wrote to Mr. Harris to that purpose, and the four proprietors once more met together the very next evening. From the first part of our conversation, joined to the behaviour of Mr. Rutherford the evening before, I began to flatter myself that the auspicious moment was at length arrived when our differences would be adjusted. I declared, with the utmost sincerity, that the moment they desisted from *studied interruptions*, I should, on my part, not only conduct the Theatre to the best of my abilities for the general advantage, but in the minutest points study to do every thing agreeable to their wishes. An accommodation now seemed to have taken place, but at length their latent intention disclosed itself. There was one point still behind. They made a claim of signing the articles of agreement with performers. Harris's Let. p. 30. That this was not according to *the common usage and nature of* such *partnership*, the case of our immediate predecessors was an obvious instance; Ibid. that it was not according to *the express letter of our article*, was clear on the face of that article; Ibid. nor was it even reconcileable to *common sense and common equity*, where one particular partner was by article invested with the management; since if *four* had a right to sign these agreements, *fourteen* or *four and twenty*, in case of so many equal proprietors, might lay the like claim, which would be ridiculous, and would incur the very inconvenience which the article respecting the direction was calculated to prevent. Even supposing a breach of trust on my part, our article of May 14, 1767, was so strong in their favour, that if I either varied the terms of such agreements, after being proposed to *them*, or formed any contracts to which they had jointly signified their disapprobation in writing, their certain recovery of any

damages

damages reſulting from ſuch engagements would at once be my puniſhment and their reparation, which muſt effectually check or redreſs all injurious proceedings.

After much debate they left me this alternative, either to inſert *the new clauſes*, ſo long in queſtion, or to ſuffer all the *four* proprietors to become ſubſcribing parties to the articles of agreement; which laſt propoſal plainly proved, that either expedient meant the ſame thing. So far from agreeing that the article ſhould be ſubmitted *to counſel of only my nomination*, ſo jealous were they, that Harris's Let. p. 31. they not only excepted to two moſt eminent and reſpectable gentlemen, (whom they knew I had often conſulted, and who were conſequently beſt acquainted with theſe affairs) but they extended this ſort of proſcription to *all my circuit-acquaintance*; inſidiouſly mentioning at the ſame time, with an affected careleſſneſs, a gentleman whom I knew to have been a counſel of their own. Theſe were ſuſpicious circumſtances, and it is no wonder therefore that I choſe to act by advice, *and to take two or three days to conſider of it.*

The opinions I collected on this matter were, that this was only a new device to countenance an attempt to infringe the article reſpecting the management; that *when an agreement was once approved*, by virtue of that article, *the care of entering into that agreement reſted* WHOLLY *upon me:* beſides that, to perſons of ſuch a complection, any conceſſion of a material and fundamental right muſt be extremely dangerous, the rancour, the ſpleen, the pride, the malice, the duplicity, the tyranny and oppreſſion of their conduct having invariably betrayed themſelves throughout the whole ſeaſon.

From theſe juſt and prudential motives I was induced to abide by my right, and to keep ſtrictly to our article; nor indeed was it reaſonable to expect that we ſhould relax on our part, while they on all occaſions ſo rigidly enforced their power of controul. The only conceſſion that had ever been deſired by us was, by recurring to my firſt draught, to give Mr. Powell an equitable voice in the management and diſpoſal of our common property; and at the bare mention of ſuch a propoſal, (although the point was immediately given up, on their objection to it,) they had taken very great offence.

The reader being now made acquainted with the *true ſtate* of the hiſtory of the engagement of the performers, will not be ſurpriſed that *during theſe tranſactions they heard nothing from me relative to the adjuſtment of affairs for the enſuing ſeaſon.* Harris's Let. p. 32. The truth is, that they had been endeavouring, in open defiance of all compact, to adjuſt thoſe affairs themſelves. They knew therefore *it* Ibid. *was wholly owing to themſelves that they had not received an an-*

swer sooner. What then can be thought of men, who, after a vain effort to prevail on me to rescind *a part* of our article, preceded by an attempt to overthrow *the whole*, an attempt notorious to the whole Theatre, could pretend, in their Letter of May 17, that *to keep them so perfectly ignorant of my transactions could not be deemed consistent with honour, equity, or honesty?* From the 27th of April, *their own transactions* had engrossed their attention. If I would not become a mere *nominal director* of the Theatre, and allow them to *prescribe* as well as *controul*; if I would not, with no more than equal profit, take all the trouble, and resign all the power; they were resolved to seize the management themselves. The integrity of the performers, officers, and servants of the Theatre, on this occasion, does them singular honour: Neither threats nor promises could induce them to combine to rob me of my rights. It was necessary they should be employed; but they resolved, provided I would enter into agreements with them, to withstand all the sollicitations of Mess. Rutherford and Harris. I made no scruple, therefore, and I think it was the duty of my station, to keep together a company of performers, who have already been so well received, and who hope still to experience the favour of the Publick.

Harris's Let. p. 33.

Not being very sollicitous to square my actions to Mess. Rutherford and Harris's theory of *honour*, *equity*, *or honesty*, if I had not nearly finished a very long letter to them on the affairs of the Theatre, I should not (after this last insult of their's of May 17) have taken the trouble of writing to them at all. This I gave them to understand, when I transmitted it to them a day or two afterwards, informing them, moreover, that any future intelligence of my conduct and measures should be communicated to them by the Prompter, Treasurer, or some other officer of the Theatre, according as I should find it requisite occasionally to direct.

Harris's Let. p. 35.

This Letter, says Mr. Harris, was *filled with false facts, false reasoning, and false suggestions.* Those *facts*, that *reasoning*, and those *suggestions*, which he wished to conceal from the world, now appear before it in this Pamphlet. They are *true*; they are capable of the clearest proof; the transactions are recent; a cloud of witnesses, men of the most unquestionable integrity, can confirm my account of them; and their truth will, I doubt not, cover the falshoods of T. Harris with confusion.

May.

It has been a constant custom with our two young gentlemen, on every new rupture, to dip their pens in gall, and to send letters to Mr. Powell and me overflowing with scurrility and invective. Mr. Powell had very lately been favoured with one of these epistles

epistles relative to his concerns at Bristol. Mr. Harris has thought proper to publish it; but nobody who reads the letter will give the least credit to the declaration annexed to it, that *they had no design to revoke the consent they had passed for his going to Bristol.*

On the receipt of my letter (which before it was sent I had communicated to several friends, who thought it written in the most cool, decent, and dispassionate terms) they again had recourse to their pen and ink, not only threatening me in one letter with a *publick answer*, but writing another to Mr. Powell, wherein they spoke both of me and the letter in the most scandalous terms. It has been their constant endeavour to set Mr. Powell and me at variance, and many poor efforts of that kind appear in the late Letter of T. Harris, particularly in that part of it now under examination. The day of its appearance I wrote two or three lines to Mr. Powell, assuring him it had not made the least impression on me, though he had never communicated to me Mr. Harris's letter of the 24th of May. I have just received an answer from Mr. Powell, in which are the following passages. They contain a full confutation and able dissection of T. Harris, and give an account of his own conduct entirely consonant to his letter of the 21st of May, which, notwithstanding Mr. Harris's assertion to the contrary, was written without the least consultation between us, and during my absence from London.

Harris's Let. p. 36, 37.

Ib. p. 37.

Ib. p. 36.

"In regard to the letter, you say, I did not communicate to you, it was thus. You must remember, I told you I had been at Harris's house one morning, and that he and Rutherford had used every shameful argument to persuade me to join them, and every scandalous abuse against you, and how much they would do to oblige and serve me, would I desert you and side with them: that several of the first people of fashion had persuaded them *to use force and every method to dispossess so obstinate a man as you were*, and how much it would redound to my honour and credit with all those great people, and, in short, with the whole public, if I would desert you and join them. At this meeting too Harris said, however he might be disposed to part with his share, he was then determined to keep it, if for no other reason than to plague and perplex you (with much abusive language); that, *by all that was sacred, you should neither eat nor sleep in comfort*; that he would haunt you by letters at morn, at noon, and night, till he had teaz'd you out of the theatre; and, as I remember perfectly well, sat down on a sopha, and concluded all his bitter exclamations against you with these words, "*G—d d—n his blood, I'll* " *teaze him till he is weary of his life, and then*, like Job, *he'll curse his God and die.*" On this I said, I was well satisfied with your conduct, that I was sure you were a perfectly honest man, that I should never think my fortune safe but in your hands, as it was, and that I should sink or swim with you. I left them in this manner. The moment I saw you, I told you in some part what had past, and you then told me, in what manner Rutherford attacked you at Ranelagh, to disengage yourself from me, and from that moment I determined that I never would, nor I never have, nor ever will ſpeak to, or take notice, or hold converſe with either of them. The very next day after this you went to Richmond—Benſley happened to be with me in my parlour, when that letter was brought me; it was left at the door, and the man ſaid it did not require an anſwer. I opened it, and it ſhock'd me very much. I gave it to Benſley, who read it, and I told him what had paſt. He ſaid it would be quite wrong to ſhew it you; that, as I had taken a reſolution to have nothing more to ſay or do with them whatever, he adviſed me to burn the letter, and take no notice of it to you, as he thought it would make you uneaſy. I put it in the fire, before his face, and never ſince have taken the leaſt notice of either, but with the contempt you have been witneſs to. As to the converſation they quote of mine with them at that meeting, *it is a falſhood, a moſt infamous falſhood*; for every ſyllable of mine tended to prove to them my love and regard for you, and to convince them it was not in any man's power whatever to draw me from the ſide of a man I honoured, eſteemed, and loved, and in whom I placed the unbounded confidence of my future fortunes and happineſs, and which, my dear friend, I ſhall ever continue to do."

In my letter I had informed them, that I ſhould direct our attorney, Mr. Hutchinſon, to ſend them an account of the engagements I had made: from which Mr. Harris, though complaining of his *ignorance of my tranſactions*, took occaſion to ſend Mr. Hutchinſon a letter, *filled, as uſual, with falſe facts, falſe reaſoning, and falſe ſuggeſtions*, cloathed in the moſt abuſive language, abſolutely refuſing to receive any ſuch account, and *diſmiſſing* Mr. Hutchinſon from his employment as attorney to the Theatre. *Nothing worth notice occurred between this and the cloſing the ſeaſon*; cloſed, it is true, with Cymbeline, and to a very good houſe for the beginning of June. The ſneers concerning *orders*, and my *new occaſional prologue*, throw no contempt on any perſon but T. Harris.

Harris's Let. p. 38.

Ibid.

The ſeaſon cloſed on Saturday the 4th of June. On the Monday following Mr. Harris came to the Treaſurer's office, and took upon himſelf, in his own and Mr. Rutherford's name, *to diſmiſs* Mr. Garton, who had given ſecurity in a bond of 5000*l.* to *the four* proprietors. Mr. Harris ordered him, however, *to meet them at the Theatre on the 10th of June* (the Friday following) *in order that they might examine his accounts.* Before Mr. Harris quitted the Theatre, he made particular enquiries concerning the apartments in Mr. Sarjant's houſe. Mr. Sarjant himſelf, it ſeems, was not at home, but orders were left for his due attendance on the Friday following. The wardrobe-keepers alſo received the like orders.

Ibid.

June. From theſe circumſtances, as well as from ſome intimations given me of their declared intentions by Mr. Powell, I had now little reaſon to doubt of their purpoſe to diſpoſſeſs all the perſons, acting under my direction, of the Theatre by force. To proteſt againſt ſuch violence, I deſired an attorney likewiſe to attend. He accordingly

ingly did; but not being witness to their proceedings that day with Mr. Garton, the first intelligence I received of them was from Mr. Garton himself, who came immediately to my house, and informed me that Mess. Rutherford and Harris had, in spite of his resistance, (though Mr. Harris asserts there was none) taken away from him the Journal and Ledger of the Theatre by force. The threatened outrages being now actually commenced, I ran to the Play-house, where I found Mess. Rutherford and Harris, and, in the presence of Mr. Garton and the gentleman whom I had desired to attend, demanded the reason of their conduct to Mr. Garton. Mr. Harris, knowing the gentleman attending to be an attorney, refused to give me an answer: whereupon I left them for a few moments, and dismissed both the wardrobe-keepers. I fairly told them what I had done, assigning their violence in the treasury, which bespoke like designs upon the wardrobe, as my reason for it. Mr. Harris then set his foot against the wardrobe-door, which being very slightly fastened, flew open. Mr. Harris walked in, walked out, caused the door to be padlocked, and departed. For the degree of credit due to T. Harris, when he says *I attacked him in terms the most scandalous and provoking*, I appeal to Mr. Garton and the gentleman who attended.

June 10.

Harris's Let. p. 39.

Ib. p. 42.

Flushed with these exploits, and the promise of success in their endeavours to throw their own and our affairs into confusion, they went immediately to Mr. Durant, who had joined in Mr. Garton's bond of security to *all* the proprietors. That gentleman, I believe, entertained too true a sense of their conduct, to give them any hopes of his approbation of it: nor can I conceive by what argument Mr. Harris means to prove that such a procedure can *be deemed consistent with honour, equity, or honesty*. The accounts are not yet closed, and till they are duly made up, the books are the undoubted property of the Treasurer, as well as the vouchers of his integrity, for which so large a security has been given. Was it in character for men who *thought it highly necessary to look minutely into the accounts*, to offer *to sign a general release* before they had looked into them at all? Must not Mr. Durant and Mr. Garton think such *a release* from Powell and Colman *necessary for their safety*, as well as from Rutherford and Harris? Can Powell and Colman give such a release, or the detention of the books be of no concern to Mr. Garton without one, while Mr. Harris persists to keep his partners so perfectly ignorant of the state of their accounts? If Mess. Rutherford and Harris had really a right *to become their own treasurers*, would they have a right to become *our*

Harris's Let. p. 33.

Harris's Let. p. 39.

Ibid.

Ibid.

Ibid.

treasurers

treasurers also in spite of our teeth? or could we possibly
Ibid. think *our property* so SAFE, should the custody of it be transferred, *forcibly* transferred, from Mr. Garton to Mess. Rutherford and Harris? As to the first of those gentlemen, his own Bankers have repeatedly refused payment of his draughts in favour of Mr. Garton, for money advanced from out of his own private purse, to the amount of 250 *l. value received.* They pleaded indeed at first Mr. Rutherford's *order to pay none of his draughts*, but afterwards acknowledged such an order to be needless. We could not therefore entertain a very flattering idea of the security of our property in such a situation. Mr. Harris not only retains our journal and ledger (the accounts not yet closed) in his hands, but, according to the best calculation that can be made, six or seven hundred pounds more than will be due to him on his dividend
from the profits of the season. *The* [supposed] *balance of the*
Harris's Let. p. 39. *cash-book being so exceedingly small, it is incumbent* ON US AS WELL AS THEM *to examine very carefully into the disbursements.* Mr. Harris, however, not only avowedly detains the books, and delays to repay the monies he has over-drawn, but also impounds other sums of money due ONLY to the tradesmen and his fellow-proprietors; and of which he cannot himself justly claim a single shilling: and all this he does under no other pretence than because Mr. Powell and I will not
concur in his and Mr. Rutherford's arbitrarily and ille-
Ibid p. 40. Ibid. p. 41. gally *dispossessing Mr. Garton of the power of acting as our Treasurer, and agree to authorize* EITHER OF THEM *to dispose of as many India bonds as may be necessary.*

The Publick have already been acquainted, that, "in or-
True State, p. 17. "der to complete our purchase, the sum of fifteen thousand "pounds was borrowed, viz. *six* thousand for Mr. Rutherford, *five* for Mr. Colman, and *four* for Mr. Powell; for securing "which sum of fifteen thousand pounds the three fourth shares of Mess. "Rutherford, Harris, and Colman, were mortgaged, Mr. Powell "having made over the first claim on the whole of his share." By the instrument of March 31, 1767, published by T. Harris, it appears,
that in case Colman and Powell, or either of them, should not, on
Harris's Let. p. 6. *the first of July following, be prepared with the whole of his or their proportion of the purchase-money, Harris and Rutherford should jointly and equally advance and pay for him or them, so much money as should be the deficiency of Colman and Powell, or either of them, so that the sum they respectively paid down was not less than ten thousand pounds.* This agreement conveys at first sight a wonderful idea of the property of Mess. Harris and Rutherford, who could advance, independant of all foreign assistance, by means of money advanced on the security of the Patent,

Patent, or otherwiſe, the ſum of FORTY THOUSAND POUNDS! How far theſe ideas were verified at the time of the purchaſe, may be judged from the ſtate of the above-mentioned mortgage; whereby Mr. Rutherford, one of the ſuppoſed *aſſiſtant-parties*, was himſelf to borrow the ſum of *ſix thouſand pounds*, and raiſed, independent of the patent ſecurity, a thouſand pounds *leſs* than Mr. Colman, one of the parties he had bound himſelf to aſſiſt, who alſo became joint ſecurity for Mr. Powell. This idea of their great property, and our extreme poverty, was endeavoured to be more ſtrongly impreſſed by Meſſ. Rutherford and Harris in their *Slaughter's Coffee-houſe Narrative*, where it is ſtated that *Colman and Powell were deficient in their proportion of the purchaſe-money* 9000 *l. whereupon the ſum was borrowed*, AND HARRIS AND RUTHERFORD WERE SECURITIES FOR COLMAN AND POWELL. If they were aſhamed of owning the *true ſtate* of the caſe in this inſtance, how will they ever pardon my informing the world that, on laſt Midſummer-day, they failed in the payment of 2150*l.* their proportion of 5000*l.* and intereſt then due on that mortgage? As to *poor* Powell and myſelf (though Harris and Rutherford had impounded at the bankers our money juſtly due, on purpoſe to diſtreſs us) we paid down 3225*l. our* proportion of that payment. Colman, however, to his great misfortune, is reſponſible for the payment of the proportion due from Rutherford and Harris; and all the ſecurity they have yet given him, is the breaking open the Theatre, and carrying off ſeveral thouſand pounds worth of the joint property of the four patentees, which they have, as T. Harris pretends, *ſent down to his houſe in Surry-Street*. Mr. Rutherford is ſince *gone abroad*; and, after theſe occurrences, we leave the world to judge how far our monied property would be SAFE in the hands of Mr. Harris, the other WOULD-BE *comptroller of the treaſury*, who ſtill remains here. Should *he* too be diſpoſed *to travel*, upon which of theſe young gentlemen muſt Powell and Colman draw for their money? It is doubtful whether a bill of Middleſex, any more than a chief-juſtice's warrant, would extend to France or the Netherlands.

True State, p. 2.

Harris's Let. p. 48.

Meſſ. Harris and Rutherford, before they left the Theatre on Friday the 10th of June, took a particular ſurvey of Mr. Sarjant's houſe, and dropped ſome hints of ſending proper perſons to lodge in it. Their intentions of diſpoſſeſſing all the old ſervants of the Theatre, in order to introduce an entire new ſet of their own, now grew every inſtant more and more apparent. They had already plundered the treaſury, and made inroads on the wardrobe. Mr. Sarjant's houſe was a principal fort of government, and a key to the whole Theatre. The moment they became ſole maſters of that, I

June 10. 1768.

 expected

expected to hear it publickly avowed, that they had formed a separate company of performers. A person much in their councils had very lately told me, that they thought of engaging certain actors from Ireland; and in their conversation with Mr. Powell upon my last letter, they had avowed their intentions of seizing the management *by force*, desiring him to put himself at the head of their troops, and assuring him that the majority of the performers, although under engagements, would revolt from me, and act under them. Every thing, they said, was ripe for action; and they even pressed him, though to no purpose, to suffer them to submit to him their plan of operations for the campaign of the ensuing season.

May.

June 11. 1768. It was for these reasons that the *officers* of the Theatre, as well as the *performers*, were engaged under articles. By the written notices from Mess. Rutherford and Harris of February 25, and their manifesto of April 27, they had arbitrarily and illegally attempted to *dismiss* every person belonging to the Theatre. I meant to *retain* them. Mr. Sarjant, however, on whom they were now meditating an attack, being infirm and in years, it was thought proper to give him assistants to protect the possession he maintained for us, as he had done for our predecessors, on behalf of *all* the proprietors. Neither Sarjant nor his assistants were authorised or empowered to exclude the proprietors themselves; and even these precautions would not have been taken, had not the threatened outrages, already commenced, rendered them absolutely necessary for the preservation of our rights and property in the Theatre. It was determined, in such extremities, to use every method for *the* JUST *and* LEGAL *defence of it, rather than tamely to resign* MY RIGHT *to the* CONDUCT *of it to any designing and insolent intruder.*

Harris's Let. p. 7.

June 11. 1768. The event immediately justified the truth of my suspicions, and manifested the necessity of the measure: for the assistants of Sarjant had scarce received their appointments, when on Saturday the 11th of June, the very day of their *date*, Mess. Rutherford and Harris ENTERED the Theatre (though T. Harris would seem to convey the idea of *exclusion*) and brought with them one Furkins, formerly servant to Mr. Harris, and whom I had, at his instance, appointed one of our box-keepers. Furkins, they said, must remain in the house, lie there, and keep possession of it for *them*: whereupon they were made acquainted with the precautions I had taken to protect Mr. Sarjant in his possession. They said, if I objected to *one* man, they would have *ten*, and that they would return with them that very evening. They then departed, and Furkins soon followed them.

Harris's Let. p. 45.

Apprised

Apprised of these proceedings, *which Mr. Harris, in his pamphlet, has so cautiously suppressed*, and justly alarmed at the increasing danger of our property, which seemed to be destined for a sacrifice to malice and resentment; I ordered the stage-door to be shut up, leaving no ingress, except *through Mr. Powell's house in the Piazza, in which there is a door which communicates with the Theatre*. Many of my friends were acquainted with this step, and confessed the melancholy necessity for it, the moment it was taken; and the gentlemen of the Beef-Steak Society, who dined at the Theatre that very day, were witnesses of my distressful situation, and went out through the house of Mr. Powell. June 11, 1768. Harris's Let. p. 46.

The next day, Sunday June 12, (for they did not keep their promise of returning that evening) they were informed by Mr. Sarjant junior of the directions I had given. On the Monday morning, however, they sent Furkins again to make a formal demand of entrance at the stage-door. He was refused. About noon Mess. Harris and Rutherford came themselves, and sent Mr. Sarjant junior for the keys of the Theatre. I returned my compliments, and that they might go into the Theatre, whenever they pleased, through the house of Mr. Powell. So far from being averse to *enter their own premises through another man's house*, or *aware of my litigious disposition, they* absolutely *determined to go into the Theatre through the house of Mr. Powell*, together with two gentlemen who accompanied them. Mr. Sarjant junior informed them, according to my directions given for the above-mentioned reasons, that *they* ALONE *would be admitted*. They took down this answer in writing, and retired. The two gentlemen can testify their non-admittance, and they now know the cause of it. June. Harris's Let. p. 46. Ibid.

Mess. Harris and Rutherford now finding that their projected revolution in our state could not take place so silently as that in the Rehearsal, resolved upon more vigorous measures. *The time between this event and Friday morning they passed* THUS. Mr. Rutherford bargained with Sawney Macgregory, a Serjeant in the third regiment of Guards, to provide him a detachment of stout fellows to execute an enterprize of spirit. Mr. Harris engaged his friend Mr. Hyde, the Carpenter, to procure a number of ruffians armed with oaken towels, axes, iron-crows, and sledge-hammers. *Accordingly, on the 17th of June, about six o'clock*, (a pretty *decent* time of the morning!) *Mr. Harris, attended by two witnesses, again demanded admittance for himself and Mr. Rutherford, at Mr. Sarjant's door.* Mr. Sarjant was not stirring, and June. Harris's Let. p. 46. Harris's Let. p. 47.

a watch-

a watchman (who is conſtantly retained for the preſervation of the Theatre) *anſwered from within*, that they could only be admitted through Mr. Powell's houſe in the Piazza. They had begun their operations of that morning, by cauſing a padlock to be put on Mr. Powell's ſtreet-door: wherefore *T. Harris came to the play-houſe door, in Hart-ſtreet, where Mr. Rutherford was waiting for him, attended by* the troop, whom T. Harris is pleaſed to call *ſervants*, viz. Sawney Macgregory's ſoldiers out of their regimentals,(an *army in diſguiſe*) Mr. Hyde's journeymen, and, as I am told, ſome common hired ruffians from Exeter-ſtreet. Theſe *ſervants* being ordered *to* OPEN *a window*, as the *gentle* T. Harris expreſſes it, by the application of their ſledge-hammers and iron-crows broke the outſide-ſhutters, ſmaſhed the window, forced the inſide faſtenings, and found themſelves in leſs than two minutes in one of the dreſſing-rooms, the door of which they likewiſe burſt open. One of the people in the Theatre had by this time reached the place. He offered no reſiſtance to Meſſ. Harris and Rutherford; but oppoſed the entrance of the banditti that accompanied them; whereupon he was knocked down, and very narrowly eſcaped being murdered. The ſtage was co-
Harris's Let. vered with people in an inſtant. The new-comers turn-
p. 52. ed the old tenants out of doors; or, as I ſhould ſay, *put them* GENTLY *out of the window.*

June. 17. From this moment all buſineſs, then carrying on to the emolument of all the joint proprietors, was ſuſpended. *Emery*,
Harris's Let. p. 47. however, *the maſter-carpenter to the Theatre, coming* to his work, as uſual, *at that inſtant*, the new directors graciouſly
Ibid. *ordered him to be let in.* What is aſſerted by T. Harris con-
p. 48. cerning my *compelling Emery to ſign an article*, Emery himſelf abſolutely denies. Seeing them full of exultation at their ſkill in houſe-breaking, he told them no ſecurities could withſtand iron-
p. 46. crows, axes, and ſledge-hammers; but that *he thought* IT *a ſtrange undertaking.*

Meſſ. Rutherford and Harris have a very new and peculiar method of proving a fact; a method which they have uniformly purſued ever ſince Mr. Powell and I had the honour of their acquaintance. They ſit down, and write you a letter; in which, they aſſert, that you know ſuch and ſuch things to be true, relating them at the ſame time in direct contradiction to the real ſtate of the caſe; by which ingenious device they expect to overthrow all other teſtimony, and to be believed on the forged evidence of their own letters. This was their practice on the preſent occaſion. Having broken into the play-houſe, and expelled
Harris's Let. Sarjant, with all the other old ſervants of the Theatre, *on*
p. 48. *the ſame day they ſent me a letter from the Theatre*, wherein they

they pretended *to have been informed of Mr. Powell's having conveyed* A CONSIDERABLE PART OF THE WARDROBE *from out of the possession of the proper officer, and carried the same to Bristol*; and that, *greatly* ALARMED *at this information, and determined* TO MAKE THE EARLIEST ENQUIRY INTO THE TRUTH OF IT, *they had for that purpose, on the preceding Monday, ordered their servant to go to the Theatre, and attend for their coming.* Now the real truth is, that they had made an *earlier* enquiry into the truth of it. *The women's wardrobe-keeper* had told them (and would willingly swear it) *that Mr. Powell had taken* NO CLOATHS *from the women's wardrobe*: and the men's wardrobe-keeper had shewn them an inventory of what Mr. Powell had taken from *that* wardrobe. Their previous knowledge of this circumstance is one of the main points proved by Whitfield's affidavit: though T. Harris, for obvious reasons, has past it over in silence.

Harris's Let. p. 45.

What then shall we say to a man who pretends to have DISCOVERED *that many things were taken away by Mr. Powell, but that what in the whole might be wanting it was impossible for them to ascertain?*

Harris's Let. p. 42.

The world, however, agrees that, being unhappily connected with two such partners as Messrs. Rutherford and Harris, it was wrong in Mr. Powell, whatever extraordinary indulgence he might claim as a proprietor, to take three or four suits to Bristol; and wrong in me who, as director, had the care of that property, however usual and customary such a practice might be, to consent to it. It was wrong. We agree with the world; but should be more sensibly mortified by their censure on this occasion, if it fell so heavily upon ourselves as on Messrs. Rutherford and Harris. The world was apprized of the tyranny and oppression, the rancour and malevolence of our associates. We were condemned, therefore, for giving such men a *handle*; of which, however dirty, they would not fail to take hold.

So far were they from previously *consulting and advising with several gentlemen of great eminence in all departments of the law* concerning this transaction, that no sooner had they seized the theatre, expelled our common servants, stripped the wardrobe, and carried it off in carts, together with the musick, prompt books, &c. to Mr. Harris's house in Surry-street, than they ran down to Westm. Hall, to be advised how to defend their proceedings. It was there we learnt from the gentleman to whom they applied, that having now enabled themselves to treat with something in hand, they were inclined to listen to an accommodation, and our *respective counsel* appointed the very next day for that purpose. It was WE therefore who were *amused with the hopes of a fair reference*, which im-

Harris's Let. p. 47.

Harris's Let. p. 49.

mediately

mediately fell to the ground, on these two preliminaries being given in on the part of Messrs. Rutherford and Harris.

1. That all engagements made by Mr. Colman should be void.

2. That such of the servants as had offended Messrs. Harris and Rutherford should be discharged.

Whoever has gone through these sheets will, I believe, acquit me for rejecting proposals, with which it was not even in my power, had I been mean enough to have wished it so, to comply. The preliminaries of Mess. Rutherford and Harris, having been delivered verbally, no copy was suffered to be taken of those on our part, which were in writing. I should be surprized therefore, if it were *now* in Mr. Harris's power to surprise me, at his pretending to print them in his pamphlet. He has not, I dare say, *really* forgot the following two, which, to the astonishment of his own counsel, he marked with a pencil, as having a particular objection to them.

The bills, salaries, &c. now due to be paid, monies overdrawn to be paid in, yearly account immediately settled, and dividend duly made by the treasurer.

Objected to by Mr. Harris!

No power to be given to any proprietor to controul the USUAL AND ORDINARY PAYMENTS OF SALARIES AND INCIDENTAL WEEKLY CHARGES.

Objected to by Mr. Harris!

Harris's Let. p. 48. *Reflecting now very considerately on our situation, and on the past conduct of Messrs. Rutherford and Harris*, the conclusion we drew from it was this. "That finding themselves undeceived concerning their intended DESPOTISM under the article respecting the management, they had immediately *laid a plan of driving us* (me in particular) *out of the theatre*, or of rescinding that article; "*that in the execution of that plan they had persevered through the whole season*, "by repeatedly insulting me, *and paying no more regard to* Mr. Powell, "*than if* he *was entirely unconcerned in the property*; that they had endeavoured essentially *to hurt the whole property, and the profits of the past* "*season in particular*, by their constant and unremitting endeavours to "distress and embarrass us in the conduct of it; *that, in fine*, they *had* "*endeavoured*, in open violation of our articles, *to engage, to act under* "*their direction solely, every person belonging to the theatre, upon pain of* "*large penalties*; *and had at last absolutely* committed the most flagrant "outrages on the theatre, by expelling the common servants of all the "proprietors, filling it with ruffians, stiled *servants to Messrs. Harris* "*and Rutherford*, who had by the assistance of these ruffians, not only "checked all theatrical proceedings for our common interest, but car-

" ried

"ried off by cart-loads our joint property, to the amount of ſeveral " thouſand pounds!" Add to which, that theſe ruffians ſtill held poſ-ſeſſion of the theatre, drinking and *ſmoaking* on the ſtage, (a practice never ſuffered before) and behaving in ſuch a diſorderly manner, as to cauſe a magiſtrate to ſend me the following card, which gave us reaſon to tremble for the part of our property ſtill left in their cuſtody, as well as for that which they had, with ſo very little ceremony, carried away.

The CARD.

" Sir John Fielding's reſpects to Mr. Colman; ſhould be glad to ſee him this evening at eight o'clock, to meet Meſſrs. Harris and Rutherford, to ſettle ſome plan *to relieve the fears of the inhabitants in the neighbourhood of Covent Garden Theatre, relative to the miſchiefs that may happen* BY FIRE OR OTHERWISE, *from the perſons* NOW *in the houſe.*

Bow-Street, June 21, 1768.

Having no controul over *the perſons* THEN *in the houſe*, nor any deſire *to meet Meſſrs. Harris and Rutherford*, I did not attend.

While the Theatre remained in this ſtate I ventured once or twice, and Mr. Powell oftener, to take a ſurvey of the premiſes; *and never were men ſo much aſtoniſhed as we were, to find ourſelves in ſo complete a fortification.* (Harris's Let. p. 47.) The precautions I had taken to prevent the continuance of outrages already begun, were no more than putting a few additional bolts and bars to the doors and windows, that they might not be forced open, before the civil power could be called in to prevent a breach of the peace. We did not ſpeak to Mr. Hyde, the maſter-carpenter to the Theatre under the new managers, *but we obſerved how advantageouſly he and his men had been employed in cutting our boards and timber to pieces in order to bar and fortify every avenue and window in the houſe.* (Harris's Let. p. 47.) Mr. Powell's door was particularly *barricadoed againſt its owner*; (Ibid. p 6.) and the ruffians, whom fear had made outrageous and deſperate, had even broke into part of a houſe in Bow-Street, *the excluſive property of Mr. Powell and myſelf*, to redouble their fortifications. Seeing a baſket of ſhavings at one of the ſtage doors, I could not help remonſtrating to ſome of theſe new *ſervants of the theatre*, who had made it a den of thieves, on the danger of ſuch a circumſtance from *tobacco-pipes, and lighted candles.* (Harris's Let. p. 51.) One fellow, who ſeemed by his appearance unfit to be truſted with a ſhilling, told us that he and his colleagues were only *taking care of our property*; and Mr. Powell had like to have been knocked on the head by another of them, who kept guard in the box-paſſage, for *not giving the watch-word.*

So far were they from admitting perſons *who came by our order*, that Mr. Sarjant and ſon, who were ſervants of the (Harris's Let. p. 51.)

Theatre

Theatre under my direction, were repeatedly injoined by Meſſrs. Rutherford and Harris to take their things out of the theatre. Mr. Sarjant's ſon, having occaſion to leave town, took a few neceſſaries; but Mr. Sarjant himſelf always refuſed.

Harris's Let. p. 52.

Wretched and reſtleſs as T. Harris may have ſuppoſed me, I would not, triumphant as they thought themſelves, have changed ſituations at this period with himſelf and Mr. Rutherford. They were now in poſſeſſion, in excluſive poſſeſſion; but could neither legally open, or ſhut up the Theatre. They reſolved however, as being the moſt ruinous, on the latter expedient. They had before told me, as I have before told the Publick, that they ſhould not be moved at ſeeing the Theatre in flames. It was the language of Mr. Harris, echoed by all his partiſans, that he would never give up his point, while there was one brick of the houſe remaining on another; and he perſonally declared to a gentleman at the Theatre, whom he *found therein with Mr. Powell and myſelf*, that "he "had got poſſeſſion, and d—n him if he did not keep it."

Harris's Let. p. 51.

It was incumbent on me therefore, in juſtice to Mr. Powell as well as myſelf, to apply in his abſence *to counſel and to magiſtrates*; never *raving and ſtorming*, nor ever affecting *to be perfectly eaſy*, but *declaring to two perſons in particular*, I ſuppoſe they mean Meſſrs. Macklin and Woodward, that if *the theatre ſhould not open next year, I could ſupport the loſs better* than Meſſrs. Harris and Rutherford.

Harris's Let. p. 52.

June.

I applied then, it is true, to no leſs than three learned and able counſel, three of the moſt reſpectable names in each department of the law; and the only favour I ever received from Mr. Harris, in order to balance the many and ſevere injuries he has done me, is his having afforded me this opportunity of acknowledging in publick the many obligations I owe to thoſe gentlemen, as well as to many of the profeſſion (for which I have the moſt ſincere reſpect) concerned for Meſſ. Rutherford and Harris. The counſel on both ſides have all concurred in recommending pacifick meaſures; and I cannot believe that any lawyer, or other perſon of conſideration whatever, adviſed the outrages of the 17th of June, or other violences of Meſſ. Rutherford and Harris. I will not, after their example, *bandy about the beſt opinions in the kingdom*, as I think it has been extremely illiberal in T. Harris, to dwell with ſuch unmannerly iteration on one of the firſt names in the law; though I muſt do him the juſtice to believe he rather meant to render me obnoxious to the gentleman who bore it, than to dare to give any perſonal offence to the gentleman himſelf.

Harris's Let. p. 54.

Upon

Upon a full and impartial ſtate of the caſe, my counſel were of opinion, that the Theatre was entitled to the protection of the civil power, and that a magiſtrate ought, if called upon, to act on this occaſion. Only *one* magiſtrate was applied to, except George Wrighte, of Great Pulteney Street, Eſq; to whom, upon a conference on that ſubject, one of my counſel declared, that he ſaw no forcible reaſon aſſigned by the other magiſtrate for declining *to be concerned*. Harris's Let. p. 52.

The impertinence of calling Mr. Wrighte ONE——*Wright, Eſq*; together with the pitiful inſinuations of my *prevailing on him*, BY WHAT MEANS I KNOW BEST, is only to be equalled by the falſhood of the aſſertion, *that, without giving them the leaſt notice of his intentions, he iſſued his precept to the ſheriff of the county to reinſtate Mr. Charles Sarjant in the poſſeſſion of the Theatre.* Ibid.

The truth is this: Mr. Wrighte, a gentleman whoſe character is every way proof againſt the mean imputations of T. Harris, acted in the moſt honourable, the moſt regular manner. The proceedings were all ſettled by counſel. So far from NOT *giving* T. Harris, &c. *the leaſt notice of his intentions*, that after the inquiſition was taken and found by the jury, on Friday July 8, written notices thereof, wherein the name, additions, and place of abode of the magiſtrate were given at full length, were ſent to the houſes of Meſſ. Rutherford and Harris, as well as to one Jones at the ſtage-door, ſeverally. Jones abſolutely ſaid *he would anſwer it.* One of Mr. Harris's *five attornies* (for he is perpetually ſhifting his adviſers) actually went to a gentleman concerned on our part to aſk advice on the notice. The next day, Saturday July 9, having complied with every due form, the magiſtrate iſſued his precept to the ſheriff. July. Harris's Let. p. 52.

The Theatre, now once more in its natural ſtate, yet bore evident marks of the late convulſions. Near twenty bludgeons, with which the ruffians kept guard, were left behind. Every door and drawer, which might be ſuppoſed to contain *valuable property*, had been broke open, without even demanding the keys. As to the wardrobes, it would have been impoſſible for an indifferent perſon to conceive that any proprietor could poſſibly have left them in that ſtate: for, not to mention the folly of removing any part of the cloaths from drawers and preſſes remarkably well calculated for their preſervation, and apartments wherein they were alſo *inſured from fire*, ſome of the richeſt and moſt valuable were thrown together like foul linnen; and plainly proved the pillagers ſo intent on what they carried away, that they were regardleſs of the condition of what they left behind.

Such are *a few plain facts, selected from a multitude of grievances, with which the* malignity of T. Harris *has furnished me.* The *true state* of our differences is now before the Publick, whose eyes I have never once endeavoured to divert *from taking a steady view of my conduct, or the* MOTIVES *for it.*

Harris's Let. p. 2.

Ibid. p. 54.

Neither in this, nor in my former Narrative, have I once thrown out the name of Mrs. Lessingham, but when truth extorted it from me. To T. Harris and his colleague alone it is owing that her name, as well as their own obscure names, have been rendered thus publick. I neither inflamed our private differences, nor commenced this paper-war: but if Mess. Rutherford and Harris chose to circulate libels, false as they were malicious, in print and in manuscript, I was bound to give them an answer; and if the disclosure of the truth brought any part of the publick censure on Mrs. Lessingham, as well as themselves, not I, but her illiberal friends, were the cause of it. A fine lady perhaps may be allowed a competent portion of vanity and caprice, and some little inclination to mischief; but I have too sincere a regard for the sex to believe, that there ever resided in a female bosom so black a heart, a heart so rancorous and malevolent as that of T. Harris. To her therefore, however offensively she may have acted, I bear no resentment; nor do I wish to draw upon her that of the Publick. She, as well as Mr. Rutherford, has, I dare say, often been misguided. Mr. Harris must be humoured; and has in his nature, among many worse qualities, the tyranny of a school-boy, who will have every thing his own way. To him I ascribe some letters she has sent me; for as they contain *those gentle and complacent arguments*, with which the *private correspondence* of the *gentle* and *complacent* T. Harris so much abounds, they must have been forged in the same mint of falsehood and scandal. To him also I ascribe *her serving me and Mr. Powell on the 23d of June with a copy of a writ* on account of her salary, when he knew that he had himself locked up the money, with which that, as well as many other payments, ought to have been discharged.

Harris's Let. p. 1.

Revenge, mean revenge, is the passion of a little mind. I do not wonder therefore that the malice of T. Harris should extend to my friends; and that there is not a single performer, officer, or servant, for whom he has even suspected me to entertain the least regard, or who have done their duty by obeying my orders, as director of the Theatre, whom he has not endeavoured to ruin and deprive of their bread, by expelling them the play-house. There is not one among the few inclining to him or his colleague, whatever provocation they may have given me, to whom I have offered the slightest injury.

 I con-

I consider his Address to me at the end of his pamphlet with the contempt due to a man, who calls upon me to treat with him in publick, because *my* DESIGNS UPON HIS PROPERTY *are so* DANGEROUS *and so* NOTORIOUS, *he cannot* TRUST HIMSELF *again to treat with me in private.* He may perhaps command *a proper authority from Mr. Rutherford*, which he therefore slides (as a thing of course) into a parenthesis: but he is to be taught that there is another person, whom he contemptuously omits to mention, (even in a parenthesis) whose authority is as requisite as Mr. Rutherford's, his own, or mine, to conclude upon the terms of any treaty concerning our common property: I mean Mr. Powell. Harris's Let. p. 55. Ibid. p. 56.

In regard to Mr. Rutherford, it is certain, whatever authority he may have given Mr. Harris to negotiate this treaty, that he did also authorize, by a letter from abroad, a gentleman of known character and reputation in his profession, to declare that Mr. Rutherford's share in the Theatre was to be sold; and to demand as the price of it, *the balance of the cash-book last season being so exceedingly small,* ONLY *eighteen thousand five hundred pounds:* to get more indeed, if practicable, but not to treat for less: and considering that I by my *weak or wicked mismanagement have* ONLY *lessened the customary profits near one half*, this demand cannot be thought very unreasonable from a malecontent proprietor, who may naturally wish that the purchaser should make him some compensation for the injuries he has sustained by the *mismanagement* of Mr. Colman. Harris's Let. p. 59. Ibid p. 37.

The use, however, which T. Harris makes of the name of *his colleague*, naturally leads one to observe the confidence and singularity of his present conduct. He and Mr. Rutherford *jointly* compose one negative. Mr. Rutherford goes abroad; one moiety of the negative vanishes; and the other moiety (by a very strange kind of logick) becomes an affirmative.

I shall pass over in silence his three first proposals; but as to the fourth, the only one which seems either *plain* or *intelligible*, or has the least colour of that *fairness* or *equity* to which he pretends, *I do hereby aver to the* PUBLICK, *for* TO THE PUBLICK ALONE I NOW ADDRESS MYSELF, *that whenever T. Harris and his Colleague will prefer their bill in Chancery against us, respecting* OUR PRESENT ARTICLES AND PAST TRANSACTIONS, *neither I nor Mr. Powell will make any delay in putting in a full and sufficient answer. And I now, in this public manner, call upon them to file this long-threatened bill against us: And I do hereby pledge my honour*, not to T. Harris, but TO THE PUBLICK, *that no means or endeavours of mine, or Mr. Powell, shall be wanting to bring it to a short and speedy conclusion.* Harris's Let. p. 56.

It

It now only remains to aſſure that Publick, whoſe protection we have already ſo often experienced, that we are determined to open the Play-houſe at the uſual time; and then to ſubmit it to their tribunal, whether they will ſuffer the inſolence and tyranny of T. Harris to interrupt their amuſements, as well as to oppreſs us and the reſt of their ſervants in Covent-Garden Theatre.

AUGUST 16, 1768,

FINIS.

A

NARRATIVE

OF THE RISE AND PROGRESS OF

THE DISPUTES

SUBSISTING BETWEEN

THE PATENTEES

OF

COVENT-GARDEN THEATRE.

LONDON:

PRINTED FOR MESSRS. FLETCHER, AND ANDERSON, IN ST. PAUL'S-CHURCH-YARD.

MDCCLXVIII.

A P O L O G Y.

AN advertisement having appeared in the Public Advertiser of January 27, signed George Colman, importing that a state of the differences subsisting between the proprietors of Covent-Garden theatre would be speedily published; T. Harris and J. Rutherford, two of the patentees and proprietors of the said theatre, conceiving themselves to have been greatly injured, both in person and property, by the said George Colman, think it incumbent on them, as well in justification of themselves as out of respect to the publick, to prevent, as far as lies in their power, any misrepresentation of facts in which they have been concerned. They hope, therefore, it will not be deemed impertinent in them to submit their own narrative of the case, supported by indubitable and authentic evidence, to the impartiality of the publick; on whose protection and encouragement, the success of the theatre, and the security of their property in it, immediately depend.

T. HARRIS.
J. RUTHERFORD.

A NARRATIVE

OF THE DISPUTES BETWEEN THE

PATENTEES OF COVENT-GARDEN THEATRE.

THE patents and properties belonging to Covent-Garden theatre being on ſale, purſuant to the late Mr. Rich's will, T. Harris and J. Rutherford, two of the preſent patentees, formed a deſign of purchaſing them, and entered into a treaty with Mr. Rich's executors for that purpoſe.

On farther deliberation, they judged it expedient to invite ſome third perſon, of abilities and experience in theatrical affairs, to join with them in the intended purchaſe. Mr. William Powell, an actor of known and acknowledged merit in his profeſſion, was accordingly

B thought

thought of, and made acquainted with their defign. But, as Mr. Powell was then under an engagement to the patentees of Drury-Lane, he thought it an obftacle to his entering into that propofed; nor could he, on the matureft confideration, find any other means of obviating this difficulty than that of inviting George Colman, Efq; a friend of his, to be, in like manner, jointly concerned in the affair. This, therefore, he propofed; reprefenting, at the fame time, what great advantages would be derived, particularly in the management of the theatre, from a connection with a gentleman of his extenfive reputation and abilities.

To this propofal Harris and Rutherford, thinking the concurrence of a fourth perfon unneceffary, were fome time averfe, till the confideration of Mr. Colman's talents as a dramatic writer, and his known familiar intercourfe with the ftage, induced them to acquiefce; in hopes of reaping at leaft fome of thofe many advantages on which Mr. Powell fo warmly expatiated.

On the 31ft of laft March, therefore, the parties entered into articles, for proceeding in the treaty begun by Harris and Rutherford; who were thence empowered to purchafe, on the joint account of all four, the faid patents and properties of the theatre, at a fum not exceeding fixty thoufand pounds; which fum was to be advanced in equal proportions by each party; who were accordingly to become jointly poffeffed of, and interefted in, the patents and properties fo purchafed, and to be jointly and equally concerned in the management of the theatre. By the fame articles alfo they feverally engaged to execute proper deeds and inftruments for that purpofe when the purchafe fhould be compleated.

On the 30th of April following, Harris and Rutherford actually contracted for the patents and theatre; depofiting at the fame time the fum of ten thoufand pounds, their feparate property, in part of the purchafe chaſe money; the remainder of which was to be paid on the firſt of July then next enſuing.

The contract being thus made, the four parties ſoon after met together, in order to ſettle the form of articles, to be entered into, in conformity to their preceeding agreement; when, to the great ſurprize of Harris and Rutherford, Mr. Colman propoſed that he himſelf ſhould be inveſted with the whole and ſole management of the theatre. Manifeſt, however, as was the abſurdity of any perſon's ſubjecting ſo conſiderable a ſhare of property to the uncontroulable diſpoſal of another, Mr. Powell aſſented to this ſtrange propoſal; by which he was to embark fifteen thouſand pounds in an undertaking, with the conduct of which, even in the greateſt emergency, he was to have nothing to do.

It muſt be owned that Harris and Rutherford entertained at that time no doubt either of Mr. Colman's capacity or inclination to conduct the theatre to the beſt advantage; but, as it was impoſſible for them to be aſſured that no ſiniſter accident might render their interpoſition neceſſary to the ſecurity of their property, they conceived no men of common ſenſe could ſtand excuſed for diveſting themſelves of the power of ſuperintending it. Add to this, that Harris and Rutherford gave Mr. Colman repeatedly to underſtand that, as they ſhould engage in no other employment, they intended, in conjunction with him, to make the management of the theatre at once their occupation and amuſement. They objected to Mr. Colman's propoſal, therefore, not only as abſurd in itſelf, but as being contrary to their known intentions in the purchaſe of the theatre, and inconſiſtent with the terms of agreement on which that purchaſe was made. Willing nevertheleſs to indulge Mr. Colman in his deſire of appearing the acting manager, the following articles were at length agreed to.

ARTICLES OF AGREEMENT, RESPECTING THE MANAGEMENT OF COVENT-GARDEN THEATRE.

WHereas Thomas Harris, John Rutherford, George Colman, and William Powell, by certain articles of agreement, dated the 31ſt day of March laſt, did agree to purchaſe of the repreſentatives of John Rich, Eſquire, deceaſed, two patents for exhibiting the atrical performances, and the ſeveral leaſes of Covent-garden theatre, and the rooms, buildings, conveniencies, furniture, cloaths, ſcenes, decorations, muſic, entertainments, and all things belonging to the ſaid theatre, and the ſaid Thomas Harris and John Rutherford, were thereby authoriſed to treat for and purchaſe the ſame, at a ſum not exceeding 60,000*l.* and the purchaſe-money was to be advanced by the ſaid parties equally, and they were to become jointly poſſeſſed of, and intereſted in the premiſes ſo to be purchaſed, and were to be jointly and equally concerned in the management of the ſaid theatre, and were to execute proper deeds and inſtruments for that purpoſe, when the ſaid purchaſe ſhould be compleated. And whereas the ſaid Thomas Harris and John Rutherford, have accordingly contracted and agreed with the repreſentatives of the ſaid John Rich, for the purchaſing of the ſaid patents, leaſes, premiſes and things, at and for the ſum of 60,000*l.* and ſuch purchaſe is to be compleated on the firſt of July next. Now the ſaid ſeveral parties having peruſed, and fully underſtanding the purport and contents of the ſaid contract, do approve of and confirm the ſame, and having alſo in conſequence thereof taken into their conſideration the management of the ſaid theatre, they have for the better and more eaſy conducting the buſineſs thereof, as well as for their joint and equal benefit and advantage, agreed, and do hereby mutually declare and agree,

I. That

I. That notwithstanding any thing contained in the said agreement already made between the said parties, the said George Colman shall be invested with the direction of the said theatre, in the particulars following, viz. That he shall have the power of engaging and dismissing performers of all kinds; of receiving or rejecting such new pieces as shall be offered to the said theatre or the proprietors thereof; of casting the plays; of appointing what plays, farces, entertainments, and other exhibitions, shall be performed; and of conducting all such things as are generally understood to be comprehended in the dramatic and theatrical province.

II. That the said Thomas Harris and John Rutherford, shall be desired to attend the comptrollment of the accounts and treasury relative to the said theatre.

III. Provided always and in as much as the said Thomas Harris and John Rutherford, will have leisure to attend to the affairs of the said theatre, and the said William Powell is to be engaged as an actor or performer on the stage, (for which purpose separate articles are intended to be entered into between him and the other parties) in which his time and attention will be chiefly employed and taken up, so that he will not be able to apply himself in the managing the business of the said theatre. It is therefore hereby further agreed, that the said George Colman shall from time to time, and at all times hereafter, communicate and submit his conduct, and the measures he shall intend to pursue, unto them the said Thomas Harris and John Rutherford; and in case they shall at any time signify their disapprobation thereof in writing unto the said George Colman, then and in that case the measures so disapproved of, shall not be carried into execution, any thing before contained to the contrary notwithstanding. Yet nevertheless with respect to the said William Powell, it is intended and agreed that he shall at all times give his advice and assistance relative to any part of the business of the said theatre, when thereunto desired.

desired by the other parties. Witness the hands of the said parties this 14th day of May, 1767.

Witness
JAMES HUTCHINSON.

THOMAS HARRIS.
JOHN RUTHERFORD.
GEORGE COLMAN.
WILLIAM POWELL.

It is presumed that nothing can be more clear and explicit than the restrictions contained in the third clause of the above articles; and that Mr. Colman understood them in the most literal sense, will fully appear when we come to exhibit his letter of the first of November following.*

On the 28th of the same month, it was judged proper for the patentees to enter into the subsequent agreement severally, respecting them all as proprietors of theatrical entertainments, and respecting Mr. Powell in particular, as to the services expected of him in his profession as an actor.

MEMORANDUM OF AN AGREEMENT BETWEEN THE PATENTEES OF COVENT-GARDEN THEATRE, AND MR. WILLIAM POWELL.

MEmorandum, it is agreed this 28th day of May 1767, between George Colman, Thomas Harris, and John Rutherford, Esquires, and William Powell, the intended purchasers of Covent-garden theatre, and the patents, leases, matters, and things thereunto belonging, as follows,

* Inserted in the course of the narrative.

viz.

viz. That the ſaid William Powell ſhall and will be employed as an actor or performer in the ſaid theatre or playhouſe, for the benefit and advantage of all the ſaid parties, for and during the term and ſpace of ſeven years, from the firſt day of September now next enſuing; and the conſideration thereof ſhall be paid out of the intereſts and profits of the ſaid theatre, at and after the rate of 400*l.* per annum, at ſuch times and in ſuch proportions as the ſaid William Powell ſhall think fit and require the ſame, and ſhall alſo have a benefit every ſeaſon during the ſaid term, clear of all deductions and expences whatſoever. And it is hereby further agreed, that in caſe any other performer or player to be engaged by the ſaid parties, ſhall have a larger ſalary than is hereby agreed to be paid or allowed to the ſaid William Powell, then and in that caſe ſuch addition ſhall be made to the ſaid ſalary of the ſaid William Powell, as will exceed the ſalary of ſuch other perſon or perſons. And it is further agreed, that neither of the ſaid parties ſhall, after the firſt day of October now next enſuing, during his intereſt and concern in the ſaid theatre, act, or write or have any ſhare, intereſt or concern in for or upon any other ſtage, theatre or playhouſe whatſoever. And alſo that any of the parties producing any new play, farce, entertainment, or other exhibition, or any alteration of an old play, farce, &c. ſhall have and be entitled to the common and uſual emoluments accruing to authors from ſuch production, excluſive of the other parties.

Witneſs
JAMES HUTCHINSON.

GEORGE COLMAN.
THOMAS HARRIS.
JOHN RUTHERFORD.
WILLIAM POWELL.

On the firſt of July the contract with Mr. Rich's executors was compleated, the remainder of the money paid *, and the proper aſſignments executed.

* It ill becomes a man, who confers a voluntary obligation, to remind the perſon obliged of the favour done him. T. Harris would therefore have been ſilent, with regard to the

 pre-

It will hardly be ſuſpected by any reader, poſſeſſed of common-ſenſe or acquainted with the principles of common juſtice, that any one of the parties, ſubſcribing to articles ſo very explicit and determinate, ſhould take upon him, almoſt immediately, to act in direct contradiction to them.

At the meeting of the company before the opening of the theatre, however, Mr. Colman's behaviour began to appear in a very extraordinary light. It was very natural for Harris and Rutherford to ſuppoſe that Mr. Colman, who was perſonally known to the performers, would introduce the principal of them, at leaſt, to his brother patentees, on their firſt appearance at the theatre. So far, however, was he from doing this, that when they were advancing to ſpeak to him, as he was ſeated on the middle of the ſtage, he roſe up, and with a petulance he could not conceal, deſired them to withdraw, leſt they ſhould interrupt the rehearſal; leaving them to introduce themſelves to the company, and take their own ſeats where they might think proper.

Diſreſpectful as this behaviour appeared, it would have been thought too inſignificant a circumſtance to be here taken notice of, did it not lend a clue to the maze of Mr. Colman's future proceedings; all which afford the moſt circumſtantial evidence that he had, even ſo early as the opening of the theatre, formed a deſign of acting as if the other proprietors had ſubſcribed to his firſt romantic propoſal of being ſole manager, inſtead of his having engaged " from time to time, and at all times, hereafter to " communicate to and ſubmit his conduct, and the meaſures he ſhall

predicament in which Mr. Powell ſtood at the time of this payment, had not Mr. Powell been pleaſed, more theatrically than gratefully, to deny that when he had none but perſonal ſecurity to offer for a conſiderable ſum of money which he borrowed on this occaſion, T. Harris did agree to give the lender a real ſecurity of his own; without which the money would not have been advanced. Of this the fact itſelf is an inconteſtible proof.

" intend to purſue to T. Harris and J. Rutherford." Mr. Colman indeed ſoon grew too impatient of even the appearance of controul, to ſubmit any thing to the judgment of his colleagues; and though, after much expoſtulation he aſſented to a weekly meeting, for adviſing about the buſineſs of the theatre, it laſted only a few weeks; nor was it of any effect while it did laſt; as Mr. Colman was neither pleaſed to lay open his whole plan, in order to know the opinion of Harris and Rutherford concerning it, nor to act in conformity to their opinion when he did know it *.

It was not till Thurſday the 29th of October, however, that Mr. Colman openly and avowedly diſclaimed their right to lay him under any reſtraint; which he then did, in the moſt poſitive terms; declaring that he would never diſcloſe to them any of his future intentions, but would be reſponſible to the publick only, and not to them, for the conſequences †.

* Mr. Colman has endeavoured to juſtify this proceeding, by pretending that Harris and Rutherford were too little converſant in theatrical matters to adviſe him on theſe occaſions. But though we ſhould grant that the want of experience in what is doing behind the curtain, prevents a perſon's knowing what will pleaſe before it, was Mr. Colman ignorant of their inexperience in this particular before? Did he not know they were neither authors nor actors by profeſſion, when he ſigned the articles ſubjecting himſelf to their controul? —It is not for Harris and Rutherford to determine how far the above plea is valid; they are but too well convinced however that an impartial review of the boaſted ſkill and abilities, Mr. Colman has diſplayed in the management of Covent-Garden theatre this ſeaſon, will afford ſmall proofs of the proficiency he made in the ſtudy of theatrical management, for many years behind the ſcenes at Drury-Lane.

† As to Mr. Colman's particular motives for ſuch a declaration at that time, we ſhall conſider the validity of them, when compelled to examine into the propriety of his conduct as a theatrical manager. At preſent we are only ſtating the facts, which may enable the publick to judge of the rectitude of his behaviour, as a man.

In this resolution he persisted, in spite of all remonstrances, till the Sunday following; when, notwithstanding he had declared, and that even on the Saturday night preceding, he would have no farther communication with them, he addressed to them the following epistle:

TO THOMAS HARRIS, ESQ;

AND

JOHN RUTHERFORD, ESQ;

GENTLEMEN,

I Have seen Mr. Powell; but after what has past, a personal intercourse between us cannot be expected. According to our articles, I shall from time to time submit to your consideration the measures I propose to pursue in the management of the theatre, and any measures against which you shall jointly protest in writing, according to our articles, shall not be carried into execution.

G. COLMAN.

Nov. 1, 1767.

Surely nothing can be more plain than that Mr. Colman, at the time of writing the above letter, understood the articles he had entered into, in the most literal sense; and that he had then no conception of making that artful distinction between the *letter* and *spirit* of them; which he afterwards judged it expedient to do in his letter of January 5 following*.

* Inserted in the course of the narrative.

What

What conſtruction can then be put on his conduct, in calling together the principal performers the very evening of the day in which he wrote this letter, in order to perſuade them that he was ſolely inveſted with the abſolute management of the theatre? Yet, inconſiſtent as ſuch behaviour muſt appear, this he did without having ſeen or heard from Harris or Rutherford; inviting the ſaid actors to a tavern, where he diſingenuouſly communicated to them the ſubſtance of the firſt clauſe of the articles before inſerted †, to give colour to his pretenſions; entirely ſuppreſſing the third clauſe, by which his power was ſo expreſsly limited.

This tranſaction, of courſe, reduced Harris and Rutherford to the neceſſity of reading to the company, aſſembled on the ſtage next morning, the whole of thoſe articles. In conſequence of which lecture, Mr. Colman did apparently take ſhame to himſelf, and declare, in the preſence of Meſſrs. Woodward, Smith, Gibſon and others, that he would for the future ſubmit the meaſures he intended to purſue, to the conſideration of Harris and Rutherford, agreeable to the tenor of their articles, and the ſubſtance of the letter he had written them the preceding day.

The reconciliation which enſued on this declaration, gave Harris and Rutherford ſome reaſon to hope that affairs would now be carried on in an amicable manner, and conformably to thoſe intentions, with which they engaged in ſo conſiderable an undertaking. They were very ſoon ſurprized however with the information of Mr. Colman's having, on his own authority, and without their knowledge or conſent, taken upon him to engage Mr. and Mrs. Yates; the former at ten pounds a week, with a benefit, and the latter at five hundred pounds for the ſeaſon, with a like benefit ‡.

† See page 4.

‡ Not that Harris and Rutherford would have objected to the expence of this engagement, or to any other conducive to the entertainment of the publick, could that have been

 effected

The ſurprize of Harris and Rutherford, at this information, was by ſo much the greater, as all the four proprietors, in a conſultation held ſome few days before on the ſubject, had been unanimouſly of opinion, that as their company then ſtood, it was impoſſible, without breaking through the eſtabliſhed cuſtoms of the theatre, to avail themſelves properly of the ſervice of thoſe excellent actors. Add to this, that, having a right to think their conſent neceſſary to Mr. Colman's forming an engagement of ſo much expence and conſequence, they could not help regarding it as another groſs breach of the articles ſubſiſting between them*.

To this act of Mr. Colman's, nevertheleſs Mr. Powell, not only aſſented, but even affected to juſtify it: from what motives we preſume not to ſay; as we ſhould be very ſorry to impute any action to a ſiniſter deſign,

affected in any proportionable degree. They by no means wiſh to ſacrifice the amuſements of the town to their private emolument; but it is to be obſerved, that when a company is full, the engagement of additional performers, even of the greateſt merit, muſt create great confuſion, and at leaſt render thoſe uſeleſs who would otherwiſe have ſupplied their places. There is no doubt that Mr. and Mrs. Yates would in any circumſtances be a valuable acquiſition to either theatre, although, from their too late engagement the preſent ſeaſon at Covent-garden, they have had (particularly Mr. Yates) fewer opportunities of diſplaying their reſpective talents, and conſequently of being ſo uſeful as their great reputation might give reaſon to expect.

* It has been pretended by Meſſrs. Colman and Powell, that Harris and Rutherford, though not privy to the engagement of Mrs. Yates and her huſband, did afterwards aſſent to that meaſure; of which their acquieſcing in the payment of their reſpective ſalaries is a proof.—It may be aſked however, in anſwer to this plea, what could Harris and Rutherford have done to any purpoſe after the contract was actually made? Had they put an abſolute negative, as they were empowered to do, on the fulfilling ſuch contract, would not Colman and Powell have had a very plauſible, if not a juſt, pretence, to charge them with a penurious reluctance to contribute their utmoſt to the entertainment of the town? a pretence which, they beg leave to aſſure the publick, never had, nor ever ſhall have, any foundation either in their principles or conduct.

which

which may be fairly attributed to an ingenuous one. If the public however, take into consideration, that Mr. Powell became entitled as an actor, to the addition of one hundred pounds to his yearly salary, in consequence of Mrs. Yates's receiving five hundred, we leave them to make what comment they please on Mr. Powell's conduct in this particular*.

Perhaps they may be assisted in making such comment by Mr. Powell's subsequent behaviour.

Certain it is, that Mr. Powell carried his assent to Mr. Colman's proceedings a very unwarrantable length; a remarkable instance of which soon after presented itself; when, at a meeting of all the proprietors, the latter proposed his taking out of the treasury of the house, a sum between sixty-four and seventy pounds, on account of his having inserted a few lines in the comedy of the Rehearsal †, and his intended alteration of the tragedy of King Lear; in which proposal Mr. Powell most readily acquiesced.

As it was impossible also for Harris and Rutherford to know how far the projected alteration of King Lear might entitle Mr. Colman to that sum; and, as they were willling to allow of every emolument due to him as a

* In order to obviate any suspicion of sinister views in Mr. Powell, it has been given out that he could not take the advantage above-mentioned, of the agreement with Mrs. Yates, because Mr. Woodward had likewise a greater salary. But it is to be remarked that Mr. Woodward's engagement with the theatre was antecedent to the formation of the articles with Mr. Powell; by virtue of which he was entitled to a larger salary than any other performer or player hereafter "TO BE engaged" in the service of the house. See memorandum of those articles, p. 6.

† A customary liberty taken from time to time with this play in representation; and particularly by the celebrated manager of Drury-lane, who, we are assured, never charged a single farthing to his brother patentee for such services.

writer, they did not directly oppofe the propofition then made; yet could not help mentioning the impropriety of taking out the money till the altered play was produced *.

In return for this complacency on the part of Mr. Powell, Mr. Colman, at the very fame meeting, as readily affented to the former's moft unreafonable demand of a benefit, to indemnify him for the lofs he fhould fuftain in not acting at Briftol theatre the enfuing fummer. Nay Mr. Colman went fo far as to infift warmly on the reafonablenefs and equity of fuch demand; notwithftanding it was exprefsly ftipulated in the articles which they mutually entered into on the 28th of May, that none of the parties fhould after the firft day of September then next enfuing, be concerned in any other theatre whatever †.

The abfurdity, not to fay the infolence of this proceeding, could not fail to ftrike Harris and Rutherford in a very peculiar manner, and to fuggeft a fufpicion that Meffrs. Colman and Powell had formed the defign of taking an advantage of their ignorance of playhoufe cuftoms and artifices, to difpofe of the general property of the theatre at their own pleafure, and to lofe no opportunity of converting it to their private emolument. How far fuch a fufpicion was juftified by the above facts, is fubmitted to the determination of the publick.

* Mr. Colman did neverthelefs appropriate the faid fum, although he did not produce the play, nor indeed appear to have it ready, even on the fecond of January following; when he was exprefsly required, by letter from Harris and Rutherford, either to produce the play or repay the money into the treafury of the theatre; neither of which he thought proper to do: fo that the money thus appropriated by Mr. Colman, (i. e. near feventy pounds) ftands at prefent as an equivalent for the few fpeeches inferted in the Rehearfal; a performance which on the fecond night of its exhibition did not bring feventy pounds into the houfe.

† See the copy of thofe articles, page 7.

With

With regard to Mr. Powell's acting at Briſtol; Harris and Rutherford conceiving that his advice reſpecting the management of the theatre, might in the ſummer-time be diſpenſed with; they, in order to ſhew their unwillingneſs to deprive him of any pecuniary advantage which they could reaſonably afford him, at length aſſented to his going, notwithſtanding they conceived it derogatory from the character of a patentee of one of the Theatres-Royal in London, to think of ſuch an expedition*.

The next irregularity committed by Mr. Colman, was productive of the moſt flagrant proofs of his being determined to break through every reſtraint his articles laid him under; and of acting not only without the approbation of Harris and Rutherford, but in direct oppoſition to their moſt poſitive and legal remonſtrances. This was on occaſion of the performance of the play of Cymbeline; which, on account of ſome perſonal altercation that had paſt relative to the caſting of the parts†, had been by mutual conſent for ſome time laid aſide. The duty of the patentees however, requiring the exhibition of that play for one night‡, Mr. Colman laid hold of that opportunity to order its repetition; notwithſtanding he knew ſuch a repetition muſt be extremely diſagreeable to Harris and Rutherford; as tending to revive the diſputes which that play had before occaſioned: a conſideration that would doubtleſs have had ſome weight with Mr. Colman, had he duly ſtudied the peace and good order of

* Harris and Rutherford would indeed have given Mr. Powell formal leave in writing to go to Briſtol; but to this Mr. Colman objected; the money ariſing from a benefit, appearing both to Colman and Powell the more elegible object.

† Mr. Colman wanting Miſs W— to play the part of Imogen; which Harris and Rutherford conceived would be better ſupplied by Mrs. L—, who had played it the preceeding ſeaſon at Drury-lane. On Mrs. Yates's joining the company however, and refuſing to give up the part, it was aſſigned to neither.

‡ December 28.

the

the theatre; circumstances of much greater consequence than either the profits arising to the proprietors, or the entertainment afforded the publick by the exhibition of the play in question *. Harris and Rutherford therefore, thought it necessary on this occasion to send Mr. Colman the following card, after the play had been given out for the second time.

TO G. COLMAN, ESQ;

MR. Harris and Mr. Rutherford present their compliments to Mr. Colman, are much concerned that he directed Cymbeline again to be given out. — Mr. Colman is well acquainted with their sentiments on the subject, and how much it is their desire that play should, for the present, be postponed.——Doubt not he will conduct this affair accordingly.

Monday 28 Dec. 1767, 11 o'clock at night.

Mr. Colman still persisting in his design, another earnest remonstrance, desiring him for their mutual quiet to desist from his purpose, was made him the next day; which proving ineffectual, the following prohibition was sent him in form.

TO G. COLMAN, ESQ;

SIR,

WE absolutely disapprove the performance of Cymbeline at our theatre untill farther consideration.

Wednesday. 30 Dec. 1767.

T. HARRIS,
J. RUTHERFORD.

* Especially as it was frequently exhibited at Drury-lane.

To

To the above formal prohibition was annexed the following letter.

SIR,

OUR right to forbid the representation of the above play we draw from the articles entered into between us; from your letter of the first of November last, which runs thus, "*any measures against* "*which you shall jointly protest in writing, shall not be carried into* "*execution*;" and from your solemn declaration to the same purpose the succeeding day, in presence of Messrs. Woodward, Smith, Gibson, &c. — It is with the less regret that we write in this absolute manner, as our repeated desires on this occasion have failed to make the least impression.

We are, Sir,

Your humble Servants,

T. HARRIS.

Sent away at 12 o'clock at noon. J. RUTHERFORD.

In answer to the above, about an hour after, Harris and Rutherford received the following laconic epistle from Mr. Colman, with Mr. Powell's approbation, as under annexed.

TO T. HARRIS, ESQ;

AND J. RUTHERFORD, ESQ;

GENTLEMEN,

I Have juſt received your mandate, and will print it as a reaſon to the publick, for performing no play to-morrow.

Dec. 30, 1767. G. COLMAN.

GENTLEMEN,

GREAT part of our boxes being taken for the play of Cymbeline, great damage muſt accrue to MY property, by your method of proceeding, and I muſt appeal to my friends and the public for redreſs. I moſt ſincerely concur with Mr. Colman's ſentiments above, and ſhall abide by his determination.

I am your humble ſervant,

W. POWELL.

Juſtly alarmed at the above threats of Meſſrs. Colman and Powell to ſhut up the theatre, Harris and Rutherford took proper meaſures to prevent their deſigned interruption of the public entertainments, and ſent notice of it to Mr. Colman, as follows:

TO

TO G. COLMAN, ESQ;

SIR,

IF you refuse to give directions for a play to-morrow night, we shall :—Whether they will be obeyed or not, is for future consideration. What you are pleased to call our mandate, can be no reason for shutting up the theatre, as you have the whole circle of the drama (Cymbeline excepted) from whence to elect the play.—Whatever damages may arise, we doubt not will be at your peril, as they can only ensue from your committing a breach of the most solemn and legal engagements.

We are your humble servants,

Wednesday, 30 Dec. 1767,
4 o'clock.

T. HARRIS.
J. RUTHERFORD.

It is presumed the above letters need no comment: and we leave the publick to judge of the conduct of a man, who could thus determine to abandon * the management of the theatre, merely because he

* And that Mr. Colman did abandon the theatre is evident, from his leaving Powell to give out the play at his own indiscretion, and the prompter's notice to Harris, dated the same evening.

TO T. HARRIS, ESQ;

SIR,

BY Mr. Powell's order, the Clandestine Marriage will be reheased to-morrow at ten.

Your most obedient servant,

JOSEPH YOUNGER.

was

was required to act in conformity to thofe articles, by which fuch management was put into his hands.

We will even fuppofe, for a moment, the above prohibition on the part of Harris and Rutherford to have been merely a groundlefs and capricious difplay of that authority which the negative claufe in their articles confeffedly invefted them with. Yet furely as it was the firft prohibition of the kind, and Mr. Colman had the whole ftock of plays to apply to, one only excepted, nothing can excufe him for this rafh and precipitate refolution! But if, on the other hand, fuch prohibition was founded on motives which every man of fenfe and fenfibility muft feel the force of, while the refolves of Mr. Colman were the mere effect of fpleen and refentment *, his behaviour muft furely appear not more abfurd than criminal.

But though Mr. Colman thus precipitately withdrew himfelf from the theatre, he left Mr. Powell to give out the play in difpute; which was accordingly acted on the thirty-firft of December, in open defiance of Harris and Rutherford, and in direct breach of the articles fubfifting between the patentees.

On this proof of Meffrs. Colman and Powell's total difregard to their engagements, Harris and Rutherford grew naturally more and more alarmed at the apparent danger of their property. They judged it immediately expedient therefore to audit the accounts of the theatre, and to enquire into the ftate of the wardrobe; to which latter there had been lately made very confiderable and expenfive additions. To this end they ordered the treafurer to prepare his accounts, and wrote the following letter to Mr. Powell.

* And that of the moft unmanly refentment; of which there might, and will, be produced the moft "damning proofs," if Mr. Colman fhould carry his indifcretion fo far as to make it neceffary.

TO

TO W. POWELL, ESQ;

SIR,

WE desire you will present our compliments to Mrs. Powell *, and acquaint her we desire she will be pleased to send every thing in her possession appertaining to the theatre, to the wardrobe-keeper's office, as we intend forthwith to examine the state of both wardrobes: that you will also inform her we are much obliged to her for the trouble she hath hitherto incurred; but request she would not make any farther purchase on account of the theatre, as we shall give directions to the treasurer to pay nothing but incidental charges, until previously consented to by us.

T. HARRIS.
J. RUTHERFORD.

Dec. 31, 1767.

Mr. Powell's reply to the above requisition.

TO T. HARRIS, ESQ;

AND J. RUTHERFORD, ESQ;

GENTLEMEN,

YOUR directions to Mrs. Powell cannot be complied with. The unappropriated cloaths belonging to the theatre, have ever been kept

* Mrs. Powell having obligingly taken the trouble to make many considerable purchases for the use of the theatre.

out

out of the houſe, under the care of one of the proprietors. They are now in my poſſeſſion, always free for your inſpection, and forth-coming for the proper uſe of the theatre. However you may eſteem Mrs. Powell for the care and trouble ſhe has taken to herſelf concerning the property, I believe every gentleman that has made an advance in the purchaſe, when they are acquainted with it, will think themſelves greatly obliged to her.—Whatever *your* doubts may be for the ſafety of that part of your property in my poſſeſſion, I know not; but this I know, that my conduct has hitherto been ſuch as not to have my honeſty or Mrs. Powell's called in queſtion; ſo that you may be aſſured your property is ever ſafe with either of us.

Your humble ſervant,

1 Jan. 1768. W. POWELL.

P. S. Mr. Colman by our articles is inveſted with the theatrical as well as dramatic direction of the theatre, and the care of the women's wardrobe, and that of the men's, was deſired by Mr. Colman to be taken by Mrs. P----- and myſelf, without any objection on your part, and therefore we ſhall pay every attention to the department, for the good of the property, and the pleaſure of the publick. — And you muſt give me leave to tell you, that you ſhall find I am not that CYPHER, even according to our preſent articles, as you ſeem by your treatment to imagine.

I am yours, &c.

W. POWELL.

It is here to be obſerved, that Mr. Powell founds his right, of refuſing to deliver the cloaths in his wife's poſſeſſion into the cuſtody of the wardrobe-keeper, on a pretended cuſtom. He ſays, "the unappropriated cloaths belonging to the theatre have *ever* been kept out of "the houſe, under the care of one of the proprietors." This may, indeed have poſſibly been the caſe with ſome former proprietors; but how are Harris and Rutherford bound to follow their example? They think the property in queſtion would, for many reaſons, be better depoſited in the hands of the wardrobe-keeper; and conceive the publick will be alſo of their opinion, that the delivery of them when required into the proper office would have been a ſtronger proof of the honeſty Mr. Powell boaſts of, than his peremptorily declaring the requiſition could be complied with. As to Mr. Powell's being treated as "a *Cypher*," certain it is that Mr. Colman treats him as ſuch, in his letter of the firſt of November; wherein he ſo explicitly recognizes the reſtraining power of Harris and Rutherford, and makes not the leaſt mention of Mr. Powell, as if he was indeed a CYPHER, and there was no ſuch patentee exiſting.

We cannot help taking notice alſo of the ſtreſs Mr. Powell lays in particular on the PRESENT *articles*. It is certain the *preſent articles* are not well calculated for the game Meſſrs. Colman and Powell ſeem diſpoſed to play into each other's hands. But can either of them be ſo abſurd as to ſuppoſe, that Harris and Rutherford will ever enter into *future* articles, with perſons who have diſplayed ſo conſcientious a regard to the obſervance of the *preſent*?

The impertinent inſinuation, thrown out by Mr. Powell, reſpecting ſuch gentlemen as intereſted themſelves in the purchaſe of the theatre, would be here paſſed over with contempt; had it not been immediately followed by a ſtill more impertinent application to ſeveral of Harris and Rutherford's particular friends: of which application Meſſrs. Colman and Powell thought proper to give them the following notice.

TO MESSRS. HARRIS AND RUTHERFORD.

GENTLEMEN,

BEING confcious of the rectitude of our conduct, we are willing and defirous to fubmit it to your moft intimate and particular friends; for which purpofe we have fummoned the underwritten gentlemen to the King's Arms tavern in Cornhill next Tuefday at one o'clock, when if you pleafe you may attend.

We are,

GENTLEMEN,

Your humble fervants,

G. COLMAN.

Jan. 1, 1768. W. POWELL.

C— F—, Efq; H— B—, Efq;
R— O—, Efq; T— L—, Efq;
—— P—, Efq; —— N—, Efq;
M— D—, Efq;

What ideas Meffrs. Colman and Powell may entertain of moral rectitude, the reader who hath perufed this narrative with attention, will probably be at a lofs to determine. He will very readily conceive however from the above letter alone, that they muft entertain very ftrange notions of humanity and good manners. In this appeal to the friends of Harris and Rutherford, they have dared to treat the latter as contemptuoufly as if not arrived at years of difcretion, and incapable of anfwering for their own conduct. What unparalled infolence! But even fuppofing they had a plea for this, what can juftify their impertinence in *fummoning* together a number of gentlemen of refpectable characters, to a common tavern, to trouble them with a difpute in which few of them were concerned, and none could with propriety interfere! The mortification therefore which Meffrs. Colman and Powell met with on this occafion, was undoubtedly juft; few of the gentlemen attending, and three of them, being thofe only to whom Harris and Rutherford were known, treating the fummons they had received with the contempt it deferved; as appears by the following letter left for Meffrs. Colman and Powell at the place of meeting.

FOR G. COLMAN,

AND W. POWELL, ESQUIRES.

To be left at the King's-Arms tavern Cornhill.

GENTLEMEN,

WE have each of us a fummons to attend you on the affairs of Covent-garden theatre. But as we cannot poffibly have any right to interfere in this matter, muft beg leave to decline the meeting. Meffrs. Thomas Harris and John Rutherford, are gentlemen, who, in our opinion, will never act contrary to the principles of honour and right. As our friends, therefore, we are ever ready to support them to the utmost of our abilities.

We are,

GENTLEMEN,

Your humble servants,

Jan. 5. 1768.

C. F——.
H. N——.
T. L——.

This attempt * to prejudice Harris and Rutherford in the opinion of their friends having failed, the impatience of Mr. Colman could no longer be kept within bounds; but broke out the same day, in the following extravagant letter, written in answer to some remonstrances of Harris and

* An attempt as basely designed as meanly executed; Colman and Powell, ignorant of the real connections of Harris and Rutherford, going to enquire of their sollicitor for the addresses of those gentlemen to whom they supposed Harris and Rutherford obliged. To this purpose Mr. Hutchinson's card of the 30th of December, 1767.

" Mr. Hutchinson presents his best compliments to Messrs. Harris and Rutherford, and begs leave to acquaint them he has just now had a visit from Mr. Colman and Mr. Powell, to know the adresses of Mr. O— Mr. N— and Mr. F—, in order, they say, to lay a state of the affairs before them and the other gentlemen, who have advanced money upon the security of the theatre."

Let our readers compare this disingenuous behaviour, particularly in Mr. Powell, with that of T. Harris, who, wanting to borrow no money on the security of the theatre for *himself*, yet lent that security for *Powell*; and we may leave them to their own reflections on it.

Rutherford

Rutherford againſt his unjuſtifiable proceedings*, and the danger they thence apprehended to the intereſt of the theatre.

TO MESS[rs]. HARRIS

AND RUTHERFORD.

GENTLEMEN,

THE intereſt of the theatre is in no danger but from *your* conduct and *your* partialities. Mr. Powell, who has a right to give his advice and attendance when called on, perceives that it is not poſſible for us to keep our doors open, if the director is liable to ſuch frequent and ſtudied interruptions: and we are adviſed that no court can ever be led ſo far to miſconſtrue the articles between us, as to ſuppoſe the giving you a power that muſt be ſo prejudicial to our common intereſt, could be the intention of it. I ſhall continue to act in a manner conſiſtent with the ſpirit of it, and wiſh you to do the ſame. As to the rectitude of your conduct, or of our own, I ſhall ſubmit that matter to the publick: before whom I ſhall lay a full ſtate of the caſe in a very few days †.

Jan. 5, 1768. G. COLMAN.

* Particularly in regard to his exhibiting the Merchant of Venice when Miſs Macklin was indiſpoſed, in oppoſition to the remonſtrances of Mr. Macklin againſt it; to the diſcredit of that performance, and the great confuſion of the actreſs, who played on the ſhorteſt warning the capital part of Portia.

† This has been the conſtant threat of Colman, from the very commencement of the diſputes; relying doubtleſs on his literary abilities for the ſupport of his cauſe, and well

The reader is desired to compare this letter with that received from Mr. Colman on the first of November, and then to judge whether any sufficient reason can be given for the total change in the writer's sentiments concerning the spirit of the articles alluded to.

Mr. Colman here alledges it to be Mr. Powell's opinion, that the doors of the theatre cannot be kept open, if the director is liable to such frequent and studied interruptions. Now the truth is, that, whatever right was invested in Harris and Rutherford to control Mr. Colman in his management, he never did suffer them to interrupt him in fact, except in deferring the exhibition of Cymbeline before Mrs. Yates's admission into the company.

They did indeed sometimes take the ineffectual liberty to remind him of the irregularity of his proceedings, in not properly acquainting them from time to time with his intended measures. They endeavoured also to persuade him to take proper methods to render Mr. Yates, Mr. Macklin, and some other performers of known merit and popularity, more useful in the theatre, and of course more conducive to the entertainment of the publick.

If they objected also to any part of his actual conduct, it was only in the way of general advice and remonstrance; which could not, with any propriety be construed into an interruption of his management; much less a studied one, and such as obliged him to shut up the theatre *.

knowing the reluctance of Harris and Rutherford to trouble the publick on so improper an occasion as the squabbles of individuals. Nothing, indeed, but the absolute necessity of removing the unjust aspersions cast on them, and of preventing the dissipation of their property, could have made them break that respectful silence, which they have hitherto imposed on themselves, out of the profoundest regard to the publick.

* Nothing can be more absurd and inconsistent than such a pretence, if it be considered that even their absolute and formal prohibition of the repetition of Cymbeline, notwithstanding

It was never denied by Harris and Rutherford that Mr. Powell had a right to give his advice, when called upon by the other three parties; but they never conceived that they were under any obligation to take that advice; and much leſs that it was to be taken by any one of thoſe parties, in oppoſition to the other two. Nothing of this kind appears from the letter of the articles: but perhaps counſellor Powell hath diſcovered ſuch a latent meaning in the ſpirit of them, in the ſame manner as Mr. Colman's other ſagacious adviſers have convinced him, that the tenor of thoſe articles is now totally different to his conceptions of them three months ago.

That the power with which Harris and Rutherford are inveſted by the ſubſiſting articles, muſt be prejudicial to the common intereſt of the parties, Mr. Colman and his adviſers ſeem too readily to take for granted. At preſent this aſſertion muſt be merely problematical, as that power has never in any ſingle inſtance been efficaciouſly exerted. It can never ſurely be obviouſly deducible from the terms of the agreement. If it were, how comes it that Mr. Colman, a gentleman bred in the ſtudy of the law, ſhould enter into ſuch abſurd articles? But that no ſuch inference can be drawn, is boldly preſumed, on the aſſurance of ſome of the firſt and ableſt council, learned in the laws of this kingdom; whoſe opinions have been taken on this occaſion, and who are unanimous that a court of Equity would, on a hearing of the cauſe, decree a ſpecific performance of the articles in queſtion.

A copy of one of theſe opinions was accordingly tranſmitted directly to Mr. Colman, in hopes that it might influence him to come to ſome

withſtanding it induced Mr. Colman to retire for a while from his directorſhip, was yet of no interruption of the buſineſs of the theatre; that play being re-exhibited on the night for which it was given out, and repeated afterwards.

reaſonable terms of accommodation with Harris and Rutherford, and induce him to admit in fact of their having what they had an indubitable right to, a negative voice in the management of the theatre, and the diſpoſal of their common property.

This opinion * was accompanied by a letter from Harris and Rutherford, of which the following is an extract.

TO MESS[rs.] COLMAN,

AND POWELL.

GENTLEMEN,

INcloſed you will receive a copy of ——'s opinion on our caſe. As his abilities and integrity are well known to Mr. Colman, we have the

* The ſubſtance of which was, that, on a peruſal of the caſe of Harris and Rutherford, and the articles of their mutual agreement with Meſſrs. Colman and Powell, together with the letters which had paſſed between them, it appeared that Meſſrs. Colman and Powell had been guilty of many material and ſubſtantial breaches of the ſaid articles: And that farther it appeared from ſuch conduct, that they were determined to throw off all regard to their articles, and to act in the management of all matters relative to the theatre, as ſole and entire owners thereof, in abſolute excluſion of Harris and Rutherford, from ſuch management. It was alſo this council's further opinion, that on the filing of a bill in Chancery againſt the parties, the court would not only decree a ſpecific performance of the articles for the future, but would order Meſſrs. Colman and Powell, to make ſatisfaction to Harris and Rutherford for their reſpective ſhares of all damages which ſhould appear to have been ſuſtained by any breach of thoſe articles by them reſpectively: And, at the ſame time would order Mr. Powell and his wife to depoſite in the proper office of the theatre, ſuch part of the wardrobe as they improperly withheld in their own poſſeſſion.

greater

greater reliance upon the impreſſions they muſt neceſſarily make. This opinion, as well as others we have taken, points out the infallible remedy for redreſs; yet, like the reſt, it adviſes an adjuſtment by arbitration, becauſe our diſputes, differing from the generality, muſt be attended with the ſevereſt injury to the property litigated, excluſive of the actual perſonal expence to be incurred individually. We therefore propoſe an arbitration of our diſputes, by four gentlemen totally unconcerned in affairs of the theatre, two to be nominated by us, unexceptionable in point of rank, fortune, and reputation, and impartial, never having been in the leaſt concerned in our affairs. If you ſhall both concur in this propoſal, and nominate two gentlemen of equal conſideration and impartiality, we ſhall be ready to enter into bonds for ſubmitting to the award of the gentlemen ſo nominated.

In anſwer to this letter, and in order to invalidate the opinion therein mentioned, Mr. Colman affected to think a fair and impartial ſtate of the caſe had not been laid before the council*. And in a ſubſequent letter, from Meſſrs. Colman and Powell in conjunction, the propoſed arbitration appears to be artfully eluded, by their ſaying only in general terms, that "they were ready to refer to proper perſons "the care of framing a plan of articles which might prevent future "uneaſineſs."——

This not being thought ſufficiently explicit, Harris and Rutherford again applied to them for a more preciſe and poſitive anſwer to their propoſal; which application produced the following reply.

* Setting the caſe, however, as to the damages complained of, out of the queſtion, the above-mentioned opinion, reſpecting the ſpecific performance of the articles, was confirmed by that of other learned council, and thoſe of the firſt eminence, who gave the ſame in the moſt explicit terms; with this addition, that thoſe articles were entered into upon valuable conſideration, were expreſſed with clearneſs and certainty, nor could admit of any doubt in their conſtruction as to the rights and powers of the reſpective parties.

TO THOMAS HARRIS, ESQ;

AND JOHN RUTHERFORD, ESQ;

GENTLEMEN,

OUT of tendernefs to yourfelves, we forbore to enter into any paft tranfactions, as an enquiry of that nature muft neceffarily lay open the real caufe of the unhappy difference between us; nor indeed is any thing material to the general intereft and happinefs, but a proper arrangement of matters for the future. We propofed therefore, and we now repeat the propofal, to refer to proper perfons the care of fettling the articles in fuch a manner, that the management of the theatre may be carried on to the fatisfaction of all parties: nor have we any objection, if you think it agreeable, to fubmit our paft conduct to the confideration of the fame perfons; confident as we are, that in the opinion of any unprejudiced judge, we fhall be found to have deferved a very different treatment than we have met with from you.

We are,

GENTLEMEN,

Your humble fervants,

G. COLMAN.
W. POWELL.

The

The attentive reader will obſerve that this ſecond anſwer is couched in as vague and equivocal terms as the preceding; the doubtful expreſſion of *proper perſons* being uſed in both. Is it poſſible that men, really conſcious of the integrity of their actions, as Meſſrs. Colman and Powell here pretend to be, ſhould heſitate in approving ſuch perſons as are deſcribed in the letter of Harris and Rutherford, viz. diſintereſted men of rank, fortune, and reputation?

The uncommon effrontery of Colman and Powell, in affecting a tenderneſs for Harris and Rutherford in not diſcloſing the real cauſe of their difference, is of a piece with the reſt of their behaviour, equally contemptuous and contemptible. To have the aſſurance to pretend, and that in a private letter *, addreſſed to the parties themſelves, that the unhappy differences between them are owing to any ſingle cauſe, when they muſt be conſcious, if they had any conſcience at all, of their having given repeated and aggravated cauſes of difference! To have the aſſurance, in reply to complaints made againſt them for the violation of articles formally ſubſiſting, to propoſe the new modelling thoſe articles, or the framing of new ones! They may indeed well boaſt they are confident; for their confidence appears in this to be matchleſs. It is difficult however to ſay which is the greateſt ſubject of admiration, the exceſs of their folly or that of their inſolence, in this complicated inſtance of both, undoubtedly the greateſt inſult that ever was offered to men of the leaſt pretenſions to common underſtanding.

It is little to be wondered at, that, on Meſſrs. Colman and Powell's thus evading the propoſal of an equitable arbitration, all epiſtolary corre-

* Or are we to ſuppoſe this private letter artfully written, with a view to give ſome colour to their pretenſions and practices, ſhould it hereafter come to be neceſſarily made publick.

ſpondence between the parties, on the ſubject of their diſputes, ſhould have an end.

A meeting of their reſpective ſolicitors did indeed take place ſoon after, but proved ineffectual; ſo that things remained in this ſituation, when the accidental publication * of a looſe and deſultory ſtate of their caſe, injudiciouſly and imperfectly drawn up, induced Mr. Colman to publiſh the advertiſement, which laid Harris and Rutherford under the neceſſity of making this remonſtrance; on a candid peruſal of which, it is preſumed there is no impartial reader who will not rather wonder at their long ſilence, than cenſure them for the preſent appeal to the publick.

Having thus given an exact and faithful narrative of ſuch facts as relate to the legality and rectitude of Mr. Colman's conduct, in regard to Harris and Rutherford, we beg the reader's farther attention to a few general reflections on his behaviour as a theatrical manager, and the pro-

* By having been ſcandalouſly and unjuſtifiably exhibited by the maſter of Slaughter's coffee-houſe; where it had been caſually and unintentionally left upon the table. Great pains indeed have been taken, to repreſent this accident as a wilful miſtake of Harris and Rutherford; tending to injure the character of Meſſrs. Colman and Powell. And yet nothing could appear more plain, on the very face of the thing itſelf, than that ſuch caſe could not have been intended for public inſpection; which the ſeveral blank ſpaces left for the future inſertion of names and dates, with the references to letters and memorials not annexed to it, ſufficiently evince. It was thought incumbent therefore on Harris and Rutherford, publicly to diſclaim ſo illiberal a deſign; in doing which, however, they did not (as hath been falſely repreſented) diſavow the papers ſo left, or mean in the leaſt to exculpate Meſſrs. Colman and Powell of the ſeveral facts therein charged upon them.

priety of their exerting their undoubted right to controul him in that province.

Harris and Rutherford have ſeverely felt, and therefore are extremely ſenſible of, the diſadvantage they lie under from a comparative view of the known abilities of the reſpective patentees. They have had the frequent mortification of having their moſt legal and juſt complaints diſregarded on the prudential plea of their own intereſt. They have heard it repeatedly alledged, even by thoſe who have acknowledged the injuſtice and inſolence of Meſſrs. Colman and Powell's behaviour, that it would be yet highly indiſcreet for them (Harris and Rutherford) to interfere in the conduct of an undertaking, for which it has been inconſiderately taken for granted they were unqualified.

But, let us take the liberty to aſk, if it be not poſſible for ſuch adviſers to have impoſed on themſelves in this particular, by carrying their notions of the reputation and abilities of Meſſrs. Colman and Powell, much farther than their influence in the management of a theatre extend.

They preſume not to enter the liſts with their brother patentees in their reſpective profeſſions. But, as they pretend neither to write comedies nor to enact tragedies, ſo neither do they pretend to talents for compoſing muſic, leading the band, inventing dances, or deſigning and painting the ſcenes. Yet they conceive it little leſs unreaſonable to expect a manager to be a painter, architect, compoſer, fiddler, or figure-dancer, than to ſuppoſe he ſhould neceſſarily be either an author or actor.

The proprietors of a theatre, may certainly avail themſelves of the ſeveral talents of muſicians, dancing-maſters, architects, painters, players, poets, and even of managers, if neceſſary, on paying them a valuable

 conſideration

consideration for their services*! And while they are modest or prudent enough to make the public voice their director, in the employment of such as afford the town the highest entertainment; it is surely a strange absurdity, to suppose that men, in the least acquainted with business, should be unequal to the care and conduct of their property in a theatre.

If to this plea should be opposed an imaginary circumstance, industriously propagated about the town; viz. that the profits of the theatre this season have been greater than that of former years; and therefore actual experience ought with prudent men to prevail over speculative reasoning: Harris and Rutherford make answer, that, though it is at present impossible for them to ascertain what the profits of the season will be, they are sufficiently authorised to deny the fact: which is all the satisfaction they can at present give the reader as to this particular. For, however injuriously they have been treated by Messrs. Colman and Powell, they do not think themselves at liberty, without their consent, to expose the receipts and disbursements of the theatre, even were it in any case judged necessary.

* It may not be improper to observe here, that Mr. Colman's not stipulating for such a consideration, when he accepted of the nominal directorship of the theatre, is a corroborating proof that it was never intended he should take more trouble on himself than Harris or Rutherford: as, had it been otherwise, he would certainly have been as much entitled to a salary for managing, as Mr. Powell was to his salary for acting. Unless indeed Mr. Colman's known disregard to pecuniary emoluments may be supposed to have induced him to make a present of his services to his brother-patentees. For it will hardly be supposed, by persons convinced of the *conscious rectitude* he boasts of, that he could have any sinister views to answer by his unrequested officiousness.

At the ſame time, nevertheleſs, they cannot neglect this occaſion of gratefully expreſſing the higheſt ſenſe of the obligations conferred on them by the town, in its generous approbation of the moderate efforts exerted for its entertainment at Covent-Garden theatre this ſeaſon.

They ſhould think themſelves as highly undeſerving ſuch approbation, if they could on their part approve of thoſe little artifices, which have too frequently been made uſe of, to betray the publick into an appearance of applauding what in reality they were ſo candid as reluctantly to condemn; artifices that have been ſometimes carried to the utmoſt extravagance, to the prejudice of the proprietors, and diſguſt of the town.

If the art of theatrical management indeed conſiſt in the practice of ſuch petty expedients, to betray the confidence and impoſe on the judgment of the publick; — if it conſiſt in forcing dull performances and unpopular performers on a patient audience; the majority of which are introduced merely to keep the reſt in countenance; — if it conſiſt in keeping news-paper ſcribblers in pay to defend groſs partialities, to apologize for wilful neglect, and to enhance the feeble efforts of ignorance and inſufficiency; Harris and Rutherford confeſs they are unequal as averſe to the taſk of theatrical management. Nay, they muſt be ſo frank as to ſay, that they ſhould never have hazarded their property on the ſucceſs of ſuch an undertaking, had not they conceived it might have been conducted to advantage on a more liberal plan.

But if a ſincere deſire of contributing to the real entertainment of the publick, joined to a determined reſolution to take every juſt meaſure conducive to that end, may be ſuppoſed to qualify men long attached to the ſtage, aſſiſted by perſons of known experience and abilities, for the management of a theatre, they flatter themſelves they will not be found incapable of ſuperintending their property in that of Covent-garden,

equally

equally to their own emolument, and the ſatisfaction of the publick: under whoſe auſpices therefore, they beg leave to take refuge, and to ſubſcribe themſelves that publick's

Moſt obliged, and moſt devoted,

Humble Servants,

T. HARRIS.
J. RUTHERFORD.

THE END.

A

TRUE STATE

Of the DIFFERENCES subsisting between

THE PROPRIETORS

OF

COVENT-GARDEN THEATRE;

IN ANSWER TO

A False, Scandalous, and Malicious MANUSCRIPT LIBEL, exhibited on Saturday, Jan. 23, and the two following Days; and to a PRINTED NARRATIVE, signed by T. Harris and J. Rutherford.

By GEORGE COLMAN.

LONDON,

Printed for T. BECKET, in the Strand; R. BALDWIN, in Paternoster-Row; and R. DAVIS, the Corner of Sackville-street, Piccadilly.

MDCCLXVIII.

Although the following State of our Case has been drawn up by Mr. COLMAN, I desire to be considered as equally responsible for its Contents.

WILLIAM POWELL.

ADVERTISEMENT.

Feb. 10, 1768.

ON Thurſday laſt, after I had begun to prepare theſe Papers for the Preſs, my friend Mr. Rice, between whom and Mr. Rutherford a very ſerious difference had that day been brought to a happy concluſion, intreated me, in the moſt earneſt terms, at leaſt to ſuſpend my Publication; as he had yet hopes, by his preſent influence with Mr. Rutherford, to accommodate our differences. I conſented, and went the next morning to Richmond, where I received the following letter from Mr. Rice, the contents of which induced me to reſume my thoughts of publication; and indeed, rendered it incumbent on me to expedite it as much as poſſible; which I hope will be ſome apology for the apparent haſte and inaccuracy of the following Narrative. The attention due to it muſt, however, depend upon facts. Mr. Rice's letter is as follows; and is publiſhed at his own requeſt.

" Dear Colman,

" YOU may remember that I acquainted you before you went out of town, that the moment the affair of laſt Thurſday was over, I thought it a very proper opportunity to avail myſelf of the ſituation I then ſtood in, and told Mr. Rutherford the only advantage I would wiſh to make of the many advantages I had then given him, would be to render myſelf the inſtrument of bringing about a thorough reconciliation in the Theatre: Mr. Rutherford replied, that nothing in the world would give him greater pleaſure; and that he ſhould be the happieſt man living if thoſe diſputes were once ſettled. From the many compliments Mr. Rutherford paid me on this occaſion, and the very conciliating diſpoſition he was then in, I really was weak enough to believe him ſincere. I ſaw him the ſame evening at the Playhouſe, and we agreed to meet the next day at Mr. Harris's in Surry-ſtreet. If you recollect, I begged you not to proceed in your Publication. I went to Mr. Harris's at the time appointed, and to my great ſurprize found only Mr. Harris, who made an apology for Mr. Rutherford's not being there, but ſaid that Mr. Rutherford would meet me any where in the evening, if I would leave word where I was to be found. I mentioned the Bedford Coffee-houſe. Mr. Harris's converſation and mine was rather general, as I told him that my buſineſs was with Mr. Rutherford; that I thought I had a claim upon that gentleman, and meant to uſe it to make all the Patentees friends; and that I ſhould make a point of Mr. Rutherford's uſing his influence with *him* to bring about a reconciliation of all parties. Though Mr. Harris did not ſeem ſo well diſpoſed to a compromiſe as Mr. Rutherford, yet he did not give me the leaſt reaſon to expect the *manœuvre* of this morn-

morning. In the evening I went to the Bedford Coffee-House, and found the inclosed note * for me there; and when I went home I found a duplicate of it: I did not go to Mr. Rutherford's this morning, but waited to see him in Villiers-Street. In the mean time, the Publick Advertiser was brought me as usual, when, to my very great astonishment, I saw their Narrative advertised. Mr. Rutherford came at the time appointed in his note. It was with great difficulty I could keep my temper with him; and I told him, in the presence of Mr. Allen and a Hairdresser, that I did intend to say a great deal to him, but that the very disingenuous manner he had dealt with me, had put it out of my power to have any thing to say to him or his friend Mr. Harris; adding, "Had you told me, or even sent me word yesterday, that my interfering was quite unnecessary, as your Case was to be published this morning, I am sure I could not have been in the least offended; but, instead of that, you consented to confer about an accommodation, and concealed your intention of publishing your Narrative: Such disingenuous treatment from you I thought I did not deserve. I now renounce you both for ever, and think you a couple of people capable of doing every thing that is bad." He said, he was very sorry for my ill opinion of him; but declared, notwithstanding what had passed, that any thing I had to say in this dispute, should have more weight with him than the remonstrances or arguments of any other person. I intend to come to Richmond, and dine with you to-morrow."

Saturday Evening,
Feb. 6, 1768.

I am, Dear COLMAN,

Most affectionately yours,

WOODFORD RICE.

* Mr. RUTHERFORD's Note.

"*Mr.* Rutherford's *most friendly compliments wait on Capt.* Rice.—*Was extremely sorry that he could not wait on him in* Surry-Street *to-day*;—*but will be very happy to see him in* Newman-Street, *to-morrow at ten, to breakfast.*

"*If that should prove inconvenient to him, and he should not hear from him, will call in* Villiers-Street, *about twelve.*"

Friday Evening,
9 o'Clock.

INTRODUCTION.

BEFORE I enter upon my Narrative, it may not be improper to acquaint the Publick with the reafons that have induced me to give them this trouble; and to fhew them that filence muft have been interpreted as a tacit acknowledgment of guilt in myfelf and Mr. Powell, who could not forbear to reply to the moft grofs and open calumnies, if we entertained a proper regard for our reputations, and wifhed to be confidered as men who held their good name "as the immediate jewel of their fouls."

Contempt of flander is indeed an heroick quality, and confcious innocence is the fureft antidote to its poifon. But there are circumftances wherein the world has a kind of right to arraign our conduct; not to mention, that it requires a very uncommon fhare of philofophy not to refute fcandal and malice, when we have the means of juftification in our power.

On Saturday, the 23d of January, we were informed that there lay for publick infpection, at Slaughter's Coffee-houfe, in St. Martin's-lane, a manufcript paper, wherein we were charged, in direct terms, with the moft infamous collufion in the management of the Theatre; a collufion intended to promote our own feparate and private emolument, and confequently to defraud Meff. Rutherford and Harris, the joint-fharers in the property.

Notwithftanding thofe two gentlemen had for fome preceding weeks betrayed the moft hoftile difpofition toward us, and endeavoured to render the management of the Theatre as hazardous as it is troublefome; yet that they, or their friends, fhould think it advifable to appeal to the Publick, by drawing up a partial ftate of our differences, feemed almoft incredible. In the evening, however, we repaired to the Coffee-room, and on a perufal of the libellous paper in queftion, we found it to be more replete with falfhood, fcandal, and malice, than it had even been reprefented to us; nor indeed was it poffible for any perfon, not minutely acquainted with the facts, to difcern how much they were diftorted in order to give the leaft colour to the charges brought againft us.

* The paper was conceived in the following terms:

A short state of the case between THOMAS HARRIS, JOHN RUTHERFORD, GEORGE COLMAN, *and* WILLIAM POWELL.

" THE patents, &c. of Covent Garden Theatre, being to be sold, pursuant to the direction of the late Mr. Rich's will; Thomas Harris and John Rutherford formed a design of purchasing them, and entered into a treaty with the executors of said Rich; but afterwards thought proper to invite some one person conversant in these matters to share with them in the purchase; one who might strengthen the company as a performer, and assist them in the management thereof.—They pitched upon William Powell the player, to whom the plan was communicated.—At first his only objection was, an article subsisting between him and the patentees of Drury Lane Theatre; but he afterwards, in his own mind, got over that difficulty, and proposed a friend of his, George Colman, a dramatic author; and urged the expediency of admitting him into the treaty, by greatly exaggerating the service he would do in assisting the Theatrical Management.—At length Harris and Rutherford agreed, not only to the admission of William Powell, but also his friend George Colman. Whereon, March 31st, 1767, these four gentlemen entered into articles of agreement between themselves, for concluding such purchase; and Harris and Rutherford were impowered to conclude the treaty they had begun on their own account, and the four parties were to be equal sharers.

" April 1st, Harris and Rutherford contracted for the purchase, and 10,000 l. the property of Harris and Rutherford, was deposited on that day, the remainder of the 60,000 l. to be paid the 1st July next ensuing. And soon after, all four parties met on the subject of their future articles, when Colman proposed to have the uncontrouled management, which Powell approved; but Harris and Rutherford, (being exceedingly surprised) warmly, and reiteratedly, protested they never would consent to any other articles, but such as would give them a perfect equality of power with Colman. Whereupon, after much deliberation, the four gentlemen, on 14th May last, signed an agreement, by which Colman was appointed acting manager, with this restriction, that he was from time to time, *and at all times*, to communicate and submit his conduct, and the *measures* he should intend to pursue, unto Harris and Rutherford, who were impowered to put a negative on any such measure which they should jointly disapprove.

" Powell was to give his advice and assistance when required.

" May 28th, Powell was engaged as an actor for seven years, at 400 l. a year, and a clear benefit; and if any performer, or player, should be allowed more, then an additional charge was to be allowed Powell, so as to exceed such *future* player. 2d, None of the parties should have any concern in any other theatre.

July 1st, The contract with Rich's executors was compleated, and the money then paid; but Colman and Powell were deficient in their proportion of purchase-

* It was indorsed, " A narrative of transactions relative to Covent Garden Theatre." And at some distance was written, *in another hand*, " For the use of the gentlemen of Slaughter's Coffee-house;" which words were also written on the margin of the several leaves of the manuscript.

money 9,000l. whereupon the ſum was borrowed, and Harris and Rutherford were ſecurities for Colman and Powell.

" No ſooner were they in poſſeſſion of the theatre, &c. but Colman began to act in a moſt arbitrary and inſolent manner; he ſcarce even deign'd to conſult Harris and Rutherford in any one meaſure; he received and rejected dramatic pieces; engaging and refuſing performers, &c. &c. without ever mentioning them; and at the firſt rehearſal, inſtead of introducing them to the performers, (which were fixed by him) he forbad them the ſtage, thereby endeavouring to prevent Harris and Rutherford from ſuperintending his conduct.

" After much expoſtulation, Colman aſſented to a weekly meeting, when he, Colman, was to propoſe ſuch plays, &c. and all ſuch other meaſures, as he thought might be proper for the week following. This meeting was obſerved by all parties for a few weeks; yet Harris and Rutherford could not help ſeeing, that Colman did not, at the meetings, propoſe all the meaſures he intended to purſue; and that when he knew the ſentiments of Harris and Rutherford, he generally acted in contradiction to them.

" Fearing to throw the whole affair into confuſion, Harris and Rutherford bore this kind of treatment, and repeated inſults, from Colman, without reſenting them, as he ſtill kept, in ſome degree, the rank of decency, and did not openly diſclaim their negative power; but on Thurſday, the day of October, he, in the higheſt terms, and moſt aggravating language, openly diſclaimed their right of reſtraining him, and ſolemnly declared, that to them he would never diſcloſe his future intentions; and that he would be reſponſible to the public, not to them, for the conſequences. Though *they knew of no cauſe*, yet this appeared to them the language of paſſion or madneſs; therefore, he was again, the ſucceeding day, aſked, if he would comply with his articles, and propoſe his meaſures, &c. Accordingly he again refuſed; and being expoſtulated with again and again, he on Saturday night declared, he would have no further communication with either of them; yet, notwithſtanding all this, on Sunday November the 1ſt, he wrote them a letter, (vide copy marked A) wherein he recognizes the articles, recapitulates the ſubſtance of them, and promiſes to adhere to them for the future: but (ſtrange as it muſt appear!) he ſo ſoon forgot his promiſe, that without having either *heard from*, or ſeen ſaid Harris and Rutherford, he, on the very ſame night, and without their knowledge, or giving them the leaſt notice thereof, ſummoned all the principal performers to a tavern, and there harangued them, and acquainted them, that he was inveſted with the abſolute management of the theatre, and entirely ſuppreſſed Harris and Rutherford's right of controuling him. This conduct obliged Harris and Rutherford to read publicly on the ſtage, on Monday morning, the whole articles, when Colman, in appearance, took ſhame to himſelf, and declared, in the preſence of Woodward, Smith, and Gibſon, &c. that he would ſubmit his meaſures to their controlment.

" During theſe tranſactions, it was impoſſible for Harris and Rutherford to be blind to the ridiculous partialities of Colman; yet they were of opinion, the cauſes of them were of ſuch a nature, that as men, they could not take notice of them; but the inſtance was ſo glaring, in caſting the play of Cymbeline, that, *in duty to the public*, Harris and Rutherford were obliged to take notice of it. What can be more diſtreſſing to men who have the leaſt ſenſe of honour or generoſity, than being obliged to diſcloſe the foibles and infirmities of others! yet a conciſe and true declaration of this ſort, Harris and Rutherford find to be the only way that can clear themſelves and others, from the imputation Colman has no leſs artfully than wickedly put upon them. The uncommon effrontery Colman has exhibited in making a ſuppoſed partiality to a certain actreſs, his great plea of complaint, and even carrying his aſſurance to ſuch a height, as to ſummons the friends of Harris and Rutherford, with others who were ſtrangers to them, and then wickedly depending on alarming and frightening them with falſe accounts of their conduct reſpecting the above lady, the *narrators* hope will be deemed a ſufficient occaſion for their ſetting that affair in a clear light.—Colman had conceived a violent pique and reſentment againſt the above-mentioned actreſs, the cauſe of which ſhall not be here related; but whilſt others are conjecturing, Colman muſt burn with ſhame, as that lady's conduct had ever been moſt unexceptionable in the theatre. Harris and Rutherford could not help frequently expoſtulating on the injuries he delighted to inflict on her; in particular, although the whole theatre deemed her, as the company then ſtood, (*Mrs. Yates being not then engaged*) the propereſt perſon to have the part of Imogen in the play of Cymbeline: yet he, (Colman) at once to gratify his reſentment to her, his luſt of acting contrary to the opinion of Harris and Rutherford, and his ſpirit of gallantry, inſiſted moſt heartily, that that character ſhould be given to a certain *young* actreſs; but with much ado he was ſhamed from his purpoſe, and he pledged his honour, that the firſt mentioned lady ſhould have the character.—It may not be improper to remark here, that after Mrs. Yates was engaged, *it was univerſally acknowledged*, that no perſon in our company could ſtand in competition with her for that character.—Yet, after the conceſſions that were made by Colman, November the 2d, and the reconciliation that enſued, it was agreed by all parties, that as Colman had abſurdly made that play a matter of diſpute, it ſhould be laid aſide, and not got ready for exhibition, until approved by Harris and Rutherford; but notwithſtanding that, he has ſince, viz. on the day of thought proper to perform it in oppoſition to their written diſapprobation.

" On the day of Colman took upon him, without the knowledge or conſent of Harris and Rutherford, to contract with Mr. and Mrs. Yates as players, viz. Mrs. Yates at 500 l. per annum, and Mr. Yates at 10 l. a week, with benefits.—Though the merit of theſe two performers would at firſt ſight induce one to think, that this ſtep, though irregular, was for the intereſt of the proprietors, yet, in fact, it has turned out *very much the reverſe*; nay, it had been viewed in that light three or four days before by all the proprietors, who jointly declared their ſentiments againſt ſuch a ſtep.—Colman engaging them in this clandeſtine manner may be accounted for from the following motives:—Firſt, *being very avaricious*, and Powell and himſelf being in perfect colluſion from firſt to laſt, he, by giving 500 l. to Mrs. Yates, made an addition to Powell's ſalary of 100 l. per annum; and again, by doing an act of ſo much conſequence, without the knowledge of Harris and Rutherford, and even againſt their conſent; he thereby meant to prove to the whole theatre, that he could and would act without conſulting or regarding them; and, in conſequence, expoſe Harris and Rutherford to deriſion. That this was a powerful motive, was plain from his immediate ſubſequent boaſtings—" That he had made this engagement on his own authority."—The real loſs ſuſtained by this meaſure cannot be eſtimated at leſs than 1500 l. which may be thus made appear: The ſalaries of capital performers, that were before engaged, and now rendered uſeleſs, the addition of Powell's ſalary, the incredible

expence

expence of dresses for Mrs. Yates;—add to this, a loss which has been exceedingly heavy, though it cannot be ascertained, incurred by Colman's neglecting his duty in reviewing and getting up all other plays, except those in which the two abovementioned performers, and William Powell, had capital characters; endeavouring by such most unjustifiable means, to give colour and sanction to the step he had taken.

"The following is a proof of the glaring degree to which Colman and Powell carried their collusion. At a meeting, on or about the 20th of November last, between all the four parties, Colman proposed taking out of the treasury a sum from 64 to 70l. on account of the insertion of a few lines in the Rehearsal, and his proposed alterations of King Lear; to all which Powell concurred immediately, and warmly; but Harris and Rutherford remonstrated, that it would be more proper to take the money after the tragedy was produced. Yet, notwithstanding, Colman did take out of the treasury that sum, between 64 and 70l. since which Harris and Rutherford have neither seen nor heard of the play. At the very same meeting, Powell, notwithstanding his articles to the contrary, earnestly insisted on the equity of his having the benefit arising from some one night, on account of his not going to Bristol theatre in the ensuing summer; to which proposal Colman immediately and warmly concurred. At length, to avoid dispute, Harris and Rutherford consented that Powell should go to Bristol theatre, but Colman refused; notwithstanding he urged the propriety of giving him a benefit, and flew into a great heat and passion because Harris and Rutherford would not consent to it.

"What aggravates, to Harris and Rutherford, the very extraordinary expences for dresses, &c. is, that Colman has taken upon him, with some sinister view or other, to deposit a great part of the wardrobe, amounting to a very large sum, in the house of Mr. Powell, instead of the place appointed for that purpose in the theatre; and Powell, in the most insulting terms, refuses to bring them to the proper place, though applied to by letter.

"Through Mr. Colman's ill conduct, in the management of the theatre, in measures pursued without the knowledge, or against the consent, of Harris and Rutherford, *they verily believe* a loss not less than 3,500l. has been sustained; which sum will not appear extraordinary, to those who know the very large receipts and disbursements of a theatre, and which altogether depend on the management thereof.

"It is not so much the abovementioned *losses* that alarm Harris and Rutherford, as that they plainly perceive the ultimate views of Colman and Powell to be their total exclusion, which they purpose to bring about, by setting them, Harris and Rutherford, at so great a distance, and keeping them so ignorant of their own affairs, that they may not be able to see through the future operations of Colman and Powell; and which will unquestionably be directed for the purpose of their private emolument.

"From the foregoing case, how very unjustifiable the behaviour of Colman and Powell is, in persisting (in despite of honour and honesty, and the known original intentions of Harris and Rutherford, and their present subsisting articles) to *mismanage* their property, every reader is left to determine."

On Monday, January 25, the Prompter of the Theatre, a very honest and intelligent man, who thought himself a party aggrieved by that part

part of the paper which related to a *certain young actress*, waited on Meff. Harris and Rutherford, who both difclaimed any knowledge of fuch a paper having been expofed till within two hours before that inftant; adding, however, *that they could eafily conjecture the quarter from which it proceeded, and feeming to afcribe the publication of it to the intemperate zeal of fome particular friend.* Upon their expreffing a defire to fee the paper, the Prompter produced a copy of it; which Mr. Rutherford turned over with much apparent eagernefs and curiofity, and joined with Mr. Harris in a requeft that it might be left in their hands. It was fo, and the Prompter departed; but not without previoufly declaring, that, fince the Paper did not appear to have their fanction, he hoped they would not be offended, if he took every occafion of teftifying his contempt and deteftation of that part of it, which was relative to a *certain young actress.*

Within lefs than an hour after this interview were received, by the feveral perfons to whom they were addreffed, the two following Letters:

To GEORGE COLMAN, *Efq. and* W. POWELL, *Efq.*

" GENTLEMEN, Monday 25th Jan. 1768. One o'Clock.

" THIS inftant we are inform'd of a paper having lain for publick infpection at Slaughter's Coffee-houfe ever fince Saturday morning. We think it proper to inform you, that we were greatly furprized at the above information, being intirely ignorant that fuch a paper was left there, until now acquainted therewith. Are,

Gentlemen, Your humble Servants,

T. HARRIS.
J. RUTHERFORD."

To the Mafter of SLAUGHTER'*s Coffee-Houfe.*

" SIR,

" I AM aftonifhed to hear you have expofed a paper (indorfed " A narrative of tranfactions relative to Covent Garden theatre") that was by accident left on Saturday morning on one of your tables.

" You are required immediately to feal it up, and fend it by the bearer.

Your humble fervant,

Surry Street, Monday morning, Jan. 25th. T. HARRIS."

On the fame day, and the next morning, the following notes paffed between Mrs. Yates and Mr. Harris:

" MRS. Yates prefents her compliments to Meff. Harris and Rutherford. She has feen a copy of a paper in their names left on the table of a Coffee-houfe, wherein they are pleas'd to complain of heavy loffes fuftained in confequence of her engagement at Covent-Garden. She begs to know whether it has their fanction; becaufe, if it has, Mrs. Yates, in juftice to herfelf, will give it a publick anfwer: if, if, on the other hand, some busy meddling scribbler has made free with their names; she will treat it with the most silent contempt."

Monday, Jan. 25th, King-street, Covent-Garden.

" MR. Harris presents his compliments to Mrs. Yates : flatters himself no one but the enemies of Mr. Rutherford and Mr. Harris, or those to whom they are entirely unknown, can pretend to suppose them capable of so very mean an action as to submit a case in which they were any ways concerned, to the opinion of a Coffee-room."

Surry-street, Tuesday morning, 26th January.

The same evening Mr. Harris told the Prompter, that it was hoped he would not be too violent or acrimonious in his language concerning the written paper left at Slaughter's; for although Mr. Rutherford and himself utterly disclaimed the circulation of it, yet as malevolent persons would undoubtedly attribute it to them, such language from him would be considered as an indirect affront to themselves.

The next morning, January 26, the following Advertisement appeared in the Publick Advertiser and the Gazetteer :

" A WRITTEN paper, wherein our names were inserted, having been exhibited at Slaughter's Coffee-house, we think it necessary to declare, that it was done without our consent or knowledge.

T. HARRIS.
J. RUTHERFORD."

N. B. This was also in Publick Advertiser of 26th January.

On perusing the above Advertisement we sent them the following Letter :

To J. RUTHERFORD, *Esq. and* T. HARRIS, *Esq.*

" GENTLEMEN, Jan. 26th, 1768.

" WE are very glad to find that you have thought proper publicly to declare the written paper, so injurious to our characters, was exhibited at Slaughter's coffee-house without your knowledge or consent; but we could wish, that you had, at the same time, disavowed being the authors of it; for if you do not disclaim that also, it is a matter of great indifference to us, whether it was circulated by yourselves or your friends. We think it incumbent on you to add such a declaration to your advertisement, as otherwise, we must still consider the paper as coming directly or indirectly from yourselves. We are, &c.

G. COLMAN.
W. POWELL."

To

To this Letter we received the next day the following anſwer :

To G. C. *and* W. P. *Eſqs.*

" GENTLEMEN,

" YOU are in an error if you imagine the advertiſement we publiſhed was intended for any other purpoſe, than to contradict the inſinuations which we heard had been thrown out, that we were the circulators of the paper exhibited at Slaughter's coffee-houſe, which we neither were directly or indirectly.

" Whenever we think proper to acknowledge ourſelves the authors of any production, it will be from the ſuggeſtions of our own minds, and not at the requiſition of any man whatſoever. We are, Gentlemen, yours, &c.

Surry-ſtreet, Wed. morn. Jan. 27th, 1768.

T. HARRIS.
J. RUTHERFORD."

In the Gazetteer and Publick Advertiſer of the ſame day appeared this Advertiſement :

Speedily will be publiſh'd,

" A TRUE ſtate of the differences ſubſiſting between the proprietors of C. G. Theatre, in anſwer to a falſe, ſcandalous, and malicious libel, highly injurious to the characters of Meſſ. Powell and Colman, exhibited on Saturday, Jan. 23d, and the two following days, at Slaughter's Coffee-houſe, in St. Martin's-lane.

By GEORGE COLMAN."

In the ſame papers of the next morning appeared the following :

" GREAT enquiries having been made after the Author of a paper left by accident at Slaughter's Coffee-houſe on Saturday laſt, any perſon who has publickly expreſſed himſelf to have been injured by the exhibition of that paper, may receive information concerning the Author, by applying to either of us.

T. HARRIS, Surry-ſtreet.
J. RUTHERFORD, Newman-ſtreet."

In conſequence of the above Advertiſement Mr. Bury, an attorney of King's-Bench-Walks, Temple, waited on Mr. Harris from us, for the information promiſed in the advertiſement concerning the author ; againſt whom (he told Mr. Harris) he had orders to commence a proſecution. To this Mr. Harris replied, that Mr. Bury did not come within the deſcription of the advertiſement, and that neither himſelf nor Mr. Rutherford could give an anſwer to any perſon's attorney.

The ſame day, an hour or two after, Mr. Bury waited on Mr. Harris a ſecond time, and delivered the following Letter :

To J. RUTHERFORD, *and* T. HARRIS, *Eſqrs.*

" GENTLEMEN,

" *WE have publickly expreſſed ourſelves to have been injured* by the libellous paper left at Slaughter's coffee-houſe; we now *apply to you* for the information you have to-day promiſed by publick advertiſement concerning the author.

G. COLMAN.
W. POWELL."

At this interview another gentleman, whom Mr. Bury ſuppoſed to be Mr. Rutherford, was preſent. This application, however, proved as fruitleſs as the former. Mr. Harris ſaid that they could ſend no written anſwer, nor any verbal meſſage: and upon being aſked what was the intention of their advertiſement, again replied, that they could ſend no written anſwer, nor any verbal meſſage. Mr. Bury then obſerved, that Mr. Powell and Mr. Colman *had publickly declared themſelves to have been injured by the paper*; and aſked if thoſe gentlemen, on a perſonal application to them, (Meſſ. Harris and Rutherford) might receive the information promiſed in the advertiſement. Mr. Harris replied, that they could ſend no other anſwer than what he had juſt before given.

Upon enquiry after the manner in which the Paper came to be exhibited at Slaughter's Coffee-houſe, the fact ſtands thus.

On Saturday, January 23, about noon, as Mr. Julliott, of Henrietta-ſtreet, apothecary, was ſitting in a box at Slaughter's Coffee-houſe, reading the news-papers, two young gentlemen entered the room, and deſired to paſs him. They paſſed him, and ſat down in the ſame box. After ſome time they pulled out a book and a written paper, and called for pen and ink. The bar-maid aſked, if they did not want any *paper?* They replied in the negative, and uſed the pen and ink in making inſertions or eraſements, or both, in the manuſcript which they had juſt before produced. In about a quarter of an hour they departed; and Mr. Julliott, after having ſufficiently amuſed himſelf with the news-papers, happened to caſt his eye on the manuſcript, which lay on the table. At firſt he thought it might have been by *accident left* there; but ſeeing it indorſed, "A Narrative of Tranſactions relative to Covent-Garden-Theatre," took it for granted, from the title, that it was left there for general inſpection, and accordingly made no ſcruple to examine the contents of it; on peruſal of which he told the ſervant in the bar, that it related to the diſputes among the Covent-Garden Managers; and that he ſuppoſed that the two Gentlemen who had juſt left the room, were no other than Meſſ. Rutherford and Harris.

Mr. Julliott does not recollect that the Paper was alſo indorſed, "For the uſe of the Gentlemen of Slaughter's Coffee-houſe," at the time that he ſaw it. Mr. Preſton, the maſter of the Coffee-houſe, is confident that neither he, nor any of his people to the beſt of his knowledge or belief, added thoſe words; and a gentleman (whoſe name will be mentioned if the fact is diſputed) who peruſed the paper about two o'clock the ſame day, well remembers that it was then ſo indorſed.

It has been contended that this Paper was nothing more than the heads of a Law-Caſe, left by accident on a Coffee-houſe table. The ſubſtance of it may have been, and I believe has been, laid before Counſel;

but the very form of it, as it now ſtands, pronounces it to have been drawn up with another view. Be that as it may, it lay for three days together in the Coffee-room, as common and publick as the Daily Advertiſer; ſo that the characters of the parties vilified were equally injured, whether it was left there by accident or deſign. We have ſtiled this paper "a falſe, ſcandalous, and malicious libel." We repeat thoſe expreſſions, confident that every diſpaſſionate reader of the following narrative will aſſent to the juſtice and propriety of the terms in which we have ſpoken of the Paper. The charges of colluſion and fraud affect us too deeply to be mentioned without ſome emotion. As to the virulence and malignity of the ſtile, and the words "effrontery," "aſſurance," "void of honour and honeſty," &c. &c. we take them from whence they come, and conſider them as mere paper and packthread to make up the parcel of ſcandal. The expreſſions of contempt thrown on us on account of ſuppoſed talents, which we ſhould be proud to poſſeſs, give us no pain; and we look on the terms *William Powell the Player*, and *George Colman a Dramatick Author*, as mere words of courſe, like John Rutherford, and Thomas Harris, *Eſquires*.

Conſcious of the integrity of my actions, and that the more my conduct was known to the world, the more fully it would be juſtified, I have in ſome peeviſh moments, when provoked to the uttermoſt, threatened to appeal to the Publick; but on cooler reflection was always averſe to ſuch a proceeding; and it is not without the greateſt regret that I am now driven to publiſh letters, and lay open converſation. The reader indeed will immediately perceive that they are not ſuch as paſs between friend and friend; or, if they were, that I have not been the aggreſſor in this inſtance. My letters have been ſubmitted by my profeſt adverſaries to Counſel, and the moſt caſual expreſſions dropt careleſsly in the flow of *table-talk* have been urged againſt me as ſolemn reſolutions. Theſe very letters and converſations are alſo the baſis of the black charges brought againſt me; ſo that I do but meet the Libeller on his own ground; on which, if he uſes the arms of Falſhood for the attack, I have certainly a right to have recourſe to Truth for my ſhield.

A TRUE

A

TRUE STATE, &c.

ABOUT the latter end of laſt March, Mr. Powell deſired to ſpeak with me on particular buſineſs, and acquainted me that a couple of gentlemen had applied to him to become a joint purchaſer with them of the patents, &c. of Covent-Garden Theatre; that he could never think of embarking in ſuch an undertaking with two inexperienced young men, who perhaps might know but little of the world, and certainly could know nothing of the internal management of a Theatre; that he had not ſufficient confidence in his own abilities to ſuppoſe himſelf equal to the taſk; but that, if he had my aſſiſtance, he did not doubt of ſucceſs; concluding with a requeſt of my permiſſion to mention me to the two gentlemen, and at the ſame time declaring, that, unleſs I were included in the treaty, he ſhould decline the propoſal, fearing it might terminate in his ruin.

Mr. Powell, with my conſent, mentioned my name to the gentlemen. They objected to taking in a fourth; but Mr. Powell declared his opinion, that they would reap more profit from a fourth ſhare with Mr. Colman's aſſiſtance, than from a third without him.

A few days after, on another interview between Mr. Powell and the gentlemen, they told him that they had conſidered of his laſt propoſal; in conſequence whereof they had made proper enquiries concerning Mr. Colman, and found his acceſſion to the partnerſhip ſo deſirable a circumſtance, that they returned Mr. Powell many thanks for making ſo happy an improvement of their plan, and deſired to have a meeting on the occaſion with Mr. Colman as ſoon as poſſible.

March 30. 1767. Accordingly, on the thirtieth of March, all the four parties met at Mr. Powell's. Mr. Colman being asked by Meff. Rutherford and Harris, whether he had confidered of the affair which Mr. Powell had at their defire communicated to him, replied, that he thought himfelf much obliged to Mr. Powell for his good opinion, but could not think of availing himfelf of fuch a partiality, unlefs they concurred in Mr. Powell's fentiments; and that if they were not of opinion that Mr. Colman's advice and affiftance were effential to the welfare of the undertaking, he would by no means think of becoming a party concerned merely from the nomination of Mr. Powell. Their reply to this declaration was conceived in the moft handfome terms; and, to convince Mr. Colman that the many civil things they faid on this occafion were not words of courfe, they afterwards recurred to this fubject, and repeatedly affured him of the great value they fet upon his acceffion to their fcheme, independent of every other confideration than their thorough perfuafion of the advantage that would refult from it in the fuccefs of the Theatre. Being late, it was agreed, after a fhort converfation on the intended purchafe, that *the four* fhould have a fecond meeting the very next night, in order to come to a final determination, and to enter into articles of agreement among themfelves concerning the purchafe. Juft before their parting, Mr. Colman, addreffing Meff. Harris and Rutherford, obferved, that managing a Theatre was like ftirring a fire, which every man thought he could do better than any body elfe. "Now, "gentlemen, faid he, I think I ftir a fire better than any man in England." To this they replied, "Do you manage; let Mr. Powell act; all we "want is to have good intereft for our money."

March 31. The next evening we met again; and, at the defire of Meff. Rutherford and Harris, Mr. Hutchinfon, a gentleman whom they particularly recommended for his abilities and integrity in his profeffion, attended with an inftrument prepared for us to fign. By this agreement, Meff. Rutherford and Harris were empowered to treat for the purchafe of the Theatre, &c. at any fum not exceeding 60,000l. forty thoufand to be raifed by themfelves, and twenty by Colman and Powell, whom they were to affift with a loan of 5000l. each, to make up their proportions of the purchafe-money. On Mr. Hutchinfon's reading over this inftrument, when he came to that part of it wherein it was recited, that the four parties *fhould be jointly and equally concerned in the management of the Theatre*, Mr. Colman begged leave to interrupt him, and told him it was a fettled point that he (Mr. Colman) was to be invefted with the direction of the Theatre; whereupon, to his very great furprife, Meff. Harris and Rutherford declared, that they never had the leaft intention of forming fuch an article; that, as they had the

the turn of the fcale in the purchafe-money, they could not think of lowering their confequence in the purchafe, &c. Mr. Colman faid, that he took it for granted (as he moft certainly did) that this matter had been previoufly underftood on all fides; and that he had plainly declared to Mr. Powell, on his firft application, that he would never be concerned in the purchafe, unlefs he fhould be invefted with the theatrical direction. Mr. Powell allowed the truth of this affertion, but *faid nothing in approbation of Mr. Colman's claim of the management*; and Meff. Rutherford and Harris, feeming fenfible of his fuperior utility in this province, but unwilling to acknowledge that fuperiority under their hands, the agreement was at laft figned by each of the four parties, in the form in which it had been originally prepared.

This tranfaction paffed on the thirty-firft of March, though the manufcript paper exhibited at Slaughter's, as well as the printed Narrative, for the fame purpofes of fallacy that will appear through the whole, place it much later.

The next morning I fet out for Bath, where I remained till the third or fourth of May. In the mean time, Meff. Harris and Rutherford contracted for the purchafe, depofited 10,000l. and agreed for the payment of the remainder on the enfuing firft of July. April 1.

I have been extremely particular in the above relation, becaufe I am refolved not to fuppres or difguife the moft minute fact, that may feem in the leaft favourable to Meff. Rutherford and Harris. For a like reafon I fhall fupprefs all my reflections and refolutions declared to particular friends, till I had the pleafure of feeing thofe gentlemen again, which was not till fome days after my return to town; the fame melancholy occafion that fummoned me from Bath fooner than I propofed, having alfo fecluded me from company. In the mean time, Meff. Rutherford and Harris expreffed the greateft impatience for an interview with me, *apart from Mr. Powell.* On the very firft conference, they teftified, in the warmeft terms, their earneft defire that I fhould be invefted with the theatrical direction, complaining at the fame time of the indifcretion of Mr. Powell, to whom they afcribed the notoriety of our intended purchafe, which was now become the common talk of the town, and our names inferted in every news-paper. May, 1767.

It is but juftice to Mr. Powell to declare, that it afterwards appeared that, from the peculiar circumftances of Mr. Rich's will, his widow thought herfelf bound in honour to declare to fome other candidates for the purchafe, that fhe had given notice to the truftees of her having contracted for the fale. This circumftance, as well as the neceffary applications by each of the parties to their friends for the requifite fum, tended to make the treaty publick. One part of Mr. Powell's conduct on this

2 occafion,

occaſion, though it certainly contributed to betray our operations, is very much to his honour, though the written Narrative, with the ſame ſpirit of candour that animates the whole, endeavours to interpret it to his diſadvantage, and to tax him with a ſcandalous breach of faith to the Patentees of Drury-Lane Theatre. The truth is, that the very day after Meſſ. Rutherford and Harris had applied to Mr. Powell, he communicated the matter to Mr. Lacey, who very kindly aſſured him of his beſt wiſhes, and a continuance of the ſame friendſhip which he had ſhewn to Mr. Powell on every former occaſion. Mr. Garrick was then at Bath.

May, 1767. In a word, Meſſ. Harris and Rutherford now inſiſted on the expediency of inveſting Mr. Colman with the direction of the Theatre, and were extremely ſollicitous to ſettle this point before Mr. Powell's ſummer-engagements ſhould call him out of town. To this end it was propoſed, that we ſhould each of us conſider of that and ſome other neceſſary articles, and throw our thoughts concerning them upon paper. I did ſo; and Mr. Harris, in a few days, took occaſion to call upon me one morning *alone*. I then ſubmitted to him a paper containing a ſketch of ſome articles, and, among the reſt, one relative to the management, which was as follows:

"That George Colman ſhall be inveſted with the theatrical direc-
" tion, that is to ſay, the power of engaging and diſmiſſing actors, ac-
" treſſes, ſingers, dancers, muſicians, &c. &c. of receiving or re-
" jecting ſuch new pieces as ſhall be offered to the Theatre; of caſting
" the plays; of appointing what plays, farces, &c. ſhall be performed;
" together with the ſole conduct of all ſuch things as are generally un-
" derſtood to be comprehended under the dramatick and theatrical pro-
" vince: *Provided always that the ſaid George Colman ſhall not do any act*
" *contrary to the opinion of* ANY TWO *of the other partners in writing ex-*
" *preſſed: and that if the four partners ſhall be equally divided in opinion,*
" *that the matter in diſpute ſhall be referred to two arbitrators, one for each*
" *party; and if the ſaid two arbitrators cannot agree, that they ſhall join in*
" *appointing one other arbitrator, whoſe opinion ſhall be deciſive and final.*"

On peruſing the above rough draught of an article, Mr. Harris did me the honour to obſerve, that the footing on which I was willing to reſt my management was extremely generous, and agreeable to the candour which I had ſhewn in my whole tranſaction with them; but that he thought it neceſſary that I ſhould have *more power* than ſuch an article would give me; that he had the greateſt eſteem and regard for his friend Mr. Rutherford, whom he thought a very honeſt, good-natured man, but that there were no two perſons in the world more likely to differ in

opinion

opinion than himſelf and Mr. Rutherford ; ſo that if Mr. Rutherford and Mr. Powell ſhould happen to join in oppoſition to any of my meaſures, an obſtruction in the management muſt neceſſarily enſue ; that his brother-in-law, Mr. Longman, had told him, that he and Mr. Rutherford *might* differ, but that he and Mr. Colman *never could*; he could wiſh, therefore, that I would agree to put Mr. Powell entirely out of the queſtion, and to place the whole *negative power* in himſelf and Mr. Rutherford, and then (added he) "*You will always be ſure of* ONE *of us.*"

Although this ſcene paſt entirely between Mr. Harris and me, yet the truth of it does not reſt on my bare aſſertion ; for I recapitulated all theſe circumſtances to Mr. Harris ſome weeks ago at the Theatre, in the preſence of Meſſrs. Rutherford, Powell, and Hutchinſon. He allowed the facts, but added, that he had been miſtaken in me. I returned him the compliment.

I fell into the ſnare, and ſaid, that if Mr. Powell could be prevailed on to aſſent to ſuch an article, I had no objection to it. Mr. Rutherford, in this inſtance, as in every other, implicitly ſubmitted to the opinion of Mr. Harris. Mr. Powell, however, ſhewed *great repugnance* to giving me the direction. On my expoſtulating with him alone on this ſubject, and reminding him of his firſt application to me, and my declared reſolutions at that period, he frankly confeſſed that *he had been adviſed to the contrary*; but that, on reflection, he returned to his original intentions, and was content to put his fame and fortune into my hands.

This is the *real* hiſtory of the article reſpecting the management, which was accordingly ſigned by all parties on the 14th of May, and is as follows : May 14.

" WHEREAS Thomas Harris, John Rutherford, George Colman, and William Powell, by certain articles of agreement, dated the 31ſt Day of March laſt, did agree to purchaſe of the Repreſentatives of John Rich, eſq. deceaſed, two patents for exhibiting theatrical performances, and the ſeveral leaſes of Covent-garden theatre, and the rooms, buildings, conveniences, furniture, cloaths, ſcenes, decorations, muſic, entertainments, and all things belonging to the ſaid Theatre ; and the ſaid Thomas Harris and John Rutherford were thereby authoriſed to treat for, and purchaſe the ſame, at a ſum not exceeding 60,000 l. and the purchaſe-money was to be advanced by the ſaid parties equally, and they were to become jointly poſſeſſed of, and intereſted in, the premiſſes ſo to be purchaſed, and were to be jointly and equally concerned in the management of the ſaid Theatre, and were to execute proper deeds and inſtruments for that purpoſe, when the ſaid purchaſe ſhould be completed. And whereas the ſaid Thomas Harris and John Rutherford have accordingly contracted and agreed with the repreſentatives of the ſaid John Rich, for the purchaſing of the ſaid patents, leaſes, premiſſes, and things, at and for the ſum of 60,000 l. and ſuch purchaſe is to be completed on the firſt of July next : Now the ſaid ſeveral parties, having peruſed and fully underſtanding the purport and contents of the ſaid contract, do approve of, and confirm the ſame. And having also, in consequence thereof, taken into their consideration the Management of the said Theatre, they have, for the better and more easy conducting of the business thereof, as well as for their joint and equal benefit and advantage, agreed, and do hereby mutually declare and agree, that, notwithstanding any thing contained in the said agreement already made between the said parties, the said George Colman shall be invested with the Direction of the said Theatre in the particulars following, viz. that he shall have the power of engaging and dismissing performers of all kinds; of receiving or rejecting such new pieces as shall be offered to the said theatre, or the proprietors thereof; of casting the plays; of appointing what plays, farces, entertainments, and other exhibitions, shall be performed; and of conducting all such things as are generally understood to be comprehended in the dramatic and theatrical province. And that the said Thomas Harris and John Rutherford shall be desired to attend to the comptrolment of the Accounts and Treasury, relative to the said theatre. *Provided always, and in as much as the said Thomas Harris and John Rutherford will have leisure to attend to the affairs of the said theatre, and the said William Powell is to be engaged as an Actor or Performer upon the Stage (for which purpose separate articles are intended to be entered into between him and the other Parties), in which his time and attention will be chiefly employed and taken up, so that he will not be able to apply himself in managing the business of the theatre; it is therefore hereby further agreed, that the said George Colman shall, from time to time, and at all times hereafter, communicate and submit his conduct, and the measures he shall intend to pursue, unto them the said Thomas Harris and John Rutherford; and in case they shall, at any time, signify their disapprobation thereof, in writing, unto the said George Colman, then and in that case the measures, so disapproved of, shall not be carried into execution, any thing before contained to the contrary thereof notwithstanding. Yet, nevertheless, with respect to the said William Powell, it is intended and agreed, that he shall, at all times, give his advice and assistance relative to any part of the business of the said theatre, when thereunto desired by the other parties.* Witness the hands of the said parties, this 14th day of May, 1767.

Witness,
JA. HUTCHINSON.

T. HARRIS,
JNO. RUTHERFORD,
G. COLMAN,
WILL. POWELL.

It was at the time of the above conference that Mr. Harris first mentioned Mrs. Lessingham, expressing his desire that she might be engaged at our Theatre; but at the same time requesting that *I would not be alarmed* on this occasion, as he did not wish to have her considered with more partiality than any other Performer, either in regard to the allotment of Parts, or proportion of Salary. I very readily acquiesced in receiving her, provided she could, with any propriety, disentangle herself from her engagements at Drury-Lane; and even declared a propensity to shew her any reasonable partiality, which I did not doubt was all that would be required.

May 28. On the 28th of May was signed another Article, chiefly relative to Mr. Powell's engagement as a Performer, of which more shall be said in the sequel. By the same Article it was also agreed, that none of the parties should be concerned in any other Theatre; and that

that any of them producing any new Play, Farce, Entertainment, or other exhibition, or any alteration of an old Play, Farce, &c. ſhould have the common emoluments accruing to Authors from ſuch productions, excluſive of the other parties.

July 1.

On the firſt of July the contract with Mr. Rich's executors was compleated, and the money then paid; but in order to effect the purchaſe, the ſum of Fifteen Thouſand Pounds had been borrowed, viz. *Six* Thouſand for Mr. Rutherford, *Five* for Mr. Colman, and *Four* for Mr. Powell; for ſecuring which ſum of Fifteen Thouſand Pounds the three fourth ſhares of Meſſrs. Rutherford, Harris, and Colman, were mortgaged, Mr. Powell having made over the firſt claim on the whole of his ſhare to the perſon of whom he had borrowed the other Eleven Thouſand of his proportion of the purchaſe. By this account it will appear, that Meſſrs. Harris and Rutherford were not called upon to make good their original contract; that Mr. Powell raiſed One Thouſand Pounds more than his contract required; that Mr. Colman was not obliged to them, directly or indirectly, for a ſingle ſhilling; that he was a joint ſecurity with them for the Four Thouſand advanced to Mr. Powell, and that Mr. Colman raiſed, independent of the patent ſecurity, One Thouſand Pounds more than Mr. Rutherford, who brought but *Nine* Thouſand into the common ſtock to Mr. Colman's *Ten*. It will ſcarcely be contended that Mr. Colman could not raiſe 5000l. on his ſhare; at leaſt it cannot be urged with a good grace by Meſſrs. Harris and Rutherford, who often aſſured him how much more eaſily the money was raiſed by the uſe of his name: not that theſe particulars would be worth mentioning, if it were not to ſhew that there is not the moſt minute circumſtance in this whole tranſaction, wherein the writer of the libellous Narrative has not attempted to deceive.

July.

The purchaſe being completed, Mr. Powell, who came up to town on purpoſe to ſign the writings, returned to Briſtol; and Meſſrs. Rutherford and Harris ſet out on a tour of pleaſure to Buxton, Matlock, Harrowgate, &c. leaving all the care of preparing the Houſe and Company for the enſuing ſeaſon to Mr. Colman. Before their departure Mr. Colman ſhewed Mr. Harris a paper containing a ſketch of the alterations then propoſed in the Company, and lamented the want of his and Mr. Rutherford's and Mr. Powell's aſſiſtance and advice in the courſe of his future operations during the ſummer; on which occaſion Mr. Harris, with much politeneſs and apparent ſincerity, replied, that it was of no conſequence, ſince they ſhould have nothing to do but to approve what he propoſed.

July.

The many cares attending my new ſituation are not eaſily imagined; but I was embarked on a ſea of troubles, and was resolved to make way, if possible, with chearfulness and resolution. After a most laborious and unwearied attention to the business of the Theatre for six or seven weeks, having settled every thing in the best manner I was able, I went down to Bristol, and communicated all my proceedings to Mr. Powell, who expressed great satisfaction at the measures I had taken. In about three weeks I returned to London, expecting to meet the two other gentlemen returned from the North, and to find them in the same good humour which they maintained before they set out.

Sept. In this, however, I was cruelly deceived. They received me in the coldest manner, and instead of seeming sensible of the trouble I had taken, broke out into complaints of their not having been made duly acquainted with all my proceedings. The only material steps I had taken, were the receiving a Comedy of Dr. Goldsmith, and making an engagement with Mr. Macklin; neither of which, especially the latter, I should have done merely on my own judgment, had it not been almost next to impossible to have obtained their opinion; as their motions were quite uncertain, and I never received a letter from either of them, till a few days before I went to Bristol. Of these measures, however, they declared their entire approbation; but before we parted, Mr. Rutherford took a fresh occasion to differ with me, and rendered a very trivial concern a matter of great importance, *by peremptorily insisting* that the arrangements which I had made in that instance should not be pursued. What rendered this unexpected opposition the more shocking to me, was, that it was introduced by observations rather unfavourable to the rest of my conduct, for which I was weak enough to expect a very different return. Mr. Rutherford continued to *insist* on my waving the point, which at that time was not only unadvisable, but impracticable. I professed, therefore, that I should most steadily adhere to it; and on those terms we parted.

It is but justice to Mr. Harris to declare, that he acted with the utmost candour on this occasion. He undertook to be a mediator, and used every method to conciliate the mind of each party. At length Mr. Rutherford was prevailed on to wave his opposition, by the interposition of his friend, and the following letter from me.

"DEAR SIR,

"WARM as I am, I can see and feel the impropriety of it in myself, as well as in others; and I do assure you, that I have entirely forget any little asperities on your part, and am most heartily sorry for whatever might have the air of violence on mine. Any arguments in favour of the contested point, arising from considerations of generosity, prudence, or necessity, I leave to your cool reflection; and I now request it as a favour, that all which hath passed on this subject, may be buried in silence and oblivion; and that you will give a chearful assent to the measure, if it be

for

for no other reaſon than merely to oblige your friend, who will lay hold of every occaſion to convince you, that he is, with the utmoſt regard and eſteem, dear Sir,

Your moſt affectionate humble ſervant,

Sept. 8, 1767. G. COLMAN.

To J. RUTHERFORD, *Eſq.*

The charges of my forbidding them the ſtage on the firſt rehearſal, and neglecting to introduce them to the performers, if they did not betray a ſtrange diſpoſition to jealouſy and ill humour, would ſcarce deſerve notice. All I can ſay is, that I never intended to give them the leaſt offence, or to be deficient in any due attention to them; nor did they themſelves at that time ſeem to entertain ſuch ſuſpicions: for it was on the ſtage that Mr. Rutherford and I firſt met after the above little difference: it was on the ſtage that he took me by the hand, aſſuring me that he was perfectly ſatisfied, and how ardently he deſired the continuation of a good underſtanding between us: to which I was ſo ſincerely inclined, that I concealed the whole tranſaction from Mr. Powell; and the curtain drew up on the 14th of September, with ſeeming content on all ſides, and the moſt entire harmony in the cabinet of the four kings of Brentford.

The above difference, however, proved to be a prologue to the ſcenes of diſputes that were to ſucceed. A day or two after our opening the Theatre, I found the two gentlemen there together, and Mr. Harris, to my great ſurprize, in very ill humour. On enquiring the cauſe, he ſaid that an inſult had been offered to Mrs. Leſſingham; concerning which he would make no farther enquiry, as he *would not know* from whom it proceeded. That lady having been engaged on the recommendation of Mr. Harris, I verily believe that Mr. Powell, as well as myſelf, was inclined to treat her not only with reſpect, but even with partiality, as far as it could be conſiſtent with the general intereſt. I ventured therefore to vouch thus much, and deſired to know the preſent matter of complaint, which proved to be her having been aſſigned a dreſſing-room up ſtairs. I told him that this was the firſt word I had ever heard of it: that my attendance on matters merely dramatick and theatrical, was more than ſufficient buſineſs for me; and that the care of dreſſing-rooms, ward-robe, &c. had been kindly undertaken by Mr. and Mrs. Powell. Upon this he took me apart, and repeated his expreſſions of diſſatisfaction with more warmth than before. My ſecond anſwer was no other than the firſt; whereupon Mr. Harris in ſome meaſure turned the converſation, by deſiring that Mrs. Leſſingham might have the part of Imogen. I told him that, as the Caſt Book then ſtood, it was allotted to Miſs Ward. He ſaid that Mrs. Leſſingham could play it as well. I did not deny but ſhe might; adding, that all the buſineſs

Sept.

then aſſigned to Miſs Ward muſt be underſtood to be merely on ſuppoſition; for that as I had never ſeen her play, ſhe might perhaps upon trial appear unfit for it; and that I had given her the part of Imogen, merely on account of the youth and innocence of her figure, which I thought very ſuitable to the character. I added at the ſame time, that, as a friend to Mrs. Leſſingham, I would adviſe her never to play a line of Tragedy. This Mr. Harris in ſome meaſure allowed, but did not ſeem to think Imogen ſo much out of her ſphere as Belvidera, and ſome other tragick characters. I mentioned alſo, that as Mr. Powell had a capital part in the play, it would be but a reaſonable attention to him, to conſult how far it would be agreeable to him to caſt the play in that manner: but Mr. Harris ſaw no occaſion for Mr. Powell's concurrence. This was all that paſſed on the ſubject; and this was the only time that ever the name

Sept. 16. of Miſs Ward was mentioned for the part of Imogen; nor was it then agitated on either ſide as a matter of contention between her and Mrs. Leſſingham. From this circumſtance the Publick may determine of the confidence that is due to the libellous author of the written Narrative; wherein, for obvious reaſons, mean as they are baſe, that young actreſs is brought forward as the object of diſpute. It is to be hoped, however, that theſe wicked inſinuations, falſe as they are ſcandalous, will not contribute to throw a ſtain on the character of a young actreſs, *whoſe conduct has* not only *ever been moſt unexceptionable in* THE THEATRE, but every-where elſe.

About the ſame period that the arrangement of Mrs. Leſſingham's dreſſing-room was taken into conſideration by Mr. Harris, his friend Mr. Rutherford took upon him to promiſe a ſeparate dreſſing-room for Mrs. Bellamy. Mr. and Mrs. Powell remonſtrated concerning the great want of room behind the ſcenes to no purpoſe. Mr. Rutherford ſaid he had promiſed; and if it coſt him 500*l.* to build new rooms, it muſt be done. In a word, both the ladies were obliged, and both the gentlemen were ſatisfied.

Sept. On Friday, Sept. 18, the Prompter ſurprized me, by acquainting me that Mrs. Leſſingham had returned the part of Neriſſa in the Merchant of Venice; and my ſurprize was redoubled a few hours after, by his putting into my hands the following letter:

"SIR,

"As I returned you the part of Neriſſa, I think it right to give my reaſon for it. I have as yet had no liſt of thoſe parts it is intended I ſhould play; when I have, and find I have an equal ſhare of good and bad, I ſhall have no objection to any, though the loweſt. I deſire you will acquaint the managers with this. I am, Sir,

Your humble ſervant,

J. LESSINGHAM."

To Mr. YOUNGER, *Prompter, Covent-garden.*

"Received the letter, of which this is a copy, Friday, September 18, 1767; but the letter itſelf has no date.

J. Y."

Piqued at the ſtudied inſolence of this epiſtle, but unwilling to reſent it on account of the quarter from which it proceeded, I ſubmitted the letter that very evening to Mr. Harris, who defended the propriety of it in ſuch terms as led me to ſpeak my thoughts very freely, both of the letter and its author. This was very highly reſented by Mr. Harris, by whoſe privity I then took it for granted the letter had been ſent; and I have ſince ſeen no reaſon to alter my opinion. He went directly to the Prompter, and ordered him to bring the Caſt Book to his houſe the next day. The Prompter did ſo, and delivered it to Meſſ. Harris and Rutherford, from whom, on the morning of Sunday the 20th of Sept. juſt a week after opening the theatre, I received the following letter:

"SIR, Saturday, 19 Sept. 1767.

"Upon examining the Caſt Book, we find ſeveral parts allotted to Mrs. Leſſingham, which we think improper for her to perform; and others omitted, which we think very proper for her ſphere of acting. In order to avoid miſtakes, we have either expunged or eraſed from the Caſt Book, the names oppoſite to ſuch improper parts, and deſire you will give directions to the prompter to inſert her name in lieu. There are, likewiſe, many parts of plays not caſt, which we think that lady very capable of performing, to the advantage of the theatre and herſelf, which we have ſubjoined to the liſt incloſed.

"In this, and in every circumſtance which we ſhall advert to, we ſhall endeavour to do juſtice to merit, at the ſame time that we ſhall carefully attend to propriety with reſpect to ourſelves. Are, Sir,

Your moſt humble ſervants,

T. HARRIS,
J. RUTHERFORD."

GEORGE COLMAN, *Eſq.*

"WE have deferred examining the generality of parts caſt, leſt we might interfere with the buſineſs of the theatre by detaining the book ſo long at one time; a future occaſion may preſent us with an opportunity of conveying to you our further animadverſions on that head. We are as before,

19th Sept. T. H.
J. R.

GEORGE COLMAN, *Eſq.*

	Part	Play
Theſe are in the Caſt Book.	Betty	Clandeſtine Marriage.
	Clariſſa	Confederacy.
	Imogen	Cymbeline.
	Belmour	Way to Keep Him.
	Lavinia	Fair Penitent.
	Flora	She Wou'd and She Wou'd Not.
	Lady Betty Modiſh	Careleſs Huſband.
	Sullen	Stratagem.
	Flora	Country Laſſes.
	Neriſſa	Merchant of Venice.

Lady

	Part	Play
	Lady Fanciful — — unlefs Mrs. *Bellamy* chufes it.	Provok'd Wife.
These not; but to be inferted.	Bizarre — — —	Inconftant.
	Lady Anne — —	Richard.
	Lady Dainty — —	Double Gallant.
	Leonora — —	Revenge.
	Amanda — —	Love's Laft Shift.
	Mrs. Conqueft — —	Lady's Laft Stake.
	Fidelia — —	Plain Dealer.
	Clarinda — — —	Sufpicious Hufband.
	Lady Harriet — —	Funeral.
	Berinthia — —	Relapfe.
Caft.	Florival — — —	Deuce is in Him.

" Thefe parts allotted to Mrs. Leffingham.

19 Sept. 1767. T. H.
J. R."

Here was an open act of hoftility; an act fo far from endeavouring to extenuate the infolence of Mrs. Leffingham, that it was plainly calculated to convince me that they were both determined on every occafion to countenance and fupport it. My anfwer, fent the fame morning, was as follows:

" GENTLEMEN,

" WITHOUT dwelling on the very grofs treatment which I have received from yourfelves and Mrs. Leffingham, I fhall beg leave to remind you, that while you have been confpiring to check my authority, you have exceeded the limits of your own. The article of agreement betwixt us, which invefted me with the theatrical management, empowered you jointly to object to my meafures, but not to prefcribe new ones of your own; and from the director of the theatre, to fink me into fomething lower than the prompter. You will find therefore, that in making erafements from the Caft Book, and figning a lift of parts allotted to Mrs. Leffingham, you have as little attended to the propriety you profefs, as to the refpect due to Your humble fervant,

G. COLMAN."

This anfwer was, I believe, the firft circumftance that ferved to waken them from the trance of defpotifm, into which their conftruction of the article relative to the management had thrown them. A *negative* power it left them, but gave them no *pofitive* one. They told me indeed at our next meeting, that two negatives made one affirmative. I allowed the truth of that logick; but told them, that *both together*, like the two letters in the word NO, they made but *one* negative. I taxed Mr. Rutherford alfo with want of candor on this occafion, for joining to infult me without fo much as inquiring into the merits of the caufe; reminding

minding him, at the ſame time, of the oppoſite conduct of his friend on a former occaſion. Mr. Harris then told me, he found I was an impracticable man, and deſired, or rather injoined me to put my ſhare to ſale. Mr. Powell, who till then had only lamented our diviſions in ſilence, was ſtartled at this propoſal, and frankly confeſt that he thought ſuch proceeding was injurious to our common intereſt. I told Mr. Harris that, finding I was become ſo diſagreeable a partner to himſelf and Mr. Rutherford, I ſhould retain my ſhare, on purpoſe to plague them. It was, I think, at this meeting, and on this occaſion, that Mr. Rutherford dwelling very much on the words *manly* and *gentleman-like*, I took occaſion to tell him, in a careleſs manner, that I had never in my life heard thoſe words ſo often repeated; but that I did not need his inſtruction how to behave either like a man or a gentleman. His reply to this was very violent, and ended with talking of *going out with him*, accompanying theſe laſt words with a ſtride towards the door. I told him I thought it rather extraordinary, that he was not contented with giving the affront, if any had been given; but that he alſo claimed the privilege of reſentment: however, that if he ſuppoſed I was to be terrified, he was miſtaken.—They then recurred to the paper in diſpute, and aſked if the liſt of parts contained in it ſhould be conſidered as admiſſible. I objected to all the tragedy, particularly Leonora in the Revenge; and added, that Mrs. Sullen belonged to Mrs Bulkley, and that Miſs Macklin was the original Widow Belmour. They again aſked, if I was inclined to oblige them. I told them my chief cauſe of offence was their having doubted that inclination, and having flown to acts of violence when gentle means would have been more prevalent. They then ſuddenly changed their tone and manner; Mrs. Leſſingham, ſorely againſt my judgment in many inſtances, was allowed the characters in queſtion; and we parted once more in tolerable good humour.

Such were the expoſtulations of Meſſrs. Harris and Rutherford, and ſuch were the injuries which I delighted to inflict on their favourite actreſs. But it ſeems, that I *had conceived a violent pique and reſentment againſt her, the cauſe of which ſhall not be here related.* Dark charges muſt, of neceſſity, be darkly anſwered; but whenever the lady, or her advocates, ſhall pleaſe to be more explicit, I promiſe to *ſpeak plainly* in my anſwer, if ſhe, or they, ſhall urge any thing of ſufficient importance to demand one at my hands.

I allow the charge of employing *news-papers to defend groſs partialities* *; for I was weak enough to mention Mrs. Leſſingham's having joined us, with the air of announcing a valuable acceſſion to the ſtrength of our company, by ſpecial paragraphs in the public papers. I muſt

* See Meſſ. R. and H.'s Narrative, p. 37.

alſo

alſo plead guilty to the charge of *forcing unpopular performers on a patient audience* *; for on the firſt night of her appearance, to prevent the mortification that her vanity muſt ſuffer from a thin houſe, in direct oppoſition to the opinion of Mr. Macklin, I ſupported her lame performance on the crutches of Love A-la Mode. I alſo prefixed the Stratagem, in which ſhe played Mrs. Sullen, to the Oxonian in Town, while its novelty was ſome recommendation to it. I had the more merit in theſe ſacrifices, becauſe they were made in direct contradiction to my private opinion. In the laſt inſtance, two ſtrong objections to the meaſure I purſued, ſtared me in the face: firſt, that ſhe played the part moſt wretchedly; and, ſecondly, that it was apparently injurious to a little piece, eſpecially one of ſo ſerious a caſt, to be performed after one of the lighteſt and pleaſanteſt comedies in our language.

Sept. But to return. From the moment after our meeting in conſequence of their memorable letter of September 19th, Meſſrs. Harris and Rutherford expreſſed the higheſt ſatisfaction at the conceſſions which I ſeemed diſpoſed to make, and were inceſſantly urging me to bring forward the play of Cymbeline, aſſigning as a motive, the very reaſon which they now urge for oppoſing the repetition of it, viz. that *it was frequently exhibited at Drury Lane* †. Mr. Powell alſo, being extremely attached to the character of Poſthumus, was deſirous of ſhowing himſelf in it, whoever might play Imogen. In this ſituation I could not have avoided exhibiting the play, however averſe, without diſobliging them all three, if Mr. Dall had not received orders to paint a new ſcene of Imogen's chamber; a ſcene which has ſince given the public ſo much ſatisfaction, but which then neceſſarily delayed the performance of the piece, into which it was to be introduced. Hence it will appear, that Mrs. Leſſingham, without any competition, had been avowedly in poſſeſſion of the part from the 19th of September, that is, within a week of opening the Theatre. On the 12th of October Mr. and Mrs.

Oct. Yates were engaged, the hiſtory of which tranſaction ſhall be given in its proper place. From that inſtant, I confeſs, that all my notions of Mrs. Leſſingham's playing the part in queſtion vaniſhed; for I could never ſuppoſe, that Meſſrs. Rutherford and Harris would be ſo blind to their own intereſts, or that Mrs. Leſſingham would entertain ſuch an overweening opinion of her own abilities, as to think of her entering into a direct competition with Mrs. Yates. However, I was ſoon undeceived; for on Thurſday the 29th of October, they roundly inſiſted on Mrs. Leſſingham's retaining the character, which I as roundly refuſed; but not without remonſtrating on the groſs partiality that would appear in ſuch a procedure; as well as the injuſtice to Mrs. Yates, and the af-

* See Meſſ. R. and H.'s Narrative, p. 37.

† Ibid. p. 6.

front

front to the public; for all which my reputation, *and chiefly mine*, would suffer. They treated these arguments with great contempt; upon which, finding nothing but further altercation likely to ensue, I abruptly left them; but I do most solemnly declare, that I did not then, or at any other time, *openly and avowedly disclaim their right to lay me under any restraint*; nor did I *declare, that I would never disclose to them any of my future intentions*.*

They were resolved, however, to carry this important point, if possible; and finding the *acting manager* inflexible, they not only tampered with Mr. Powell, but applied to Mrs. Yates, with whom they had a very long conference, in her dressing-room, that very evening, as will appear from the following letter, which they sent about an hour after they took their leave; and from which, together with Mrs. Yates's answer, it is not difficult to guess at the nature and subject of the conference itself.

" DEAR MADAM,

" BEING in the greatest degree desirous of proving to you, that we are not men of mere profession alone, we take the liberty to desire of you, in your note to-morrow morning, not only a favourable determination respecting the point in agitation, but that you will accompany it with such requests as will conduce to the advancement of your *Fame* or *Pleasure*; and our immediate answer thereto shall be the proof how much we are devoted to your desires. We are, dear Madam,

Your most humble servants,

Surry-street,
Thursday Evening, 29 Oct.

T. HARRIS,
J. RUTHERFORD.

" H. and R. beg the favour of your answer as soon as convenient in the morning, as we meet early on purpose to receive it."

Mrs. Yates's answer was as follows:

" GENTLEMEN,

" IT gives me great concern to be obliged to tell you, that I think it wholly inconsistent with my fame and interest, as well as my engagements to yourselves and the Publick, to consent to resign the part of Imogen to Mrs. Lessingham.—At the same time I cannot help adding, that it will distress me exceedingly, on this and every future occasion, if my mind is to be distracted by the different opinions of the several Gentlemen concerned in the management. I am, Sir, &c.

M. A. YATES.

To this she received the following reply:

" DEAR MADAM,

" WE have this instant received your favour—hope for your pardon for the trouble we have given you; and finding an application to you so ineffectual, you may dismiss all fears of our disturbing your mind by any future one. We are, and shall always be, Dear Madam, Your devoted humble servants,

Surry-street,
Tuesday morn. Oct. 30.

T. HARRIS."
J. RUTHERFORD."

* See Mess. R. and H.'s Narrative, p. 9.

Oct. 30. The next morning, while I was attending a rehearsal at the theatre, I received the following letter, to which I immediately returned the answer subjoined. From these it will appear, that Messrs. Harris and Rutherford were the first persons that threatened an appeal to the Publick, as they have, in fact, to our great astonishment, been the first who have made such an appeal.

"SIR,

"THE very gross manner in which you thought proper, yesterday, to conduct yourself, being so entirely repugnant to the articles we have entered into with you, as well as to the principles upon which you have verbally professed to govern yourself on a late reconciliation, we cannot suffer it to pass without informing you, that until you shall make the concessions due to us for such a notorious breach of good faith, we shall pursue a mode of conduct that will be influenced by the keen resentment you have inspired us with. Yet shall take no *unwarrantable* steps, nor any that we cannot justify to the Publick; who will most probably be acquainted with every part of our proceedings; and however your importance may suffer by your having overrated it, is a circumstance of which you are the sole author, and must therefore abide by the consequences.

Surry Street, Friday morning, Oct. 29th. — T. HARRIS. J. RUTHERFORD."

"GENTLEMEN,

"I NEVER did, nor ever will do any thing repugnant to our articles. The very gross manner in which you and Mrs. Lessingham have always treated me, obliges me to exert to the utmost the power those articles give me. Your keen resentment does not terrify me, nor ever shall, while I know I can justify my conduct to our royal master, the lord-chamberlain, and the publick; to all whom I am very willing to submit it.

Covent Garden, Friday morning, Oct. 29, 1767. — G. COLMAN."

This answer was received by Messrs. Harris and Rutherford, at the house of Mr. Powell, who, on every dispute, had always done every thing in his power to reconcile the parties to each other, and was then actually employed in exerting his best endeavours for that purpose. On the receipt of my letter, they both broke out into the most violent passion. One proposed *to attack my favourites*; and, in the first place, to dismiss Mr. Younger, (the prompter) *because he was useful to me in my business*. It then occurred to exercise their *negative power*, by prohibiting the exhibition of the Oxonian in Town, which was then in rehearsal; but that suggestion was, on second thoughts, opposed, because it would be doing me a favour, *as the piece would certainly be damned*.

Oct. 30. In short, the dispute now grew warm indeed, and the very same evening I received a letter from Mr. Harris, to which, on the very same evening, I returned an answer. The letter and answer are as follow:

SIR,

" SIR,

" YOU have afferted you never did any thing repugnant to our articles. Are you not by them obliged to fubmit every thing to our confideration? Have you done fo? We have neither of us any thing to do with Mrs. Leffingham's treatment of you; you fay it has been very grofs; I believe that, as well as your firft affertion, to be moft falfe. You feem determined, upon every difpute, to bring that lady's conduct into queftion, in order to avail yourfelf of it as a favourable plea with the Publick; now that I hold to be moft pitiful and infamous. You are very welcome, Sir, to my life, if you dare any how to hazard the taking it. I am going out of town this evening, at fix o'clock, and fhall return to-morrow about that time. If I hear nothing from you then, know, that your ungenerous, unmanly behaviour has made me upon every occafion of life your enemy.

Surry-ftreet, Friday noon, Oct. 30. T. HARRIS."

" SIR,

" AS Mrs. Leffingham has been the fole caufe of every difpute between us, it was very natural, as well as proper, for me to mention her name; and as to the grofs treatment with which I charged her, yourfelf, and Mr. Rutherford, I have the proofs of it under all your hands; fo that the falfhood, meannefs, pitifulnefs, and infamy, do not lie on my fide. As to my daring to take your life, God knows I dare not do it; but you and every other man fhall find that I dare on all occafions to defend my own: wherefore your profeffed friendfhip or profeffed enmity are in that refpect equally indifferent to

Great Queen ftreet, Friday evening, Oct. 30, 1767. G. COLMAN."

To THOMAS HARRIS, *Efq.*

The next evening Mr. Rutherford came to the theatre alone, and interrupting Mr. Powell during the play, in the midft of his anxieties in a new part, fpoke of me in fuch terms, that Mr. Powell thought it improper for us to meet; Mr. Rutherford, however, fending to defire to fpeak with me, I came to him. He faid that he had nothing to do with what had paft between Mr. Harris and me, but that he now came to inform me, *that I was no longer fole manager of that theatre*; of which publick notice would be given to the performers on Monday morning in the Green Room. I fmiled, and afked, if it was worth while to fend for me merely to communicate fuch a piece of intelligence? My indifference threw him into a violent paffion. He began to fwear: I walked away. He followed, and defired to fpeak with me: I refufed to have any thing further to fay to him. Oct. 31.

On the fame evening, juft after the play was over, the prompter received the following letter, to which he fent the refpectful anfwer annexed: but, refpectful as it was, *it gave the higheft caufe of offence* to Meffrs. Rutherford and Harris, from whom it drew the two letters here fubjoined to it, in which they have moft flagrantly exceeded the power given them by our articles, by affuming the power of difmiffion from the theatre.

" *Mr.* YOUNGER. SIR,

" YOU are to cauſe the incloſed paper to be immediately placed in a conſpicuous part of the Green-room, and to return us an anſwer, ſpecifying the preciſe time of your receiving the ſame. Sir, your humble ſervants,

Surry ſtreet, Oct. 31, 1767, 15 minutes paſt nine.

T. HARRIS.
J. RUTHERFORD."

The incloſed paper.

" UNTIL farther notice, any order from a ſingle manager of this theatre will be void and of no effect.

Saturday, Oct. 31ſt.

T. HARRIS.
J. RUTHERFORD."

" GENTLEMEN,

" AS I ſhall ever retain a proper reſpect for all my employers, I flatter myſelf you will, upon a moment's reflexion, not wiſh to ſo far embroil me in the unhappy diſpute at preſent ſubſiſting, as to inſiſt on my doing what muſt render me obnoxious to ſome of the parties concerned. I am with due reſpect, Gentlemen,

Your moſt humble ſervant,

Saturday, half an hour paſt 10.

JOS. YOUNGER."

" SIR,

" MR. YOUNGER, prompter of Covent Garden theatre, having given the higheſt cauſe of offence to us, we inform you, that we deſire he may have notice immediately of his diſmiſſion from our ſervice.

Surry ſtreet, Saturday Oct. 31, 1767. three quarters paſt 11 at night.

T. HARRIS.
J. RUTHERFORD."

To GEO. COLMAN, *Eſq.*

" SIR,

" THE ſalary paid to Mr. Younger, heretofore prompter of our theatre, ceaſed this day. You are therefore to forbear any future payments to him. We are,

Sir, your humble ſervants,

Saturday night, Oct. 31, 1767.

T. HARRIS.
J. RUTHERFORD."

To Mr GARTON.

Nov. 1. Mr. Powell, quite unhappy to ſee our differences running to ſuch a length, and deſirous to do every thing in his power to heal them, prevailed on a very intimate friend of mine, to accompany him the next morning to confer with Meſſrs. Rutherford and Harris on the ſubject, at the houſe of the latter, in Surry-ſtreet. I was far from wiſhing or deſiring that any friend of mine ſhould involve himſelf in my diſputes; and I now ſhudder to think, that this gentleman's kind and friendly interpoſition in my affairs, has very recently expoſed him to the moſt imminent danger of his life; the loſs of which would have deſtroyed all the future peace and quiet of my own, though I was no further acceſſary to what followed, than in being the unhappy and innocent occaſion.

The

The good offices of my friend and Mr. Powell proved wholly ineffectual. Meſſrs. Rutherford and Harris would hear of no other terms than an abolition of our preſent articles, and the execution of new ones, to be framed by their own direction. This was their *ultimatum*; and thus concluded this fruitleſs negociation of a treaty for peace. Being informed, by Mr. Powell, of their terms, I ſent them the following letter; in which I rejected their propoſal of new articles, by ſhewing that I meant to abide by thoſe at preſent ſubſiſting between us. Nov. 1.

" GENTLEMEN,

" I HAVE ſeen Mr. Powell; but after what has paſſed, a perſonal intercourſe between us cannot be expected. According to our articles I ſhall, from time to time, ſubmit to your conſideration the meaſures I propoſe to purſue in the management of the theatre; and any meaſure againſt which you ſhall jointly proteſt in writing, according to our articles, ſhall not be carried into execution.

Nov. 1, 1767. G. COLMAN."

Mr. Powell, finding their violence impoſſible to be mitigated, and thinking our property in the greateſt danger from their method of proceeding, now, for the firſt time, declared on my ſide: and foreſeeing the tumult likely to enſue, from the ſteps which Meſſ. Rutherford and Harris had declared their reſolutions of taking the next morning, thought it adviſable to prevent that confuſion as far as poſſible, by collecting as many of the performers as could be found that day, and laying before them a fair ſtate of the caſe. On this occaſion I related the ſtory in the plaineſt terms, read the letters which authenticated my narrative, and *fairly ſtated* the article relative to the management, reciting the *negative power* lodged with Meſſ. Rutherford and Harris, as well as the *poſitive* one veſted in me. *Read* the article, indeed, I could not, as I then had no copy of it. For the truth of theſe circumſtances, I appeal to all the parties then preſent. Nov. 1.

The next morning the tumult, ſo vehemently threatened on their part, and patiently expected on our own, actually enſued. About eleven o'clock Meſſ. Harris and Rutherford came on the ſtage, and interrupted the rehearſal. They aſked me, in an authoritative tone, if I had diſmiſſed Mr. Younger? I anſwered, No.—Will you diſmiſs him? No.—Some time after this, Mr. Rutherford ſaid, *Did not we* ORDER you *to diſmiſs Younger?*—ORDER me, *Sir!*—He immediately recanted the imperious word *order*, and was polite enough to ſubſtitute the gentler term *deſire*. He read the article in an audible voice on the ſtage to the performers, and afterwards aſked them if they would continue to act under Mr. Colman's management. They anſwered, YES. Nov. 2.

Mr.

Mr. Rutherford, misunderſtanding Mr. Smith, and ſuppoſing that he meant to aſſent to *their* direction, ſaid with great heat, *I am obliged to you, Sir; you are a gentleman.* Mr. Smith, however, being aſked by another performer to *what* he had anſwered *yes*, ſaid, that his YES implied an aſſent to act under Mr. Colman. *Why then, gentlemen,* ſaid Mr. Rutherford, *I will tell you one thing for your comfort; the Theatre will be ſhut up, for we ſhall apply to the court of chancery for an injunction for that purpoſe.* Soon after theſe tranſactions, Mrs. Mattocks fainted away, and I ran among others into the common Green-Room to her aſſiſtance. During my abſence, a difference aroſe between my friend and Mr. Rutherford, in conſequence whereof he and Mr. Harris left the ſtage, to which I returned a few ſeconds before their retiring to the great Green-Room.

Nov. 1. In leſs than half an hour, Mr. Powell came and told me, that Meſſ. Harris and Rutherford were inclined to a reconciliation, if I would but conſent to the diſmiſſion of Mr. Younger for five minutes. I replied, that provided his diſmiſſion ſhould be *literally* for five minutes, I would aſſent to it, ſince they thought the form ſo neceſſary to ſave appearances. I own I did not ſee why they were ſo well inclined to terms of peace, which they ſo peremptorily refuſed the

Nov. 1. morning before; but being very deeply affected at the part which my friend had taken in this affair, I was willing to do every thing in my power to promote a thorough reconciliation on all ſides. Accordingly I accompanied Mr. Powell into the great Green-Room; and being aſked by Mr. Harris *whether I would carry on the management without doing any thing contrary to the article?* I replied, to the beſt of my knowledge and belief, in theſe words: *I never* DID *any thing contrary to the article: I never* MEANT *to do any thing contrary to our article. All I deſire is to manage according to the article, and to have an uninterrupted exerciſe of the power which the article gives me.* Meſſ. Woodward, Smith, Gibſon, &c. were preſent: to them I appeal for the truth of this relation; and to them I appeal whether * *I apparently took ſhame to myſelf* on this occaſion.

The gentlemen, however, preſerved the decorums of reſentment to the laſt, and thought it neceſſary, on the very moment of our reconciliation, to commit a freſh violation of the article in queſtion, by writing the following note to the treaſurer of the Theatre:

"SIR,

"MR. YOUNGER being reinſtated as a prompter, you are to continue the payments of his ſalary as heretofore.

Monday,
Nov. 2, 1767.

T. HARRIS.
J. RUTHERFORD."

Mr. GARTON.

* See the printed Narrative, p. 11.

A reconciliation being thus effected, Mr. Harris desired, that as the play of Cymbeline had been so much the object of conversation and dispute, it might be laid aside for the present. Accordingly it was so; and the appearance of a good understanding among us was once more restored. But it was with the utmost difficulty that Mess. Harris and Rutherford preserved these appearances; for, instead of each of them favouring me with their advice in a friendly manner, they were continually sending me letters formally signed by them both. This was so directly opposite to their professions, that I expostulated with Mr. Harris on the subject, and told him, that I was in hopes we were now to have gone on as friends, without recurring, in every little instance, to the article, and reminding each other of the extent and limits of our respective power; but that if I saw him and his friend resolved to drive me, on every occasion, to the ground of the article, I would stand on that ground, and defend it to the last; for that I very well knew how much and how little power that article gave me. Mr. Harris replied, that we had all just power enough to plague each other; and, to convince me that he might easily be induced to exercise that power on his part, he added, that the breach between us had been so very wide, that it would not readily close again, without the most sincere desires and endeavours on all sides. I professed the greatest readiness to promote so desirable an end; but the gentlemen were so little inclined to meet me half-way, that they still continued the same mode of behaviour which had led me to the above-mentioned expostulation. In short, I plainly saw that they never would forget or forgive the transactions of the second of November. Nov. 2.

About the latter end of that month, while things were in this situation, Mr. Dall had finished the scene intended for Cymbeline. This redoubled Mr. Powell's impatience and anxiety to exhibit the play; and he applied to Mess. Harris and Rutherford (particularly the former) in the most earnest and submissive terms, to wave their objections to it. Mr. Harris was inexorable; Mr. Rutherford said, that we ought not to perform it *without asking Mrs. Lessingham's leave*; and referred the farther consideration of it to our next meeting. Novemb.

One little occurrence, that happened about this time, will perhaps shew the temper and complexion of these gentlemen, more than a matter of more consequence. The prompter had orders to send them every evening an account of the rehearsal settled for the next morning, and at the end of every week a plan of my arrangement of plays for the week ensuing. One of these notes was as follows:

SIR,

" SIR,

" MR. MACKLIN's withdrawing his farce having rendered it neceſſary to change the buſineſs propoſed for this week, Mr. Colman has ordered me to ſend you the freſh plan he has now *ſettled*. Your moſt humble ſervant,

J. Y."

This was addreſſed to Mr. Rutherford. The like note was addreſſed to Mr. Harris, only concluding with the word *fixed* inſtead of *ſettled*, as in the above. Mr. Harris was ſo touched at this expreſſion, that he aſked the prompter if the note was dictated by Mr. Colman. The prompter replied in the negative. Mr. Harris then commented on the word *fixed*; and obſerved, that if the buſineſs was *fixed* by Mr. Colman, there was no need of ſubmitting the plan of it to them. Being informed of this circumſtance, I enjoined the prompter to uſe the term *propoſed* or *intended* for the future; a caution which I believe he has ever ſince religiouſly obſerved.

Dec. The prompter's note of December the fifth ran thus:

Plan of Buſineſs propoſed for next Week.

Monday, Dec. 7th. (*By particular deſire*) Fair Penitent, and Fauſtus.
8th. Mahomet, and Muſical Lady.
9th. Philaſter, and Apprentice, for the Fund.
10th. Othello, and Love-a-la-Mode.
11th. Royal Merchant.
12th. Orphan, and —— Mrs. La Roche.

" SIR,

" MR. COLMAN has ordered me to ſend you the above plan of buſineſs, *propoſed* for the enſuing week, and to acquaint you that he has received notice from his Majeſty, that the firſt time he honours this theatre with his royal preſence, will be to the play of Cymbeline; for which reaſon he has ordered it to be put into rehearſal next week. I am, Sir, your moſt humble ſervant,

J. YOUNGER."

" P. S. THE author of the farce has been with Mr. Colman to withdraw it, and is to call for the copy on Monday morning; muſt therefore beg Mr. Colman may have it by that time."

Rehearſal on Monday next.

Mahomet at 10.
Muſical Lady at 12.

To J. RUTHERFORD, *Eſq.*

On the Tueſday and Wedneſday following, the letters here ſubjoined paſſed between us.

DEAR

"DEAR SIR,

"WE are very happy to receive your information, that we may ſpeedily expect the honour of his Majeſty's preſence; but we could have wiſhed his Majeſty had not been pleaſed to command Cymbeline.

As cogent reaſons might be given why that play ſhould not be performed; we ſhall never think you treat us fairly unleſs it is for the preſent poſtponed.

The appointment of the new opera for Friday next, we ſuppoſe, was an overſight in you; that being the * author's benefit at Drury Lane, would be deemed in the higheſt degree illiberal in us to produce a new piece on that night, and is a meaſure we cannot by any means aſſent to. It may be played for the firſt time on Thurſday next, as at firſt propoſed, or any other day (excepting as before) that you ſhall think moſt proper. We are, very cordially,

Dear Sir, your moſt humble ſervants,

Dec. 8th. 8 o'clock evening.

T. HARRIS.
J. RUTHERFORD."

"GENTLEMEN,

"YOUR intimation of *my not treating you fairly*, in the beginning of your letter, does not carry that air of cordiality which you profeſs in the concluſion of it. If there are ſuch cogent reaſons for diſobeying his Majeſty's commands, it would have been kind in you to have ſuggeſted them, as I muſt confeſs that none occurred to me which I durſt have ſubmitted to his royal notice. The opera cannot be ready on Thurſday, and muſt therefore be poſtponed till next week. I confeſs I never thought of the author's ſixth night; and as the firſt night of the opera ſtood for Friday, in the plan of buſineſs ſent you, it is pity it did not occur to you ſooner, as we ſhall probably be conſiderable ſufferers by the alteration; not to mention the great hardſhip on the compoſer, who is detained from Bath, to his great inconvenience.

I am, Gentlemen, your moſt humble ſervant,

Covent Garden, Dec. 9, 1767.

G. COLMAN."

"SIR,

"YOUR charging us with inconſiſtency in your *laſt*, can only be occaſioned by your haſte in reading it: *the air of cordiality which we profeſſed in the concluſion*, was in confidence that reaſons ſufficient would occur to you why Cymbeline ſhould be poſtponed.

Cymbeline not being (as we are informed) in the liſt of plays ſent to his Majeſty, and the ſcenery, decorations, caſting, &c. &c. not being yet fixed on, you may moſt certainly dare to ſubmit reaſons to his Majeſty's royal notice why Cymbeline cannot for the preſent be exhibited, if your paſſion to oppoſe our inclinations does not ſway you in a ten times greater degree, than your deſire to comply with what is pretended to be the choice of his Majeſty.

We are very ſorry the opera has not been got ready long ſince, and that the compoſer ſhould ſuſtain the injury of being kept in town; but ſtill remain of opinion, that if the opera cannot appear on Thurſday evening, as was at firſt ſettled, in regard to all our reputations, it cannot be produced before next Monday. We are, Sir,

Your moſt obedient ſervants,

Surry ſtreet, Dec. 9, 1767.

T. HARRIS.
J RUTHERFORD."

* Mr. Kenrick, author of the Widow'd Wife.

Dec. 10. The next day I met them at the Theatre, and fairly told them, that it was impoſſible for me to proceed in the management, while they ſo ſtudiouſly endeavoured to take every occaſion to make me uneaſy; that Cymbeline was in the liſt of plays ſubmitted to his majeſty at the beginning of the ſeaſon; but to convince them that I did not want to carry any points but ſuch as were conducive to the general intereſt, which I had always meant to purſue, I was reſolved to refer my conduct to thoſe who had embarked their property with us, and to their own friends in particular; that it was a wanton piece of cruelty to be perpetually trying to make my mind miſerable, when my labours rather deſerved their thanks; that I had been a voluntary ſlave in the conduct of their property; but that I was extremely hurt on their ſeeming inclined to treat me like a ſervant in every particular, except that of paying me wages.

They received this expoſtulation on my part with more temper and moderation than uſual. They declared that they had repeatedly, and on all occaſions, profeſſed how much they thought themſelves obliged to me; and no longer inſiſted on my repreſenting to their Majeſties that we could not obey their Royal Commands reſpecting the exhibition of Cymbeline. Mr. Rutherford, a day or two after, lamented the little bickering at this meeting, profeſſing the warmeſt cordiality towards me on his ſide, and vouching for the ſame ſentiments on behalf of his friend Mr. Harris.

Decemb. The rehearſals of Cymbeline were then continued without farther interruption or remonſtrance; and on Monday the twenty-eighth of December the repreſentation of the play was honoured with the preſence of their Majeſties; after whoſe departure the plays, Dec. 28. as uſual, were announced, and, among the reſt, Cymbeline again for the ſucceeding Thurſday, which occaſioned the following notes:

Monday Evening, 10 o'clock, Dec. 28th.

" Mr. HARRIS and Mr. Rutherford preſent compliments to Mr. Colman.—— Are much concerned that he directed Cymbeline to be given out this evening. Mr. Colman is well acquainted with their ſentiments on that ſubject, and how much it is their deſire that Cymbeline ſhould for the preſent be poſtponed. They doubt not he will conduct this circumſtance accordingly."

" Mr. COLMAN preſents his compliments to Meſſ. Harris and Rutherford, and is equally concerned and ſurprized at their repugnance to the repetition of Cymbeline; which is the more unexpected, as he mentioned to Mr. Harris his intention to have given it out for the next night, had it not been for the indiſpoſition of Mr. Powell. He flatters himſelf they muſt do him the juſtice to acknowledge the delicacy which has been uſed towards them in this point. As this play had unhappily been the cauſe of diſſenſion, it was laid aſide for a time, and at length reſumed and

performed

performed by the expreſs command of their Majeſties; to whoſe royal orders it would appear an indirect affront, to diſcontinue a performance, ſo likely to redound to the intereſt and credit of the theatre; at the ſame time that ſuch a conduct would be a publick confirmation of the evil reports of diſputes amongſt the managers. From this and many other conſiderations which their own good ſenſe will ſuggeſt to them, Mr. Colman flatters himſelf, that on cool reflection, they will chearfully concur with himſelf and Mr. Powell."

Dec. 29th.

"THE compliments of Mr. Rutherford and Mr. Harris wait on Mr. Colman. It is certain Mr. C. did mention his deſign of giving out Cymbeline to Mr. H. which exceedingly ſurprized him; but Mr. H. was very happy to hear it was to be deferred, both on account of the hatred he ever bears, and the unwillingneſs he has about him always to enter into altercation, and that there would be time to take Mr. R's opinion. The advice of their friends, joined to their cooleſt reflection, ſtill ſuggeſts to them the abſolute impropriety of repreſenting the play of Cymbeline again ſo ſoon as propoſed.

Their united and moſt ſincere wiſhes are, that this little difference may end here, and no more may ever ariſe; and that Mr. C. will, in ſome degree, pay attention to *their ſentiments*: ſeeing *that* will make their happineſs conſiſt in *entirely purſuing* thoſe of Mr. C.

Surry ſtreet, Tueſday one o'clock.

I was now credibly informed that, during the reheatſal of the play, wagers had been laid by ſome, who were of their *privy-council*, that Cymbeline would never be performed but *once*. We had been at great expence in the decorations, which were much approved; the play was eſteemed a creditable performance; and there was a great demand for places againſt any future repreſentation of it, not to repeat the duty incumbent on us to teſtify the utmoſt reſpect to the Royal Order by which it had been revived at our Theatre. The expences beſtowed on the play had been incurred with the conſent and approbation of Meſſ. Harris and Rutherford, in whom it was therefore the more unreaſonable to preclude our reaping the profits that might reſult from them. It appeared alſo impoſſible to keep terms with men, who were for ever ſeeking occaſions of diſpute. On theſe conſiderations I made no reply to the above note, and continued to advertiſe the play.

On Wedneſday, Dec. 30, paſt the following letters:

"SIR,

"WE abſolutely diſapprove the performance of Cymbeline at our theatre until further conſideration.

Wedneſday, Dec. 30, 1767.

T. HARRIS.
J. RUTHERFORD."

To GEORGE COLMAN, *Eſq.*

 SIR,

" SIR,

" Our right to forbid the representation of the above play we draw from the articles entered into by yourself and us; from your letter of the first day of Nov. last, (which runs thus, " Any measure against which you shall jointly protest in writing shall not be carried into execution); and from your solemn declaration, to the same purport, in presence of Mess. Woodward, Smith, Gibson, &c. on the 2d of the said November.

It is with the less regret that we write in this absolute manner, as our repeated desires, signified in the most respectful manner, have failed to make the least impression.

We are your humble servants,

Surry street, Dec. 30th.

T. HARRIS.
J. RUTHERFORD."

To GEO. COLMAN, *Esq.*

" GENTLEMEN,

" I HAVE just received your mandate, and will print it as a reason to the Publick for performing no play to-morrow.

Dec. 30, 1767.

G. COLMAN."

" GENTLEMEN,

" GREAT part of our boxes being taken for the play of Cymbeline, great damage must accrue to my property, by your method of proceeding; I must therefore apply to my friends and the Publick for redress. I most sincerely concur with Mr. Colman's sentiments above, and shall abide by his determination. I am,

Your most humble servant,

W. POWELL."

" SIR,

" IF you refuse to give directions for a play to-morrow night, we shall: whether they will be obeyed or not, is for future consideration. What you are pleased to call our mandate, can be no reason for shutting up the theatre, as you have the whole circle of the drama (Cymbeline excepted) from whence to elect a play.

Whatever damages may arise, we doubt not will be at your peril, as they can only ensue from your committing a breach of the most solemn and legal engagements.

We are, Sir, your humble servants.

Surry street, Wednesday Dec. 30, 1767,
4 o'clock, P.M.

T. HARRIS.
J. RUTHERFORD."

The following notes to the Prompter, with his minutes annexed, will shew the other particulars relative to this transaction:

" MR. Rutherford is greatly surprised that Mr. Younger did not, as usual, send him on Saturday last the plan of the ensuing week's business.——Desires that he will be careful not to omit it in future, and that he will this evening send to Mr. Rutherford the account of plays intended for the remainder of the week."

Newman-street, Wednesday noon, 30th Dec.

" N. B. I gave the plan of the week's business, as usual, on Saturday night to Sam. Besford, for both Mr. Rutherford and Mr. Harris; but sending for him on Sunday

Sunday morning, (before he had delivered them) and giving him a fresh one for each concerning the command, he thought the first of no consequence and burnt them.— I received the note above at one o'clock, and directly took the boy with me to Mr. Harris, where the porter said Mr. Rutherford was, and told him as above: he said I need take no farther trouble, he would explain it to Mr. Rutherford."

Second Letter.

"MR. Harris and Mr. Rutherford desire Mr. Younger would not fail to come down to them directly, if he can do it without injury to the representation of the opera; otherwise to come to them immediately after the opera is over."

Surry-street, Wednesday seven o'clock, 30th Dec.

"WENT directly; and on their asking what orders I had for to-morrow, told them Mr. Colman had informed me of their interdiction of Cymbeline, and that he would give no other order; but that Mr. Powell was at the house, and said he would give it out. I also told them the Merchant of Venice and Love-a-la-mode was designed for Friday, and Philaster for Saturday.——They gave me no order of any kind (except to send them word of what was to be rehearsed next morning)—but said they sent for me to have ordered a play, if Mr. Colman refused doing so, as his letter to them mentioned."

Dec. 31. Sent for by Mess. Harris and Rutherford to Surry-street: told them Mr. Powell ordered the giving out of the play last night, and sent himself the bills to the printer; and that Mr. Colman had given no theatrical orders since, though I breakfasted with him. J. Y. Prompter."

Open hostilities were now recommenced, and every effort of spleen and resentment was exerted to distress Mr. Powell and myself in the conduct of the Theatre. The *single cause of difference* was not, however, to be avowed; but * *repeated and aggravated causes* were to be supposed. The very day before, if I would but pay due attention to their sentiments, they would *intirely pursue* mine: but if not, they would not only oppose my sentiments, it seems, but endeavour to blacken and asperse both our characters with the charges of fraud and collusion: but when the reader has gone through these sheets, I will submit it to his decision, in what quarter there has been the most appearance of *collusion*.

They begun their first attack on the exchequer, and sent the following letter to the Treasurer of the Theatre: Dec. 30.

"*Mr.* GARTON. SIR,

"YOU'LL please to prepare your accounts for our inspection next Friday morning nine o'clock; and you are on no account to disburse any monies between this and that time, when you will have further directions.

SIR, Your most humble servants,

T. HARRIS.
J. RUTHERFORD."

Wednesday night,
Dec. 30th, 1767.

* See printed Narrative, p. 33.

Dec. 31. They next attempted to storm the wardrobe, as will appear by the following letters between them and Mr. Powell.

" SIR,

" WE desire you will present our compliments to Mrs. Powell, and acquaint her that we desire she will be pleased to send every thing in her possession appertaining to the Theatre to the wardrobe-keeper's-office, as we intend forthwith to examine the state of both wardrobes :—that you will also inform her how much we are obliged to her for the trouble she has hitherto incurred ;—but request she would not make any further purchase on account of the Theatre, as we shall give directions to the Treasurer to pay nothing but incidental charges, until previously consented to by us.

Your humble servants,

Surry-street, Thursday evening, 31st Dec. 1767.

T. HARRIS,
J. RUTHERFORD."

" GENTLEMEN,

" YOUR directions to Mrs. Powell cannot be complied with.—The unappropriated cloaths belonging to the Theatre have ever been kept out of the house under the care of one of the proprietors ; they are now in my possession, always free for your inspection, and forthcoming for the proper use of the Theatre. —However you may esteem Mrs. Powell for the care and trouble she has taken to herself concerning the property, I believe every gentleman that has made any advance in the purchase, when they are acquainted with it, will think themselves greatly obliged to her. Whatever your doubts may be for the safety of that part of your property in my possession, I know not; but this I know, that my conduct has hitherto been such, as not to have my honesty, or Mrs. Powell's, called in question : so that you may be assured, your property is ever safe with either of us.

Your humble Servant,

1st January, 1768.

W. POWELL."

To Mess. H. *and* R.

" P. S. Mr. Colman, by our articles, is invested with the theatrical as well as dramatic direction of the Theatre ; and the care of the women's wardrobe and that of the men's was desired by Mr. Colman to be taken by Mrs Powell and myself, without any objection made on your parts ; and therefore we shall pay every attention to the department for the good of the property and the pleasure of the publick : and you must give me leave to tell you, that you shall find I am not that *cypher*, even according to our present article, as you seem by your treatment to imagine.

I am yours,

W. POWELL."

Here it may not be improper to mention, that there had been some little altercation the preceding day, concerning a dress for Mrs. Lessingham ; that lady having taken great offence, from not being indulged with a gown and petticoat to play a chamber-maid in the Clandestine Marriage. *The directions to Mrs. Powell* we interpreted as an intended insult to her husband, and *the request to desist from further purchases* as a new mode

mode of diftreffing and embarraffing us in our affairs: but it was almoft impoffible to conceive or imagine that they meant to ground a charge of fraud or collufion in this circumftance, after they had, by the advice of Mrs. Rich, approved of keeping the unappropriated cloaths out of the wardrobe; and had not only joined with me in defiring Mrs. Powell to take the care of them, but agreed to purchafe Mr. Rich's dwelling-houfe adjoining to the Theatre for the refidence of Mr. and Mrs. Powell, allowing a very large abatement of the rent, in confideration of their re-ferving a room for the occafional meetings of the managers, and other apartments for the purpofe of lodging therein the unappropriated cloaths.

As Meff. Harris and Rutherford were now to ftand forward as acting managers, no circumftance, however minute, tending to im-prefs an idea of their importance, was to be neglected or over-looked. On the fecond of January therefore the Treafurer of the Theatre received the following: Jan. 2.

" Mr. GARTON. SIR,

" IT would have been proper in you to have advertifed the different tradefmen of the juft form of addrefs to their refpective bills——which fhould have been thus: *Harris, Rutherford, Colman, and Powell*; that being the form in which the patent, &c. is conveyed to us.

" The bills we now fend you, as far as we are concerned, you are at liberty to pay, with the refervation exprefs'd—excepting thofe which are differently fubfcrib'd.

Are, Sir, Your moft humble fervants,

Surry-ftreet,
Saturday, Jan. 2d, 1768.

T. HARRIS.
J. RUTHERFORD."

If the reader recollects the dialogue with the Prompter touching the word *fixed*, he will not be fo much furprifed at the above reprimand to the Treafurer. Proper orders, however, were immediately iffued to the tradefmen; and it is hoped that all who may hereafter be employed in the fervice of Covent-Garden Theatre, will remember to addrefs their refpective bills to Meff. Harris and Co.

The fame day I received the following:

" SIR,

" THERE is now fo much time elapfed fince you were *paid* for your *intended* alterations of the tragedy of King Lear, that we think proper to defire you forth-with to produce the play, or pay the fum you have received on that account *again* into the treafury of the Theatre.

" If you will take the latter propofed method, it will be by far the moft agreeable to

Your humble fervants,

Surry-ftreet,
Saturday Morning, 2d Jan. 1768.

T. HARRIS.
J. RUTHERFORD."

Knowing;

Knowing the unquiet ſpirits of the writers, I looked upon this letter,

Jan. 2. as well as that to Mr. Powell, to be nothing more than a freſh inſult; that their reſentments to me might keep pace with their inſtances of ſpleen to Mr. Powell. I muſt own I never expected to be called on for a juſtification of my character in a tranſaction of this nature; and I am very well convinced, that the gentlemen themſelves never thought of exhibiting ſo ſcandalous a charge, till after the ſecond repreſentation of the play of Cymbeline. This, and the other aſſertions relative to Mr. Powell's going to Briſtol, as well as the inſinuations concerning the wardrobe, and Mrs. Yates's engagement, will appear to be the moſt exceptionable parts of Meſſ. Harris and Rutherford's conduct. Paſſion is a human frailty, and therefore in ſome degree excuſable; but rancour and malice, ſupported by falſhood, are diabolical.

The affairs of the wardrobe have been already conſidered. The matters of King Lear, and Mr. Powell's going to Briſtol in the ſummer, were

Nov. 26. both agitated ſo long ago as on Thurſday the 26th of November, and the ſubſtance of what paſt was as follows:

I told them that the money ariſing from my night, as author of the Oxonian in Town, lay as yet in the office; but that as I was, by our articles, to be paid for every thing which I did in ſuch a capacity, I would, if they thought proper, take *the clear receipt* of the houſe that night, as a conſideration for my inſertions in the Rehearſal at the opening of the Theatre, and my alteration of King Lear; adding, that the alteration of Lear had given me more trouble than that of Philaſter, for which I had a night at Drury-Lane; but that as it did not abſolutely add a play to our catalogue, and as it was a work I ſhould never have undertaken had I not been engaged in the direction of a theatre, I ſhould be very well contented with ſuch a conſideration for my trouble. They aſked if I had not better refer all thoſe matters to the end of the ſeaſon. I replied, with all my heart; that I did not mean to aſk it as a favour; but that as I believed I ſhould do nothing more of that ſort this year, and as the money happened to be in the office, thoſe circumſtances had induced me to mention the matter at that time. Mr. Powell declared his opinion, that the demand was a very moderate one, and that he thought I might very reaſonably have claimed a night. I ſaid that, whenever I produced my alteration of the Silent Woman, I ſhould be undoubtedly entitled to one for that piece; but in the preſent inſtance I ſhould be very well ſatisfied with the ſum then in the office: whereupon it was unanimouſly agreed, that I ſhould take out the clear receipt, which amounted to 64 *l.* 5 *s.* more than was due to me as author of the Oxonian in Town. The above letter, inſolent as it is, does not deny my having been *paid* by their conſent; but it is particularly happy for me, that Mr. Hutchinſon,

a gentle-

a gentleman whose integrity has heretofore extorted even their approbation, was present at this scene, and can vouch for the truth of this relation.

But, says the invidious note to the printed Narrative*, This is *a customary liberty taken from time to time with this play in the representation; and, particularly, by the celebrated manager of Drury Lane, who, we are assured, never charged a single farthing to his brother patentee for such services.* If the celebrated manager of Drury Lane had ever attempted to execute my projected plan of altering King Lear, my labours on this occasion would undoubtedly have been superseded; *but that he never charged a single farthing to his brother patentee for such services* †, both he and his brother patentee know to be false; and that justly celebrated manager himself, more than once, proposed to me to join with him in *a reform of the theatre*, wherein those pieces which did not require so much alteration as to entitle the new editor to a benefit-night, were to be rewarded *by a certain sum* for each play. My revisal of King Lear falls directly under that description; and, I believe, the manager himself will allow, that I have had no more than a *quantum meruit* for my trouble; nay, I will submit to be tried by a theatrical jury, with that manager, as he ever ought to be, at their head; and I will forfeit double the sum, if my foreman does not bring me in *not guilty*. That he has been paid for his services is most certain, as it is most certain, that he has been paid no more than he has very fairly earned. He was pleased to tell me, that I should find my trouble, as acting-manager, would very well deserve 500 l. a year; and to add, that he would give my partners 500 l. a year, if they would not suffer me to be acting-manager. These were his sentiments and expressions at that time; but, as Abraham says in Harlequin's Invasion, *those happy days are over*.

The other affair stands thus:

On the 28th of May, when the article relative to Mr. Powell's salary, &c. was signed, when Mr. Hutchinson, who prepared it, first read that clause, wherein it was to be agreed, that *none of the* May 28.

* See their Narrative, p. 13.

† On a revisal of this page, and a second reference to their printed Narrative, I find, that their note in p. 13, concerning *the customary liberty taken with this play in representation*, alludes to the play of *The Rehearsal*; not to King Lear. In that instance Mr. Shuter, as well as every former *Bays*, took the same liberty, and charged nothing extraordinary for such services. But the usual *extempore* pleasantries of the actor in this character, are very different in point of quantity, not to say quality, from those written additions which they are pleased to call *the insertion of a few lines* ‡. How much of the 64l. 5s. Mess. R. and H. are pleased to charge to this account, I cannot tell; but my agreement gave me an undoubted right to receive a consideration for them: and, few and trifling as they are pleased to call these additions, on whatever occasion they shall produce the like, I will convince them I have not been over-paid.

‡ Mess. R. and H.'s Narrative, p. 13.

parties should, after the first of October, act, write, or have any concern in any other theatre, Mr. Powell absolutely refused to sign it, alledging the necessity he should be under to retain his property at Bristol, at least for some years, in justice both to himself and his family; who, notwithstanding the emoluments that might accrue from our intended purchase, would be extremely distressed and pinched in their income, till he had paid off the money, principal as well as interest, borrowed on the occasion. After two or three hours debate, he, with great reluctance, set his hand to the article; and I will venture to say, that my arguments and warmth on the occasion induced him to consent to it. At the same time, to mark our sense of his compliance in this instance, he was promised, by Messrs. Harris and Rutherford, as well as myself, that * *to indemnify him*, in some measure at least, *for the loss he should sustain by not acting at Bristol in the summer*, should be a matter of our future consideration.

May 28.

After the completion of the purchase, and our opening the theatre, Mr. Powell frequently took occasion to mention this matter, and desired to know on what footing this affair was to stand, that he might determine in what manner to conduct himself, in regard to his connections in Bristol. Mess. Rutherford and Harris, for a long time, found means to evade giving a determinate answer; but, on the 26th of November, Mr. Powell desiring a categorical answer, they told him they would give him leave to go to Bristol; that they had altered their sentiments on this head, and conceived the reputation of each patentee to be as distinct as his person, and that the actions of one individual would be no derogation to the character of another; that they were even reduced, though with great regret, to *plead poverty* on the occasion; for, as the money laid down for the purchase was not all their own, what with the payment of interest, and the large incomes they had given up by abandoning trade, their abilities to oblige Mr. Powell did not keep pace with their inclinations; besides which, it was to be considered, that both Mr. Powell and myself derived emoluments from the theatre, in which they had no share: but however,* *to show their unwillingness to deprive him of any pecuniary advantage, they assented to his going*; and ordered Mr. Hutchinson to draw up a proper form of permission, in writing, on the spot, to be immediately signed by Mr. Colman and themselves. To this, however, Mr. Colman would by no means consent, saying, that he originally opposed Mr. Powell's going to Bristol *propter dignitatem*, thinking it inconsistent with his present situation; but that if they had surmounted that obstacle, he had no stronger objections to urge against it; though he would never suffer it to appear under his hand,

* See their printed Narrative, p. 14.

† Ibid. p. 15.

that,

that, for the sake of refusing some *rascal counters to his friend*, he would suffer him to bring an imputation on them all. To shew, however, that he did not mean to counteract Mr. Powell's intention, or their permission, he proposed to add to that clause in the article relative to the parties not being concerned in any other theatre, the words *within ten miles of London*; by the insertion whereof, Mr. Powell would be at liberty to follow his own inclinations, without rendering Mr. Colman responsible for a conduct which he did not approve, and would be glad to find proper means to prevent. As to the separate emoluments of Mr. Powell and himself, he reminded Mess. Rutherford and Harris, that they were no more than they must necessarily pay to other actors and authors; and that, as Mr. Powell and Mr. Colman paid each a fourth of it themselves, their particular advantages from their labours were less than those of others in the same situation; but that, such as they were, if Mess. Harris and Rutherford would * *enact tragedies, or write comedies*, they would be entitled to the like. As to Mr. Colman's || *going so far as to insist warmly on the reasonableness and equity of Mr. Powell's demand of a benefit* on this occasion, it is absolutely false, for which I appeal to Mr. Hutchinson. Such a demand, I really think, after the transaction of the 28th of May, would have been both reasonable and equitable; but, to the best of my knowledge and belief, the mode of compensation was not mentioned, nor any such demand then made by Mr. Powell.

By this time the reader will be tolerably enabled to judge how far the narratives, printed and manuscript, *drawn up by the* AUTHORITY of Mess. Harris and Rutherford, are *supported by indubitable and authentick evidence* ‡. Their account of the engagement of Mr. and Mrs. Yates is, in point of exactness and veracity, consistent with the rest of their narration. The very date is erroneous, purposely erroneous, like that of the first material transaction between us. Their Narratives † would insinuate the engagements of Mr. and Mrs. Yates to be subsequent to the transactions of the second of November; thereby meaning to conceal, as they have always most industriously endeavoured, the *real cause* of those violent disputes, and to hold up Miss Ward as the object of contention. She never was, on any occasion, rendered an object of contention; though the note in their Narrative § relative *to some personal altercation, on account of casting the parts of Cymbeline*, expressly says, in direct contradiction to the living testimony of the whole theatre, *Mr. Colman wanting Miss W— to play the part of Imogen; which Harris and Rutherford conceived would be better supplied by Mrs. L—*, WHO HAD

* See printed Narrative, p. 35.

|| Ibid. p. 14.

‡ See Apology prefixed to the printed Narrative.

† See printed Narrative, p. 11.

§ Ibid. p. 15.

PLAYED

PLAYED IT THE PRECEDING SEASON AT DRURY LANE. *On Mrs. Yates's joining the company however, and refusing to give up the part, it was assigned to neither.* The poor flimsy fallacy of their whole representation of this matter must be evident to every person who has read the foregoing pages of this *true* state of the case. Miss Ward's claim to the character had never been set up with an air of contradiction to their sentiments; was never maintained in competition with Mrs. Lessingham; and was wholly withdrawn within eight days after opening the theatre. Mrs. Yates was engaged on the twelfth of October; actually played Jane Shore on the sixteenth; and whether the character of Imogen should be performed by Mrs. Yates or Mrs. Lessingham, was notoriously the whole subject-matter of the violent heats and animosities from the twenty-ninth of October to the second of November. Yet, say Mess. Harris and Rutherford, in their printed narrative, after having concluded their garbled account of those transactions, *The * reconciliation which* ENSUED *gave Harris and Rutherford some reason to hope that affairs would now be carried on in an amicable manner.* THEY WERE VERY SOON HOWEVER SURPRIZED *with Mr. Colman's having taken upon him to engage Mr. and Mrs. Yates:* an assertion, in respect to its chronology, which the very authority of the play-bills is sufficient to confute.

Still, however, (say they) Mr. Colman engaged Mr. and Mrs. Yates; and the † *surprise of Harris and Rutherford was the greater, as all the four,* IN A CONSULTATION HELD *some days before, had been unanimously of a contrary opinion.* The only *consultation* that I recollect on this affair was, that I had one day the honour of all the proprietors under my roof at dinner; after which the subject was started, I believe by Mr. Powell, who seemed very desirous of forming such an engagement. Mr. Rutherford also seemed to lean to his opinion: I was not wholly disinclined to it, provided we could obtain Mrs. Yates without her husband, whose assistance, excellent as he is, as our company stood, we did not so much need: Mr. Harris was wholly averse to our thinking of either.

It was then generally said that Mr. Barry and Mrs. Dancer were not to return to Dublin; and on the Saturday following the latter was publickly announced, after the play at Drury Lane, to perform there on the succeeding Wednesday. The impatience and anxiety of Mr. Powell could then no longer be subdued. He prest me in the most earnest manner to permit him to enter into a serious negotiation with Mrs. Yates; adding, that he thought I carried my punctilious delicacy towards the managers of Drury Lane much too far; that if Mr. Barry and Mrs. Dancer had crossed the water, and Mrs. Yates had still been standing out upon terms, it would perhaps have been illiberal to interfere; but

* P. 11. † P. 13.

that

that ſince the managers of Drury Lane had thought proper to take Mr. Barry and Mrs. Dancer into their houſe, ſtill leaving an opening for Mr. and Mrs. Yates, he did not think, in juſtice to ourſelves, that we ought to omit ſtrengthening our company with ſo popular an actreſs as Mrs. Yates. Theſe arguments had, in my opinion, ſo much weight, that I told him I ſhould be glad to know whether Mrs. Yates would join us *alone*. This, on his application to her, ſhe refuſed; whereupon Mr. Powell intreated me, if I had the leaſt regard for his peace of mind, or his reputation, to engage *both*. We went together to Mr. Harris's houſe in Surry Street. Mr. Harris was out of town. We then went to Mr. Rutherford's in Newman Street. Mr. Rutherford alſo not being to be found, a note was left, requeſting the favour of ſeeing him at the theatre, on earneſt buſineſs, next morning by ten or eleven o'clock. We waited till near noon, at which time we ſet out for Mr. Yates's at Mortlake, leaving the following letter from Mr. Powell for Mr. Rutherford.

Oct. 11.

Oct. 12.

" DEAR SIR, Paſt Eleven.

" SINCE I had the pleaſure to ſee you, I find that Mr. G—— has engaged B—— and Mrs. D——; and I, yeſterday, had the moſt aſſured intelligence, that they had complied to give Mr. and Mrs. Y—— their own terms, the conſequence of which you muſt ſee——that they would do every play in ſuch a manner, with B——, D——, and Y——, that we ſhould not be able to make the leaſt ſtand againſt them; and in ſuch caſe, my reputation as an actor (ſtanding alone) muſt ſink; which to prevent, I would, for my own ſake, withdraw myſelf from the ſtage, for a time, as an actor. Yeſterday I ſaw Mrs. Y——, who has generouſly given me the preference, and will not cloſe with Mr. G—— till ſhe hears from me, which muſt be this morning. The moment I came to town from Mrs. Y—— laſt night I called with Mr. Colman, at both your houſes, in hopes to have conſulted and got your conſent to engage them. I applied again this morning, but could not have the pleaſure to ſee you. We have now waited to the laſt moment; it is the very criſis of my fate and fortune; my everlaſting welfare is on the engaging theſe people; and it is Mr. Colman's ſentiments, that at all events the moment ſhould not be loſt; and I think, when you come to hear how we are beſet, you will happily concur. We are now gone to Mortlake to complete it, and hope you will ſay amen. I am very unhappy till it is done. Your's,

W. POWELL."

This letter plainly declared that *we were gone to Mortlake to complete the engagement with Mr. and Mrs. Yates:* and that this intelligence was not very unpleaſing to Mr. Rutherford; and that *he*, at leaſt, did not then *regard it as another groſs breach of the articles between us*, may be collected from the following note, which I found on my table at my return.

" I Re-

" I Received this instant (my dear friends) Mr. Powell's letter. H. dines with me; and if you have any immediate occasion to recur to us, we are to be found in Newman-street from four to six; shall be at the theatre soon after six; hope to find you both there.

Yours most sincerely,

Half past 12, morn. J. R.

To G. Colman, *Esq.* *or* W. Powell, *Esq.*

That I did not offer to carry matters with so high a hand, as the gentlemen are pleased to represent, will appear from my answer to the above note.

Monday 4 o'clock. Since returned from Mortlake.

" Dear Friend,

" THE deed is done; done on my part with fear and trembling, because we had not the good fortune to meet with you beforehand; but I think, nay am sure, it is for the best. I have particular company to dinner, or would have flown to you; but will get to the theatre as soon as my company's departure shall release me.

Yours, duly and truly,

G. C.

To J. Rutherford, *Esq.*

In the evening I went to the theatre; and, from the whole tenor of Mr. Rutherford's behaviour, which was agreeable to the spirit of his letter, I concluded, I still think not without reason, that he was very well satisfied with what we had done, thinking it a measure conducive to the interest and reputation of the theatre. Mr. Harris, however, it must not be dissembled, appeared extremely dissatisfied, construing Mr. Powell's letter as a menace, and declaring his *right to think their consent necessary to our forming an engagement of so much expence and consequence* ‡. I acknowledged that right; and assured him that Mr. Powell's letter was not intended as a menace; that, considering the tragick standing-army of Drury Lane, occasionally reinforced by Mr. Garrick himself, if we ever meant to use a bowl or a dagger this season, I thought the measure was right; but that if, after all, Mr. Rutherford and himself should declare themselves to be of a contrary opinion, Mr. Powell and myself would chearfully defray the expence of that engagement, being conscious that there was an irregularity, in having formed it without having previously obtained their assent to it. At length Mr. Powell intreated Mr. Harris, if he had any regard for his (Mr. Powell's) fame or happiness, to shew no farther repugnance to the measure; whereupon Mr. Harris declared he would never say any thing farther against it. How far Mr. Harris has kept his word, or how far Mr. Rutherford's subsequent conduct has been agreeable to

Oct. 12.

‡ Printed Narrative, p. 12.

his

his behaviour at that period, the reader is left to determine; and their objection to this engagement, on account of the expence of it, may be estimated by their conference with Mrs. Yates, as well as their letter to her, on the 29th of October. Whether this engagement has enabled us to add to the publick entertainment, the Publick will judge for themselves.

But here again occurs another instance of collusion; for * *Mr. Powell became entitled to the addition of* 100 *l. to his salary: and it* † *is to be remarked that Mr. Woodward's engagement was antecedent to Mr. Powell's article; by virtue of which he was entitled to a larger salary than any performer hereafter* TO BE *engaged.* The reader is desired to observe, that Mr. Powell's article with us, as a Performer, was signed, as appears by the date, on the 28th of May, some weeks before we were in possession of the patents; and I will appeal to Mr. Hutchinson before-mentioned, who drew the article, and whose name appears as a witness to it, as well as to the *consciences* of all the parties who signed it, whether the whole scope and intention of that article was not to secure to Mr. Powell the first salary in the theatre. In what manner a court of law might construe the words TO BE *engaged*; and how far the casual circumstance of Mr. Woodward's being in articles with the preceding patentees, at a higher salary, might render him an exception; I will not pretend to decide: but before Mr. T. Harris ventures another *comparison* ‡ *between Mr. Powell's disingenuity and his own generosity*, we would advise him not to insist on the above construction. Mr. Woodward's excellence in his profession is very well known: but does he, excellent as he is, deserve a superior salary to Mr. Powell? And will any reader of common sense conceive it to be the meaning of any of the parties concerned, to rate Mr. Powell lower than Mr. Woodward?—This, however, is the ground of the black charge of collusion between Mr. Powell and Mr. Colman, by which sinister method they were to add 100 l. to Mr. Powell's salary; fifty of which they were of necessity to pay themselves, and to divide the remaining fifty between them. Add to which, that estimating Mr. Yates's salary at 300 l. which added to that of Mrs. Yates's, amounted to the gross sum of 800 l. Mr. Colman and Mr. Powell, by a most refined stroke of policy, contrived to pay 200 l. each out of their pockets, for the sake of receiving five and twenty. Hence appears the great utility of the narratives of Mess. Harris and Rutherford, who *thought it incumbent on them, as well in justification of themselves, as out of respect to the Publick, to prevent, as far as lies in their power,* ANY MISREPRESENTATION OF FACTS.

* Printed Narrative, p. 13. † Note to ibid. ‡ Note to ibid. p. 26.
‖ See Apology to their printed Narrative.

The

The relation of these transactions, which naturally fell under the charges of *collusion* and *fraud*, carried on between me and Mr. Powell, has necessarily turned the tide of my narrative, which will now run on, as it began, in the regular course of time.

Jan. 1. 1768. On the first of January the treasurer of the theatre received the following letter:

"SIR,

"YOU have our permission to pay the accustomed weekly salaries, and the incidental charges of music, properties, and supernumerary performers; but you are not to pay any other sum of money whatsoever (Mr. Harris's fourth part of the balance of cash excepted) unless certified for payment under our hands. We are,

Sir, your most humble Servants,

Surry Street, Wednesday, Jan. 1st. 1768.

T. HARRIS.
J. RUTHERFORD."

To Mr. JONATHAN GARTON, *Treasurer of Covent-Garden Theatre.*

As Mess. Harris and Rutherford had, on former occasions, declared, that, sooner than suffer the sordid consideration of interest to controul them, they would see the theatre in flames; we began to think it highly necessary to call in some cool and dispassionate persons, whose interposition might adjust our differences; and to prove that we were in earnest in such an appeal, we thought it the most unquestionable mark of candour, to show ourselves willing to refer the consideration of our differences to the particular friends of Mess. Rutherford and Harris. Indeed we the more readily recurred to this method, having proposed it, as the reader may recollect, not without success, on a former occasion. To avoid, however, the most distant appearance of any clandestine transaction, the following letters, to their friends and to themselves, were dispatched at one and the same instant.

"SIR,

"AS you are a particular friend and acquaintance of Mr. Rutherford, your presence is earnestly requested at the King's Arms tavern in Cornhill, next Tuesday at one o'clock, to meet some other persons on affairs immediately relative to the most essential interests of Covent-Garden Theatre. We are,

Sir, your most obedient humble Servants,

Jan. 1st. 1768.

G. COLMAN.
Wm. POWELL."

To CHARLES FOULIS, *Esq; at Woodford-Row, Essex.*

Others to the same purport, *mutatis mutandis*, to the under-mentioned gentlemen, viz.

Richard Oswald, Esq; Philpot Lane.
Mr. Palmer, Att. at Law, Do.
Mr. Longman, Pater-noster Row.
Mr. Neale, Banker, Lombard Street.

GEN-

"GENTLEMEN,

"BEING conſcious of the rectitude of our conduct, we are willing and deſirous to ſubmit it to your moſt intimate and particular friends; for which purpoſe we have ſummoned the under-written gentlemen to the King's Arms tavern in Cornhill next Tueſday at one o'clock, when, if you pleaſe, you may attend. We are,

Gentlemen, your humble Servants,

Jan. 1ſt. 1768.

G. COLMAN.
Wm. POWELL."

Charles Foulis, Richard Oſwald, *Matthew Duane*,
Henry Bullock, Thomas Longman, —— Neale, ——Palmer, Eſquires.
To Meſſ. RUTHERFORD *and* HARRIS.

The gentlemen whoſe names are printed in *Italick characters*, were concerned for the party who had advanced the money to Mr. Powell. On my own part I ſummoned *nobody*; and Meſſ. Rutherford and Harris took care, that on their parts *nobody* ſhould appear, except the agents of Mr. Oſwald, over whom they could have no influence. On the 5th of January, however, Mr. Powell and I met the other gentlemen at the King's Arms, in Cornhill, when we received the following letter.

"GENTLEMEN,

"WE have each of us a ſummons to attend you on the affairs of Covent-Garden Theatre. As we cannot poſſibly have any right to interfere in this matter, muſt beg leave to decline the meeting.——Mr. Harris and Mr. Rutherford are gentlemen who, in our opinion, will never act contrary to the principles of honour and right, *or to the tenor of their articles*.

As our friends, we are ever ready to ſupport them to the utmoſt of our abilities.

We are, Gentlemen, your moſt humble Servants,

Tueſday morning,
Jan. 5th. 1768.

CHARLES FOULIS.
H. J. NEALE.
THOMAS LONGMAN."

To G. COLMAN, *and* W. POWELL, *Eſqs*.

The words, *or to the tenor of their articles*, appeared on the receipt of the letter to be added after the reſt; and to corroborate our ſuſpicions, they do not appear in the copy exhibited in the printed Narrative*.

Jan. 5.

This event afforded great matter of triumph to Meſſ. Harris and Rutherford, as appears by the ſtile of their letters that immediately ſucceeded it. For our parts we cannot, to this moment, account for their exultation on this occaſion; for what could more teſtify the weakneſs of their cauſe, than their unwillingneſs to ſubmit it to their particular friends, without any thing on my ſide, but the plain merits of the queſtion? We are alſo equally at a loſs to account for the conduct of the gentlemen whoſe names appear at the bottom of the above letter; who not only peremptorily refuſed to hear the caſe, which might probably have led to an accommodation; but took upon themſelves to prejudge a matter, of which they could not poſſibly know more than one ſide of the queſtion.

* See the Narrative, p. 26.

In the mean time Meſſ. Rutherford and Harris, delighting themſelves with the idea of my diſappointment, amuſed themſelves with preparing an additional uneaſineſs and inſult for me at my return. To this purpoſe they took care that I ſhould find an irritating letter on my table, which I was weak and peeviſh enough to diſtinguiſh by an anſwer, which produced, the very ſame evening, a reply more inſolent than their original epiſtle. They are here ſubjoined, according to the order in which they were written.

" SIR,

" WE diſapprove of the Merchant of Venice having been murdered on Friday night laſt, which we ſhould have prevented, had we been conſulted.—You know, Sir, it is at your *riſk* that you order any play, farce, &c. &c. to be exhibited, or that you take any one meaſure, without previouſly ſubmitting it to our conſideration.

We diſapprove of the Recruiting Officer for next Wedneſday, unleſs Miſs Macklin is well enough to play Sylvia; fearing ſome actreſs (and the pleaſure of the Publick) may be as much injured by that character, as Mrs. Bulkley was by playing Portia.

We diſapprove of the tragedy of the Orphan, that play having been too often repreſented this ſeaſon, to be again performed ſo ſoon.

We wiſh not to go on in ſacrificing the pleaſure of the Publick, the intereſt of the theatre, and our whole company of performers, to *one or two of your favourite tragedians.*

Surry Street, Jan. 5th. 1768. T. HARRIS. J. RUTHERFORD."

" N. B. We fear the Publick may think the comedy of Every Man in his Humour too often repeated."

To G. COLMAN, *Eſq.*

" THE intereſt of the theatre is in no danger but from *your* conduct and *your* partialities. Mr. Powell, who has a right to give his advice and *aſſiſtance* when called on, perceives, that it is not poſſible for us to keep our doors open, if the director is liable to ſuch frequent and ſtudied interruptions; and we are adviſed, that no court can ever be led ſo far to miſconſtrue the article between us, as to ſuppoſe, that the giving you a power that muſt be ſo prejudicial to our common intereſt, could be the intention of it. I ſhall continue to act in a manner conſiſtent with the ſpirit of it; I wiſh you to do the ſame. As to the *rectitude* of our conduct, or your own, I ſhall ſubmit that matter to the Publick, before whom I ſhall lay a full ſtate of the caſe in a very few days.

Jan. 5, 1768. G. C.

" SIR,

" THAT the advantage of the theatre is in imminent danger, we cannot but imagine, as we conceive the entertainment of the Publick, and all our own particular intereſts, to be very much injured by your paſt conduct, your unjuſtifiable partialities, and your *colluſion* with Mr. Powell. Our proofs we refer to the place where they may be exhibited with efficacy; to urge them to you, however cogent, we are too well convinced would have no effect; and it is the more to be lamented

that

that we cannot ſay you want abilities, but that you *reſerve* them for your own private ſeparate emolument, and are endeavouring *our deſtruction*; but your *diſhonour*, and Powell's *ruin*, cannot fail to be the iſſue of your conduct, as this day's meeting muſt have rendered obvious to you.

As to your charge of *ſtudied interruptions*, we totally diſclaim it; being conſcious that we can prove, to every impartial perſon, that we have never made *them*, but with a view to our joint and reſpective intereſts; and we cannot be prevailed on to believe that the Publick will ever eſpouſe the cauſe of a man who has acted *uniformly inconſiſtent* with *his articles*, and derogatory to the profeſſions which ought to be more binding to him than articles, his moſt ſolemn reiterated promiſes. It would be but *manly* in you both to exonerate yourſelves from obligations you every moment lay under to us, (preſume you are acquainted that Mr. R. has propoſed to diſcharge his part of the loan to Mr. Oſwald) by finding any one man of property who will take the *burthen* of being ſecurity for you both from us, who are fearful of the conſequence, before you perſiſt in inſulting thoſe who have made you both what you are in reſpect to the theatre.

We dare not take upon us to ſay what may be the *deciſion* of a court of judicature; but whatever *that* may be, we ſhall ſubmit to it with the utmoſt reſpect and reverence.

Sir, your humble ſervants,

Tueſday even. 8 o'clock,
Jan. 5, 1768.

T. HARRIS.
J. RUTHERFORD."

G. COLMAN, *Eſq.*

The next morning, (for now every hour teemed with freſh inſults) Mr. Powell received the following. Jan. 6.

"SIR,

"IN *colluſion* with Mr. Colman, you have *dared* to endeavour the alienating the confidence of Gentlemen, whom you *ſuppoſed* we were indebted to.

Should we retaliate ſuch *infamous* behaviour, and prevail on one of the firſt men in the kingdom to undertake a relation of the whole of your *baſe* conduct reſpecting us, to a noble lord, to whom, *we know*, you are indebted for your All, (excepting the ſum we ſtand as ſecurities for) how *ought* you to tremble for the conſequence?

This from your humble ſervants,

Surry ſtreet, Wedneſday Jan. 6, 1768.

T. HARRIS.
J. RUTHERFORD."

To W. POWELL, *Eſq.* at a Muſick Shop *in Ruſſel ſtreet, Covent Garden.*

In the above letter it is remarkable, that the gentlemen could not reſtrain their indignation within their letter, but ſuffered it to overflow, even to the direction; and remembering Tully's maxim, *ex officina nil liberale*, contemptuouſly reproached Mr. Powell with lodging *at a muſick ſhop*.

The ſame evening I was honoured with the following: Jan. 6.

"SIR,

"THE cruel neceſſity we lay under of holding correſpondence with you is exceedingly diſtreſſing and dangerous, which we are convinced of from the meeting

 of

of the players, whom you clandestinely convened, and read to them our private letters, though wrote to you in personal confidence, and in the most unguarded manner, some of them on points to which we could only be responsible as man to man.

You have often threatened us to retire from the management. You have often threatened us to appeal to the Publick; nay, you absolutely have had the effrontery to dare an appeal *to our friends*: the issue of *that* appeal, we believe, still lives in your memory. With respect to the Publick, *our reliance* on their protection cannot be exceeded by *your own*; and we have now by us a *narrative* of our whole proceedings with you, from the first moment to the present time, all ready for publication; but we have been advised by our friends not *immediately* to publish it; and if *you* do appeal to them, (the Publick) it can only be occasioned by your depending on your art to work upon the *passions* of mankind, and because you dare not wait to abide by their *judgment*, as must be the case in a high court of judicature.

You will urge, perhaps, how much we are obliged to *you* for the trouble you have given yourself, in taking upon you the whole management of the theatre, and to Mr. Powell for procuring the purchase of all our wardrobe, necessaries, and keeping them afterwards in his own house. From the above circumstances severe injuries have, in the opinion of us both, already arisen to our fortunes, and (the barrier being now entirely destroyed, which was formed for our safety) we dread the future ones.

It is not for us to determine the spirit of our articles from the *letter* of them: that we will not presume to do; but you are conscious—we say, Sir, *you know* that it was our constant, repeated, and uniform declaration, that we would never be concerned with you in the theatre, without having both of us an equality of power with you in the management thereof.

We observe it to be your constant method, when we have objected to a play, that you have ordered a weaker one. *You have no right to order a play for representation before it has been proposed to us.* What can be expected from the play of to-night, weak in itself, and having been already repeated this season to bad houses? The play of to-morrow stands almost in the same predicament. If you say in excuse, *there is no better business ready*, we are very sorry the pleasure of the Publick should be so neglected.

Sir, your humble servants,

Surry street,
Wednesday Jan. 6, 1768.

T. HARRIS.
J. RUTHEFORD."

The two plays referred to in the conclusion of this letter, were the Confederacy, and the Recruiting Officer, acted on the first two nights of the revival of Orpheus and Eurydice. It is a pity the gentlemen chose, in this instance, to prognosticate; for had they staid till they had an account of the *receipts* of those nights, which were very considerable, they might have known *what might be expected from them.*

Agreeable and entertaining as it was, we had neither leisure nor inclination to maintain so polite a correspondence. We desisted, therefore, from taking any notice of their letters, and a kind of sullen silence ensued for some days. In the mean time, the avaricious Colman and collusive Powell were digging in the mine for the benefit of Harris and Co.

Co. who, while they were eating the bread of our induſtry and the publick munificence, and the manna was yet in their mouths, like the Iſraelites in the wilderneſs, murmured againſt their feeders.

On the 11th of January, the correſpondence was renewed with an aſſumed air of candour and moderation, which, however, they not being able to ſuſtain, the correſpondence broke off a ſecond time. The riſe, progreſs, and concluſion of this reſumed correſpondence, will appear from the following letters; to which we ſhall ſubjoin a few ſhort obſervations, naturally ariſing from the letters themſelves, as well as from the comments on them in the written and printed Narratives. Jan. 11.

" GENTLEMEN,

" INCLOSED you will receive a copy of Mr. Hoſkins's opinion on our caſe. As his abilities and integrity in the law are well known to Mr. Colman, we have the greater reliance upon the impreſſion they muſt neceſſarily make. This opinion, as well as another we have taken, points out the infallible remedy for redreſs; yet, like the reſt, it adviſes an adjuſtment by arbitration, becauſe our diſpute (differing from the generality) muſt be attended with the ſevereſt injury to the property litigated, excluſive of the perſonal expence to be incurred individually. We therefore propoſe an arbitration of our diſpute by four gentlemen, *totally unconcerned in affairs of the Theatre*; two to be nominated by us; unexceptionable in point of rank, fortune and reputation; and impartial, never having been in the leaſt concerned in our affairs.——If you ſhall both concur in this propoſal, and nominate two gentlemen of equal conſideration and impartiality, we ſhall be ready to enter into bonds for ſubmitting to the award of the gentlemen ſo nominated.——You will ſee we could not accept or even anſwer the propoſals you made, becauſe you had, without our knowledge, taken upon you to determine who ſhould be judges of our cauſe; yet reſerving to yourſelves the liberty of receiving or rejecting their award.

" In caſe you ſhall liſten to this propoſal, we ſhall not remit the ardor with which we are now proſecuting our ſuit in Chancery, until the bonds of arbitration are ſigned. (We mention this, that you may not afterwards imagine there had been duplicity in our conduct.)

" If you ſhall not liſten to this propoſal, we ſhall, beſides proſecuting our ſuit immediately, take ſuch ſteps, however violent, as will more ſpeedily prevent your managing our property againſt our conſent; being well aſcertained, that for whatever damages may accrue, you will be reſponſible. And we ſhall have this additional ſatisfaction ariſe to our minds, (which we doubt not will alſo have its weight in a court of judicature) that we are not the authors of the train of miſchiefs which muſt enſue your refuſal.

Gentlemen, Your humble ſervants,

Surry-ſtreet,
Monday, 11th Jan.

T. HARRIS.
J. RUTHERFORD."

To GEO. COLMAN, *and* WM. POWELL, *Eſqrs.*

" UPON peruſal of the caſe of Mr. H. and Mr. R. and the articles of agreement therein ſtated, and the letters which have paſſed between them and Mr. C. I am of opinion that Mr. C. and Mr. P. have been guilty of many material and ſub-

 ſtantial

ſtantial breaches of the articles; and particularly with regard to Mr. C. in ordering the play of Cymbeline to be performed, after it had been expreſsly and poſitively forbidden by Mr. H. and Mr. R. by writing under their hands, and even after Mr. C. himſelf, on a *conſultation* with them, had agreed to diſcontinue it. As alſo in employing and taking into the ſervice of the Theatre Mr. and Mrs. Yates, (eſpecially at ſo large ſalaries) not only without the conſent of Mr. H. and Mr. R. but even contrary to a reſolution wherein he (Mr. C.) himſelf joined with Mr. H. and R. a few days before.——And with reſpect to Mr. P. in taking great part of the wardrobe from the Theatre into the particular poſſeſſion of himſelf or his wife. And it ſeems to me, from the conduct of Mr. C. and Mr. P. hitherto, as if they were determined to throw off all regard to the articles, and to act in the management of all matters relating to the Theatre, as ſole and entire owners thereof, in abſolute excluſion of Mr. H. and Mr. R. from any further concern therein, than to receive their ſhares of the clear profits thereof.

" I am alſo of opinion, that if a bill was to be filed by Mr. H. and Mr. R. againſt Mr. C. and Mr. P. and his wife in the court of Chancery, that court would decree *a ſpecific performance* of the articles for the future, and would order Mr. C. and Mr. P. to make ſatisfaction to Mr. H. and Mr. R. for their reſpective ſhares of all *damages* which ſhall appear to have been ſuſtained by any breaches of the articles by them reſpectively; and would order Mr. P. and his wife to depoſite in the proper apartments of the Theatre the parts of the wardrobe which they have improperly taken into their poſſeſſion. And unleſs matters can be in ſome manner *amicably* adjuſted to the ſatisfaction of all parties, and *a plan agreed upon for preventing future diſputes*, I ſhould adviſe Mr. H. and Mr. R. forthwith to file a bill in Chancery againſt Mr. C. and Mr. P. and his wife, for the purpoſes above.

Lincolns-Inn, Jan. 9th, 1768. EDMOND HOSKINS."

Monday afternoon, ſix o'clock.

" GENTLEMEN,

" I HAVE juſt received your letter with the paper incloſed, both which I ſhall communicate to Mr. Powell, and doubt not but he will ſpeedily concur with me in giving you a proper anſwer. In the mean time I ſhould conceive, from Mr. H's opinion, that he has not yet had *a full and impartial ſtate of the caſe* laid before him. I am Your humble ſervant.

G. COLMAN."

To Meſſ. HARRIS *and* RUTHERFORD.

" GENTLEMEN,

" HOW far we have or have not been guilty of any breach of our articles is not for you or ourſelves to determine; but we are ſo fully perſuaded of the integrity of our actions, that we are not in the leaſt fearful or unwilling to ſubmit them to a court of judicature, my Lord Chamberlain, or the Publick; nor are we at all intimidated by your menace of more violent meaſures. Yet as our diſſenſion (however trivial the cauſe from which it ariſes) may be ſerious in its conſequence——we are ready to refer to proper perſons the care of framing a plan of articles which may prevent future uneaſineſs. We are, Gentlemen, Your humble ſervants,

Jan. 13th, 1768. G. COLMAN.
W. POWELL."

To Meſſ. HARRIS *and* RUTHERFORD.

GENTLEMEN,

" GENTLEMEN,

" WE wiſh that your reply to our propoſal had been formed in terms more preciſe and clear, that we might not have loſt time in deſiring your elucidation of your own writing. We will repeat to you (if poſſible in more preciſe terms than before) the queſtion we propoſe. Will you, with us, ſubmit your and our paſt conduct to four gentlemen, now and heretofore totally unconcerned with the Theatre; two nominated by you, two by us; unexceptionable in point of rank, fortune, and reputation; and abide by their determination, whether as to award of damages on either ſide, *ratification of preſent articles, abolition thereof, and formation of new ones.* (if judged neceſſary and equitable) *and as to all matters relative to the future government of the Theatre?*

Your humble Servants,

Surry Street,
Wedneſday, Jan. 13th. 1768.

T. HARRIS.
J. RUTHERFORD."

To G. COLMAN, *and* W. POWELL, *Eſqs.*

" GENTLEMEN,

" OUT of tenderneſs to yourſelves, we forbore to enter into any paſt tranſactions, as an enquiry of that nature muſt neceſſarily lay open the real cauſe of the unhappy difference between us; nor indeed is any thing material to the general intereſt and happineſs, but a proper arrangement of matters for the future. We propoſed therefore (and we now repeat the propoſal) to refer to proper perſons the care of ſettling the articles in ſuch a manner, that the management of the Theatre may be carried on to the ſatisfaction of all parties; nor have we any objection, if you think it eligible, to ſubmit our paſt conduct to the conſideration of the ſame perſons; confident as we are that, in the opinion of any unprejudiced judge, we ſhall be found to have deſerved a very different treatment than we have met with from you.

Your humble Servants,

Jan. 14th. 1768.

G. COLMAN.
Wm. POWELL."

" GENTLEMEN,

" OF late we have wrote you in the moſt clear, preciſe terms, upon an affair of the utmoſt importance to our property. That part of your anſwer which, at another time, would have excited our mirth, now cauſes our indignation.—Out with your tenderneſs!, we totally diſclaim it, and contemn your pretences to it. In our preſent ſituation, all we could wiſh is, that the whole of our paſt tranſactions were known to the world.

We now refer to our former queſtion for your plain and unevaſive anſwer, and ſubjoin the following:

Have you fixed on two gentlemen under the deſcription we propoſed? and, will you direct your attorney to meet ours, and form ſome inſtrument that may effectually bind all parties to abide by the award?

If you deſire that we ſhould nominate firſt, we have no objection. It is unmanly to give us evaſive anſwers.—One to the purpoſe, or none. We are,

Gentlemen, your humble Servants,

Surry Street,
Friday morn. Jan. 15th. 1768.

T. HARRIS.
J. RUTHERFORD."

To G. COLMAN, *and* W. POWELL, *Eſqs.*

 GENTLEMEN,

" GENTLEMEN,

" THE ftile of your letters makes it as impoffible to hold an epiftolary correfpondence with you, as to maintain a perfonal intercourfe.—If you will be pleafed to favour us with the name and addrefs of your attorney, we will appoint one to attend him.

Your humble Servants,

G. COLMAN.
Wm. POWELL."

To Meff. H. *and* R.

" GENTLEMEN,

" MR. Coulthard, of Breams-Buildings, Chancery-Lane, is our follicitor, to whom we refer you for our future intentions.

Your humble Servants,

Surry Street,
Friday evening, Jan. 15th. 1768.

T. HARRIS.
J. RUTHERFORD."

To G. COLMAN, *and* W. POWELL, *Efqs.*

" GENTLEMEN,

" AS the delay of payment of our tradefmen muft be very detrimental to the credit and intereft of the Theatre, we defire to know your refolutions concerning the bills now in your hands, which ought to have been difcharged fome time ago; and the rather, as the non-payment of thofe bills is the only obftacle to the fatiffying Mr. Ofwald's claim of intereft due to him on his mortgage.

Your humble Servants,

Jan. 16th,
1768.

G. COLMAN.
Wm. POWELL."

To T. HARRIS, *and* J. RUTHERFORD, *Efqs.*

" GENTLEMEN,

" WE received your's of the 16th inftant. It is thought advifable you fhould have notice, that on the firft general fettlement of our accounts, each refpective proprietor will be deemed to have received fo much money as the orders iffued by him, or by his direction, may amount to, in part of his proportion of the dividend due to him on the profits of the theatre. We are, Gentlemen,

Your humble fervants,

Surry-ftreet,
Frid. Jan. 19, 1768.

T. HARRIS.
J. RUTHERFORD."

GEO. COLMAN, *and* WILL. POWELL, *Efqrs.*

" S I R,

" WE have inclofed to you (except two or three) all the bills in our poffeffion, either figned, or an obfervation made thereon.

For the credit of the theatre we have paffed thofe bills to you, but think proper to referve to ourfelves the right of claiming for any prejudice that may have arifen to our property by the payment of thofe bills.

We think proper alfo to advife you, that the orders for admiffion to the theatre, iffued by the proprietors, or by their direction, as well thofe heretofore given as thofe which may be hereafter given, we fhall expect to be accounted for as cafh by the refpective proprietors.

We

WE are extremely ſorry that any diſputes ſhould contribute to the increaſe of trouble in your office, and ſhall take every opportunity of rendering your ſituation as ſecure and agreeable as poſſible, and are, Sir, Your moſt humble ſervants,

Surry-ſtreet, T. HARRIS.
Tueſd. Jan. 19, 1768. J. RUTHERFORD."

To Mr. GARTON.

After a peruſal of the above letters, wherein it is propoſed to ſubmit to arbitrators, *the abolition of the preſent articles, or formation of new,* the reader will think it ſtrange, that Meſſ. Rutherford and Harris ſhould complain of our ASSURANCE, in *propoſing the new-modelling preſent articles, or the framing of new ones* † ! Strange, however, as it may appear, their agent declared to our own, that Meſſ. Harris and Rutherford had no intention to aſſent to the abolition or formation of articles.

The day after Mr. Garton received the letter, directing him to charge as caſh the orders for admiſſion to the theatre, iſſued by the ſeveral Proprietors, or by their direction; Mr. Garton, at my deſire, waited on Mr. Harris, to know if He and Mr. Rutherford meant to reſtrain the Performers from occaſionally giving orders to their friends, as uſual? Mr. Harris replied, that it was an eſtabliſhed privilege, of which neither Mr. Rutherford nor himſelf ever wiſhed or intended to deprive them. So that the only perſons who were not to be allowed that privilege were, it ſeems, the Proprietors themſelves.

In the firſt of the above letters, Meſſ. Harris and Rutherford, with the ſame ſpirit of openneſs and ingenuity that has ſhone through all their conduct, tranſmitted to me a copy of a learned counſel's opinion, without ſending me, at the ſame time, a copy of the caſe whereon that opinion was given; and how far I wronged thoſe gentlemen in *affecting to think,* ‡ *that a fair and impartial ſtate of the caſe had not been laid before the counſel*; thoſe who have compared this plain tale with their tales, may eaſily determine. The client who deceives his counſel, ultimately deceives himſelf; but the truth is, that the chief object in view was, to draw from ſome eminent counſel ſuch an opinion, as might ſerve to bow my mind to truckle to the ſlavery which they would impoſe upon me; for the reader muſt, by this time, be convinced, that in the ſhort ſpace of my theatrical direction, every method of inſult and intimidation has been uſed to drive me to ſacrifice our property, and the credit and intereſt of the theatre, to their partialities, and the caprice and vanity of Mrs. Leſſingham; of which my ſubmitting to take the part of Mrs. Sullen, in the Stratagem, from Mrs. Bulkley, in favour of

† Printed Narrative, p. 33.

‡ Ibid. 31.

Mrs. Leſſingham, is an inſtance of which I ſorely repent, and for which I am ſtill, to uſe one of their favourite figures, *burning with ſhame*. The caſe laid before their counſel, as plainly appears from the references to it in the opinion, contained the ſame charges, ſupported by the ſame evidence, that are urged againſt us in their printed and manuſcript libels. Their Narratives, indeed, and the caſe ſubmitted to counſel, are materially, and ſubſtantially, one and the ſame; firſt tranſmitted to counſel by a hackney-writer of one ſort, and then dreſſed up for publick inſpection by a hackney-writer of another.

Still, however, it is urged *that the court of Chancery would decree a ſpecifick performance of the articles.* I do not doubt but it would. But give me leave to aſk thoſe gentlemen, and even their counſel, what is *a ſpecifick performance* of the articles? Is it that I am not to carry on the ordinary buſineſs of the Theatre without previouſly ſubmitting *at all times*, every minute particular to their conſideration and controul? Is not the acting manager to appoint, or, from the contingencies of ſickneſs or other accidents, to alter a play appointed for repreſentation, without their previous concern? Is he not to caſt the parts of a ſingle play, beſpeak a ſingle dreſs, or occaſionally ſubſtitute Mrs. Bulkley for Miſs Macklin, without ſending at eight or nine o'clock in the evening to Mr. Rutherford in Newman-ſtreet, and to Mr. Harris in Surry-ſtreet? If this be *a ſpecifick performance*, as the above letters conſtrue it to be, it leaves the director leſs power than is commonly and neceſſarily lodged in the Prompter: and I cannot ſuppoſe that the wiſdom and equity of the nobleſt court of judicature in the world will ſolemnly decree ſuch *a ſpecifick performance*, as the nature of the caſe renders impoſſible to be put in execution.

Granting, however, for argument ſake, that the court would even decree *a ſpecifick performance* of that ſort, for which *the narrators* contend, give me leave to aſk another queſtion: Muſt not *their negative power* be always exerciſed in the *firſt* inſtance? and can they, after having openly or tacitly concurred in a meaſure, capriciouſly retract that concurrence? After having not only approved, but *deſired*, the repreſentation of Cymbeline; after having conſented to the expenſive decoration of it; had they a right, not only on the eve of its repreſentation, but even after the repreſentation of it at the Command of Their Majeſties, to prohibit the repetition of it? If this be, as they aſſert, their † *indubitable right to a negative voice*, by the ſame indubitable right they might reſtrain me from opening our doors; and after the lengths to which they have proceeded, I ſhould not be at all ſurprized at their attempting to exerciſe their *negative power* in that manner.

† Printed Narrative, p. 30.

But

But then *the Court would order Meſſ. Colman and Powell to make ſatisfaction to Harris and Rutherford for their reſpective ſhares of all* DAMAGES *which ſhould appear to have been ſuſtained by any breach of thoſe articles by them reſpectively.* Undoubtedly; and it would be pleaſant to be called on for *damages* in the preſent inſtance in any court of judicature. It is a cauſe worthy to come on before Trappolin. Make out a panel from the pit, and aſk any twelve on the jury, what *damages* they think have ariſen to Covent-Garden Theatre this ſeaſon from the addition of Mr. and Mrs. Yates to the company? aſk the Treaſurer of the Theatre, what *damages* have ariſen from the repreſentation of Cymbeline? aſk the ward-robe-keepers, and other officers of the Theatre, what *damages appear to have been ſuſtained by any breach of articles by Meſſ. Colman and Powell reſpectively?* If in all theſe inſtances, nothing but neceſſary expences, fairly brought to account, appear on one hand; if great *benefit* to the property appears to have ariſen on the other; alas! poor Powell, what will become of thee? alas! poor Colman, what will become of thee! *Solventur riſu tabulæ: Tu miſſus abibis.*

The words *effrontery* and *aſſurance* are favourite terms in the polite vocabulary of Meſſ. Harris and Rutherford. They aſſert they *verily believe* they have incurred a loſs of no leſs than 3500*l.* by Colman's *miſmanagement.* What does the world think of their *modeſty?*

To talk of *damages* is a very ſerious matter. Suppoſe, by a capricious diſplay of their *negative power*, damages ſhould ariſe; would not the other proprietors, would not every performer of the Theatre, if injured by ſuch conduct, have a right to call judicially upon Meſſ. Harris and Rutherford to make good ſuch damages?

As to the real intention of the reſtrictive clauſe in the article, and the declared object of it, at the time of its execution, it was merely to reſerve a proviſional power of reſtraint, which they then declared would probably not be exerciſed once in ſeven years, and very poſſibly would never be exerciſed at all. Nay, they avow themſelves that they † *entertained no doubt of Mr. Colman's capacity or inclination to conduct the theatre to the beſt advantage*; ſo that the negative clauſe was added, only leſt any *ſiniſter accident might render their interpoſition neceſſary to the ſecurity of their property*‡.—*Nec Deus interſit, niſi dignus vindice nodus*—ſeems to have been the meaning of all parties. Has the *dignus vindice nodus* yet occurred? And has any SINISTER ACCIDENT *rendered their interpoſition neceſſary*, except the repreſentation of the character of Imogen by Mrs. Yates, inſtead of Mrs. Leſſingham?

† Printed Narrative, p. 3. ‡ Ibid.

The truth is, and they have confessed it, that the two *gentlemen managers* meant to avail themselves of the talents of William Powell *the player*, and George Colman *the dramatick author*. To this end they chearfully subscribed, although not indefinitely, to my abilities for the province of director; and Mr. Powell did not scruple to give up his share of the *positive power*, thinking it safely lodged in my hands. Still, however, they had secured to themselves a *negative power*, which, instead of reserving till the end of *seven years*, the reader has seen they not only exerted, but *exceeded*, before the end of *seven days*. The force of the restrictive clause is not questioned; and it is certain, that if they chuse to counteract their own interests for the sake of abridging my authority, they have frequent opportunities to embarrass me in the theatrical management. **How comes it then*, say they in triumph, *that Mr. Colman*, A GENTLEMAN BRED IN THE STUDY OF THE LAW, *should enter into such absurd articles?* The history of the memorable visit with which I was honoured by Mr. Harris, on my return from Bath, is a full answer to their question. There are quirks in morality, as well as quirks in the law; but I did not conceive that I was dealing with a petty-fogger in either.

As to my management of the theatre, of my merit or demerit in that particular, the Publick are the most competent judges; but it ill becomes my fellow-patentees to suggest matter of reproof on that subject to the person who is said to be their *historiographer*; and it ill becomes him to revile me for my *gratuitous* services, while he is said to be himself a candidate to represent us all four as a *stipendiary* manager. Mr. Spatter, if it be Mr. Spatter, is "one of those wretches who *miscall* themselves authors; a fellow, whose heart, and tongue, and pen, are equally scandalous; who tries to insinuate himself every where, to make mischief, if there is none, and to increase it if he finds any." Mr. Kenrick, the ingenious author of the Widowed Wife, and of the candid and gentleman-like Review of Dr. Johnson's Shakespeare, has been pleased to pay me a very particular compliment in the prologue to his most excellent dramatick performance; and I will refer it to that gentleman, unless perhaps he may be thought *partial*, whether Mr. Spatter, or myself, is the fittest person to be employed in the direction of a theatre. Mr. Spatter perhaps may flatter himself with the hopes of expelling me from the management, and of seating himself, by the assistance of his friends, in the vacant chair; but Mr. Spatter is mistaken. Let him, if he pleases, make rules for experimental philosophers in his trade of brass-rule-maker: let him make rules for authors in his profession of Monthly Reviewer; but never, while Mr. Powell and myself are concerned in the property, shall he *openly* make rules for the management of Covent Garden theatre.

* Printed Narrative, p. 29.

We are told, however, that † *the proprietors of a theatre may avail themselves, not only of players, poets, &c. but even of* MANAGERS, *if necessary, on paying them a valuable consideration.*—Here the *cloven-foot* appears: and to confirm this doctrine, it is observed, that ‡ *Mr. Colman's not stipulating for such a consideration, when he accepted of the* NOMINAL DIRECTORSHIP *of the theatre, is a corroborating proof that it was never intended he should take more trouble than Harris and Rutherford: as, had it been otherwise, he would certainly have been as much entitled to a salary for managing, as Mr. Powell was to his salary for acting.* Here we cannot help observing in our turn, that the *acting manager*, in the beginning of the Narrative, is reduced to the *nominal director* at the end. That I have as reasonable a claim to a salary for managing, as Mr. Powell for acting, is most certain; and indeed in some respects the claim is more reasonable, as the acting-manager incurs, in many instances, an unavoidable expence: but that *it was never intended I should take more trouble than Harris and Rutherford*, is false on the very face of the article. After their interpretation of Mr. Powell's article, I am not in the least surprized at their candid construction of the disinterestedness of mine; and the insinuation of *sinister views in my unrequested officiousness*, is as true as it is generous. How far I was officious, or how far I was requested to take the office, is now before the Publick.

They are pleased to call *the more than ordinary profits of the theatre this season, an imaginary circumstance.* That the *receipts* of the theatre this season have been larger than ordinary, is NOT *an imaginary circumstance*, but *a real fact*: and if *the disbursements* have also been larger than ordinary, owing to our *moderate efforts*, as Mess. Harris and Rutherford are pleased to call them, to entertain the Publick, those gentlemen ought to know, that the first expences of *setting up in business* are not to be calculated as the average expences of the current year.

* *Sensible as they are of the disadvantages they lie under*, Mess. Rutherford and Harris do not, however, seem averse to enter into *a comparative view of the abilities of the respective patentees*; and have employed the latter pages of their publication to convince the town of their error, in having been pleased to bestow so much § *generous approbation on such moderate entertainment, as they have received at Covent Garden Theatre this season.* We hope, however, that our united efforts, *moderate* as Mess. Harris and Rutherford are pleased to call them, will still continue to be honoured with the GENEROUS APPROBATION OF THE PUBLICK. We flatter ourselves, that a fair comparison between the Narratives of Mess. Rutherford and Harris, and our own, will not inspire our patrons with

† Mess. H. and R's Narr. p. 35. ‡ Note to Ibid. p. 36. * Ibid. p. 35. § Ibid. p. 37.

any refentment of our proceedings. They may now judge, which TWO of the patentees have been ‡ *in perfect collusion from first to last*; which have been § *very avaricious*; and whether perfonal pique to Mrs. Leffingham on my fide, or perfonal attachment to Mrs. Leffingham on the part of Meff. Harris and Rutherford, has appeared in the *rife* and *progrefs* of our *difputes*. Her name, which is fcarce diftantly alluded to in their Narratives, makes a very confpicuous figure in our State of the Cafe; and might have been rendered ftill more capital. On the whole, if we fhall not have appeared to have acted ‖ *in defpite of honour and honefty*, if we fhall have appeared to have fpared neither expence nor pains in our efforts to entertain, we hope ftill to be favoured with the profperous gale of the publick favour; and although it is not eafy to keep the helm in fuch a boifterous fea, yet we hope, by *plain failing*, to be able to run before the wind, and that the fhip will live in a ftorm.

As to THEIR *fincere defire of contributing to the publick entertainment*, that cannot be queftioned; not only as it is their immediate intereft, but as they have fo notorioufly manifefted that defire by their loud and vehement complaints of * *the heavy loffes fuftained by the engagement of Mrs. Yates, and the incredible expence of her dreffes*, as well as other theatrical decorations: not to mention their affignment of principal characters to Mrs. Leffingham, inftead of Mrs. Yates.

† *Abfurd* as it is *to fuppofe men in the leaft acquainted with* BUSINESS, *unequal to the care and conduct of their property in a Theatre*, it is a moft certain fact, that from a particular innate modefty, or fome other commendable motive, Meff. Harris and Rutherford have never once fhewn themfelves at all difpofed to interfere in the *executive* part of the management. Their talent is legiflation. While Powell and Colman were feen every day, and almoft every hour in the day, toiling in the drudgery of rehearfing, and decorating the intended performances; while they, like petty kings, were *ftaged and hacknied in the eyes* of the whole Theatre; in the mean time Meff. Harris and Rutherford *kept, like Eaftern monarchs, from their fight*; never attempting to affift the director in his management, but now and then, to render his fituation more agreeable, ¶ *exerting their undoubted right to controul him in that province*; occafionally exercifing, and fometimes *exceeding*, their *negative power*; but never difturbing or degrading their high and mighty councils, by treating with authors or actors, *getting up plays*, or *purchafing old cloaths*.

Feb. 10. 1768. But they are to be *affifted by perfons of known experience and abilities*; and it was not till this very moment that I have learned from Mr. Becket, fent to me for that purpofe, that thefe *perfons*

‡ See Introduction, p. 4. § Ibid. ‖ Ibid. p. 5. * Ibid. p. 4, 5.
† Meff. H. and R.'s Narr. p. 37. ¶ Ib. p. 35.

of

of known experience and abilities are Mr. WILLIAM KENRICK, and Mr. HENRY WOODWARD; the firft of whom has commiffioned Mr. Becket to inform me, that Meff. Harris and Rutherford, though *they flatter* ‡ *themfelves they will not be found incapable of fuperintending their property*, intend, however, for the future, to abfent themfelves entirely from the Theatre; and that he (Mr. Kenrick *) is to be the reprefentative of Mr. Harris, and Mr. Woodward of Mr. Rutherford; in which quality Mr. Woodward and Mr. Kenrick are, in behalf of Meff. Harris and Rutherford, to *put* THEIR *negative* on fuch of my meafures as they fhall pleafe to difapprove. How far a court of law will warrant this proceeding, and whether a manager, like a militia-man, can act by a fubftitute, I will not take upon me to decide; but whether this new arrangement is not intended as a frefh infult, we fubmit, with the reft of our cafe, to that awful tribunal, THE PUBLICK.

Covent-Garden,
February 10, 1768.

GEORGE COLMAN.
WILLIAM POWELL.

‡ Meff. H. and R's Narrative, p. 37.

* It is not improper to mention here, that Mr. Lockyer Davis, of Holborn, bookfeller, called on me on Monday afternoon, immediately from Mr. Kenrick, to acquaint me, that Mr. Kenrick had authority from Meff. Harris and Rutherford to fay, that, *notwithftanding the publication of their Narrative on Saturday*, they were difpofed to enter into a treaty for an accommodation, if I was inclined to liften to it. I anfwered, that I could liften to no terms of accommodation till I had publifhed a ftate of the cafe, in juftification of my character.

GEORGE COLMAN.
WILLIAM POWELL.

A
LETTER
FROM
T. HARRIS,
TO
G. COLMAN, &c.

[PRICE ONE SHILLING AND SIX-PENCE.]

A

L E T T E R

FROM

T. HARRIS, TO G. COLMAN,

ON THE AFFAIRS OF

COVENT-GARDEN THEATRE.

TO WHICH IS PREFIXED,

AN ADDRESS TO THE PUBLIC.

"Me tradente, dolos, geftus artemque nocendi
"Edidicit; fimulare fidem, fenfufque minaces
"Protegere, & blando fraudem prætexere rifu;
"Plenus fævitiæ, lucrique cupidine fervens:
"Doctus & unanimes odiis turbare fodales:
"Solus habet fcelerum quicquid poffedimus omnes."

MEGÆRA LOQUITUR.

L O N D O N:
PRINTED FOR J. FLETCHER AND CO. IN ST. PAUL'S CHURCH-YARD; AND SOLD BY J. WALTER, AT CHARING-CROSS; AND J. ROBSON, IN BOND-STREET.
MDCCLXVIII.

TO THE PUBLIC.

THE meaſures, which Mr. Rutherford and myſelf have been lately compelled to take for the ſecurity of our intereſts and property in Covent Garden theatre, have been ſo groſly miſrepreſented in the news papers and in common converſation, that we ſhould be wanting both to ourſelves and the public, did we not once more ſolicit their attention to a plain and genuine narrative of our proceedings.

We are not inſenſible that names, intereſts and diſputes like ours, deduce all their little conſequence with the world, from their accidental connections with its occaſional amuſements.

Had the differences, therefore, which have ſo long ſubſiſted between us and our fellow-proprietors been merely of a private and domeſtic nature, we ſhould as readily acknowledge the impropriety as impertinence of a repeated appeal. But, as the rational entertainment of the town, to which we are under the higheſt obligations, may poſſibly be interrupted by the continuation of our diſputes; we yield, though reluctantly, to the diſagreeable neceſſity of exculpating ourſelves from the aſperſions, of having contributed to ſuch interruption, any farther

than

than by a juſt and reaſonable aſſertion of our legal right to the joint management of our common property. This it muſt be owned has been productive of all thoſe ill effects which naturally ariſe from the oppoſition of determined reſolution to captious inſolence and inveterate obſtinacy.

How Mr. Colman will ſtand excuſed for wilfully protracting the eſtabliſhment of our company on an equitable and amicable footing, I cannot pretend to ſay; but, however lightly he may regard his duty to the publick, we cannot but think it ours to ſatisfy all thoſe, who may honour us with their attention to the affairs of the theatre, that neither this protraction, nor the diſagreeable conſequences that are juſtly to be apprehended from it, can fairly be imputed to Mr. Rutherford or myſelf.

To this end, alſo we look upon the preſent appeal as no leſs expedient than exculpatory; having, to our great mortification, but too much reaſon to fear that no private mode of reconciliation will ever take place with Mr. Colman. In the mean time, it is with equal mortification we daily ſuffer under the miſtaken imputations of wilful ignorance or accidental miſrepreſentation.

Hence we conceive ourſelves under the neceſſity of openly making our future propoſals of accommodation in the face of the publick; hoping that, while ſuch neceſſity pleads an excuſe on our part, Mr. Colman will, on his, pay too great a reſpect to that public, to have recourſe to his uſual artifices of evaſion and prevarication; of which indeed he appears to poſſeſs a ſecret fund altogether inexhauſtible.

The eye of the world, is not ſo eaſily deluded as the ear of a friend; if Mr. Colman therefore has any thing of that regard for truth and juſtice he pretends, he will have now an opportunity of diſplaying it; and

and of encouraging at leaſt a laudable ſuſpicion that our paſt differences have been more owing to miſunderſtanding than malevolence.

As to thoſe perſonal failings, indeed, which he hath induſtriouſly contrived to drag to light, and depoſit at our door; their production will ever be imputed at beſt to ſpleen and petulance in him; while we might ſurely plead the preſcription of youth and inadvertency, at leaſt to many; which, however they may ſtand as items in our account, cannot certainly be applied as arguments in his cauſe.

Not that with regard to myſelf, who have been more particularly pointed at, I fear to meet him even on this ground, with all my imperfections. But as the juſtification of offences, from example, forms but a weak plea for committing them, ſo the preference to be gained by compariſon, conſtitutes but a very ſlender degree of merit. Beſides this I humbly apprehend theſe are enquiries ſtill more beneath the notice of the publick, than even our injudicious ſquabbles about the property and management of the theatre.

The tale I have to tell is ſimple, and perhaps tedious; but I choſe to tell it as nearly as I could in Mr. Colman's own manner, and to addreſs it to himſelf; becauſe it is on him I would have it make an impreſſion. The facts alſo are ſimple as related; the motives of which, however, may have been ſometimes ſo complicated, as to baffle my ſagacity. I have indeed been more attentive to the order and certainty of the facts, than to the propriety of any concluſions drawn from them: being ſenſible that although partiality may pervert, and ſophiſtry elude the ſtrongeſt reaſoning, the evidence of fact is irreſiſtible.

When we firſt engaged in this unproſperous aſſociation, and at the flattering inſtances of Mr. Powell, admitted Mr. Colman to a ſhare in our intended purchafe, it is well known we received and treated him him with a deference and credulity that all our inexperience, of which he has been pleafed to remind us, can hardly find an excufe. We confefs that our implicit confidence in him, and the character given us of him by his friend, betrayed a moft unworldly weaknefs and ignorance of mankind. We own we were *little hackneyed in the ways of men*, and much lefs in the ways of men, whofe verfatile genius and theatrical talents, enable them to affume a new character with every new purpofe they have to anfwer. But what epithet fhall we beftow on that principle which tends to extract profit from fuch ignorance?

If, in the formation of our articles, we have, on our part, left openings, into which the infinite pliability of the law can infinuate itfelf at pleafure: if we have weakly impofed reftrictions clear enough in their fpirit, but whofe letter may be melted down to nothing, by the indeterminate conftructions of refinement; let Mr. Colman enjoy the honour of having outwitted us, and let it be our fhame, as it is our misfortune, to have given him the opportunity.

But that this is not the cafe, there is the greateft prefumption to believe; fince it is the opinion of two of the firft lawyers in this kingdom, that the articles are expreffed with clearnefs and certainty, nor admit of any doubt in their conftruction. It is remarkable alfo, that although Mr. Colman pretends he has conftantly acted by the advice of counfel, he never produced to us a written opinion of any fuch counfel, in his favour; which, when we fhewed him that of ours, he certainly ought to have done, if he had any, or wanted really to come to an accommodation!

This was a fatisfaction in which he would or could not condefcend to indulge us: in the mean time, we found we were dropping apace into flavery. Nay, we were even told by our oppreffor, that we were

 already

already ſlaves. But this need not have been told us; we ſaw plainly the very ſhadow of power vaniſh from us; and were ſtruck with a ſerious alarm leſt our property ſhould alſo take the ſame courſe. We ſaw ourſelves involved in a vaſt and inſupportable expence, laviſhed away, in defiance of our moſt ſolemn proteſts, upon ſuperfluous ſervants, greedy favorites, and a numerous ſtanding army of undiſciplined and uſeleſs performers, under various titles and denominations.

We did not, indeed, then foreſee that the new and coſtly trappings, with which Mr. Powell was every night adorning himſelf, were to anſwer a double intent. It did not ſuggeſt itſelf to us, that they were deſigned, not only to figure on the ſtage of Covent-Garden, but to exhibit the patentee of a royal theatre in becoming ſplendor on that of Briſtol.

The menacing proſpect of our affairs, however, awakened us to a very ſerious attention. We found our theatre intemperately pouring forth the contributions of the public bounty, as faſt as it received them; and this in a manner that made us tremble for the continuance of thoſe ſupplies.

Nor was this all: ſome other practices had begun to manifeſt themſelves, which gave us the moſt ſenſible uneaſineſs. We had entered upon our office, with ſanguine hopes of attracting the favourable regards of the public, by a diſintereſted and impartial attention to the productions of men of genius. We fondly hoped, that by this conduct we might have the merit with the town, of reſcuing our ſtage from thoſe imputations which had been caſt upon it under former management.

Theſe were the conſiderations that firſt recommended Mr. Colman to our ſociety; and it was from a juſt diffidence of our own abilities

for

for the above important taſk, and a too flattering eſtimation of his, that we admitted him into our treaty, and inveſted him with the office of acting manager, under due reſtraint and controul. We underſtood him to be a gentleman of education, with an eſtabliſhment, that ought to have ſet him above every ſervile office or ſordid conſideration; and with expectations that appeared to do honour to our connection with him. Inſtructed by ſo able a maſter as the ſucceſsful manager of Drury-Lane, we conceived the talents of both in ſome degree congenial. Strangers to the friendly arts by which the tutor nurſed the rickety reputation of his pupil, we falſely imagined the latter ſafely arrived at the goal of fame; and looked upon him as qualified to conduct others, by directing the incipient efforts of genius to their proper end and deſign.

How theſe hopes have been fulfilled, ſeveral ingenious and inſulted writers too well know; we too ſenſibly feel; and the undeluded publick will be able, in ſome degree, to judge from the following ſheets. The reaſons on which we ground our late proceedings; the neceſſity we lay under of making a forcible entry into our theatre; the ſuſpicion of peculation and miſmanagement within thoſe doors which were barricaded againſt their owners; the flagrant verification of thoſe ſuſpicions; and the unneceſſary and illegal diſpoſſeſſion of two of our ſervants, by the formal and ridiculous proceſs of a third; can now no longer with propriety be with-held from the publick. The intelligence belongs to them; it is at their tribunal our cauſe muſt be ultimately decided: to them therefore we ſubmit the merits of it, and rely on their judgment and candour.

To Mr. Powell we would wiſh to ſay as little as poſſible. A perſon who has made an abſolute ceſſion and ſurrender of his faculties to another, and blindly delivered himſelf over to his arbitrary guidance, may be ſaid to ſuffer a kind of moral death, and under ſuch an entire

ſuſpen-

ſuſpenſion of volition, can ſcarcely be conſidered as reprehenſible for the turpitude, or commendable for the rectitude of his actions.

Under this predicament ſtands Mr. Powell, a man who conſigns his name to pamphlets he never penned, ſubſcribes letters and manifeſtos which if he had read, he could not comprehend ; and who, in the aſſumed office of ſuperintending the wardrobe, is ſo delicate in his truſt, that he conveys it with him to the theatre at Briſtol ; as if the preſervation and ſecurity of his finery depended on his carrying it about with him on his back.

To conclude ; we beg leave to call the public to witneſs, that notwithſtanding the juſt reſentment we cannot but feel, at ſuch repeated inſtances of oppreſſion, we deſire nothing ſo much as a fair and equitable accommodation. And that the terms of it may be no longer liable to miſconſtruction or miſrepreſentation, we have in the following pages openly tendered to Mr. Colman ſuch overtures, as in our judgment ſeem beſt calculated to adjuſt our differences.

If theſe are fair and equitable, as we hope they are, and mean they ſhould be, the town will know on which party to lay the blame ; if, when the theatrical ſeaſon ſhould open, our doors ſhall be found ſhut. We need not be told how ſeverely we ſhall ſmart, as well as our contending brethren, from ſuch a circumſtance ; but we have too long laboured under oppreſſion to bear it with patience any longer. On the contrary, we are determined to oppoſe it, at the hazard of loſing every thing we poſſeſs ; rather chuſing to be deprived of the laſt ſhilling of our property, in the juſt and legal defence of it, than tamely to reſign our right to the conduct and diſpoſal of it to a deſigning and inſolent intruder.

4

A LETTER

A

L E T T E R

FROM

T. HARRIS,

TO

G. COLMAN, &c.

SIR,

MR. Rutherford and myſelf, having ſo often in vain ſolicited your attention to our complaints, and invited you to a fair and amicable diſcuſſion of the ſeveral grievances, that gave riſe to thoſe complaints; we muſt now in mere deſpair drop all private correſpondence with you, and reſign every hope of gaining upon your nature by thoſe gentle and complacent arguments; which we have hitherto adopted in preference to all others, and from which, nothing but the neceſſity of ſelf-defence ſhould have tempted us, in the conduct of our diſpute with you, to have departed. But, to our inexpreſſible mortification, and regret, you have dragged us into public controverſy: and, to my particular diſadvantage it is, that I now find myſelf, by the abſence of my colleague, diveſted of that aſſiſtance, and ſupport, which a communication of opinions, as well as of ſufferings, would elſe have afforded me. The libellous, and unmanly

 inſinu-

insinuations, with which you have filled the public papers, and your St. James's Chronicle in particular, on that and other occasions, have obliged me to trace the stream of abuse to its source; though I have not attempted to interrupt its current; having derived this unintended benefit from it, that, while you was proving to the world you had no wit but malevolence, you have incautiously made it appear that you have no argument but scurrility.

I am now, sir, by Mr. Rutherford's absence, left to defend myself alone: yet, fortified by the integrity of my intentions, I fear not to call you forth at the tribunal of the publick; thither I recur for protection, and there our injuries, and your artifices, cannot escape discovery. 'Tis true, I enter upon this undertaking with great disadvantages; your uncommon talents, established practice, and perfect initiation into the logick, which can make "*the worse, appear the better reason*," are well known. Against these I have nothing to oppose but a few plain facts, selected from a multitude of grievances, with which your oppression has furnished me.

I shall proceed however at once to a plain and candid enquiry into your conduct, from our first interview, to the date of this letter; and from this enquiry, I think it will be seen, that even before we signed our first contract, you had formed a latent design, a regular plan of cunning and dexterity, to work yourself into the sole direction of Covent-Garden theatre, in the most absolute and arbitrary sense of the word; and this at the expence of the peace, and the property of your associates. An end like this was of necessity to be accomplished by any means, that sophistry, feigned friendship, secret collusion, or open violence could devise and execute. You are not to be told, sir, how many turns and windings are made by men who would establish a reputation for cunning, in order to escape the vigilance of their observers; but you are to be told (and it may be matter of useful information to you) that in weaving this web and labyrinth of deceit, they generally leave a clue behind

behind them; which, if once an honeſt man gets hold of, he ſeldom fails to unravel their operations, and trace them up to the point from whence they ſtarted. Such a leading thread you have undeſignedly put into our hands. This is the pamphlet you are pleaſed, by a figure in ſpeech, to which you are but too much accuſtomed, to call a *True State* of our differences. I ſhall ſo far verify the title you have given it, as to make frequent uſe of the ſame words for guiding the reader to the truth, which I have great reaſon to fear were employed by you for very contrary purpoſes.

In page twelve of that pamphlet, you ſay that, "*At a meeting between* " *all the parties on the 31ſt of March, Mr. Hutchinſon attended with an in-* " *ſtrument prepared for us to ſign; on his reading over that part of it, wherein* " *it was recited, that the four parties ſhould be* equally concerned *in the* " *management of the theatre, Mr. Colman begged leave to interrupt him, and* " *told him it was a* ſettled *point that he (Colman) was to be inveſted with* " *the direction of the theatre, whereupon, to Mr. Colman's very great ſurprize,* " *Meſſrs. Harris and Rutherford declared they never had the leaſt intention* " *of ſuch an article.*"

You ſay true, ſir, we never had the leaſt intention of inveſting you with ſuch a general indeterminate authority; we declared ſo then; and we more earneſtly proteſt againſt it now.

" *Mr. Colman ſaid he took it for granted, that this matter (of giving him* " *the ſole diſpoſal of our property) had been previouſly underſtood on all ſides.*"

The fact is, that we never heard a word of your being the abſolute director of the theatre, but from your ſaying, "*You could ſtir a fire better than any man in England.*" That indeed we laughed at, as a conceit of intended wit and pleaſantry, but could not imagine that you meant it a ſerious and concluſive argument to which we had agreed: but you further

urge in the ſame page, "*That you had plainly declared to Mr. Powell on*
"*his firſt application, that you would never be concerned in the purchaſe,*
"*unleſs you ſhould be inveſted with the theatrical direction.* Mr. Powell
"allowed the truth of this aſſertion.

And is your declaration to Mr. Powell, that you would, or muſt be inveſted with the arbitrary management of our property, a reaſon that we ſhould be ſo mad as to accede to it, in order to gratify your luſt for power? * Mr. Powell aſſerted too, when he introduced you to us, that you was a fair honeſt man, that you would lay down a plan of management that would raiſe and retrieve the reputation of our theatre, throw all competition in the other houſe at a diſtance, and advance the profits of the ſeaſon by one fourth part more than under the late direction. But theſe flattering aſſertions of Mr. Powell's, though repeatedly backed by your teſtimony, are no better a proof of your being actually poſſeſſed of theſe talents, than your declaring you would be abſolute in the theatre, was a demonſtration that we had made you ſo. We have often ſince reflected upon the variety of ſhapes you aſſumed in order to procure our conſent to inveſt you with the ſo much deſired direction of the theatre. Simile, pun, jeſt, anger, rage, complacency, nay even adulation, all had their peculiar exertions; but, at length, finding you could neither ſooth, wrangle, or menace us into the weakneſs and ſervility required, you dropped the attack, made a ſudden tranſition in your manners, and uttered ſolemly this declaration, "*God knows my heart, I never*
"*wiſh, nor ever can be* arbitrary, *it is not in my nature.*" We then immediately ſigned our firſt inſtrument of partnerſhip, which left our powers in the management of Covent-Garden theatre, as equal as our intereſts were in the property of it.

* For my own part, I ſhould think ſuch a declaration muſt be conſidered as a proof that we had not then given up our rights, and a very probable preſumption that we never have; for ſurely you would not threaten to take that from us, which we had already reſigned; on the contrary, ſuch an avowed ſpirit of reſentment would be moſt likely to put us upon our guard againſt it.

ARTICLES of AGREEMENT, Quadripartite, made and agreed upon this thirty-firft day of March, One thoufand feven hundred and fixty-feven, between Thomas Harris of Holbourn, in the county of Middlefex, Efquire, of the firft part; John Rutherford of Newman-ftreet, in the in parifh of St. Mary le Bon, in the fame county, Efquire, of the fecond part; George Colman of Great Queen's-ftreet, near Lincoln's-Inn-Field, in the county aforefaid, Efquire, of the third part; and William Powell of Great Ruffel-ftreet, in the parifh of St. Paul, Covent-Garden, Gentleman, of the fourth part, as follows:

WHEREAS the faid Thomas Harris and John Rutherford, by James Hutchinfon, their agent, are in treaty with Prifcilla Rich, the widow and reprefentative of John Rich, late of the parifh of St. Paul, Covent-Garden, Efquire, deceafed, for the purchafing two feveral patents for exhibiting theatrical performances, and of fundry leafes granted of Covent-Garden theatre or playhoufe, and of the rooms, buildings, conveniences, and appurtenances thereunto belonging; together with all and fingular the furniture, fixtures, fcenes, decorations, wardrobe, mufick, entertainments, matters and things whatfoever, which the faid Prifcilla Rich is now poffeffed of, or intitled to, as appertaining or belonging to the faid theatre, or to any theatrical performances and exhibitions, either as executrix as aforefaid, or in her own right, or for or in behalf of herfelf, and any other perfon or perfons whomfoever: And alfo, all deeds, books, papers, writings, contracts, and fecurities thereunto belonging: And whereas the purchafe-money required by the faid Prifcilla Rich, is fixty thoufand pounds; now therefore, it is hereby mutually agreed, by and between all the faid parties to thefe prefents, and they do hereby for themfelves feverally and refpectvely, and for their

their ſeveral and reſpective heirs, executors, and adminiſtrators, covenant, promiſe, and agree to, and with the other, and others of them, his and their reſpective executors, adminiſtrators, and aſſigns, in manner following, (that is to ſay) That the ſaid Thomas Harris and John Rutherford ſhall be, and are hereby authorized and impowered to proceed in the ſaid treaty, and to contract and agree for the purchaſing of the ſaid premiſes at any price or ſum not exceeding ſixty thouſand pounds; and to that end to ſign and execute any deeds or writings that may be neceſſary and proper in their own names, but for the joint account and benefit of all the ſaid parties.—That upon concluding the ſaid treaty, and ſigning any ſuch contract or agreement as aforeſaid, all the ſaid parties ſhall and will be, and become joint owners and proprietors, and be jointly and equally intereſted and concerned in the ſaid patents, leaſes, and premiſes, both for profit and loſs, and ſhall be jointly and equally concerned, and employed in the management of all the theatrical performances to be exhibited in conſequence of ſuch purchaſe.—That all the ſaid parties ſhall and will, well and truly pay and advance their ſaid ſeveral ſhares and proportions of the ſaid ſixty thouſand pounds, or ſuch other ſum of money as aforeſaid, and that at ſuch time or times as the ſaid Thomas Harris and John Rutherford ſhall agree to pay the ſame, as well as of all other ſum or ſums of money, coſts, charges and expences attending the ſaid purcaſe.—That in caſe the ſaid George Colman and William Powell, or either of them, ſhall not at ſuch time or times as aforeſaid, be prepared with, and actually pay down the whole of his or their proportion of the ſaid purchaſe money, they the ſaid Thomas Harris and John Rutherford, ſhall and will, jointly and equally, advance and pay for him or them, ſo much money as ſhall be the deficiency of the ſaid George Colman and William Powell, or either of them, ſo that the ſum they reſpectively pay down be not leſs than ten thouſand pounds, and the ſaid Thomas Harris and John Rutherford, or ſuch of them as ſhall make up ſuch deficiency, ſhall be allowed to deduct out of the reſpective ſhares of the profits belonging to the ſaid George Colman and

William Powell, intereſt for the ſame, at and after the rate of five pounds per centum per annum, until payment thereof, and his or their part, ſhare and intereſt, in the premiſes ſhall ſtand and be a pledge or ſecurity until all ſuch principal and intereſt ſhall be fully paid.—That upon the ſaid treaty and agreement with the ſaid Priſcilla Rich taking effect, all the ſaid parties ſhall enter into and execute the neceſſary and proper deeds, inſtruments, or writings, as well for the better effectuating this agreement, as for the managing and carrying on the undertaking of the exhibitions and performances in conſequence thereof. Provided nevertheleſs, and it is hereby mutually agreed, that in caſe of the death of any or either of the ſaid parties to theſe preſents, before the intended agreement with the ſaid Priſcilla Rich ſhall be carried into execution, then and in that caſe, theſe preſents, and every matter and thing herein contained, with reſpect only to the party or parties ſo dying ſhall be void and of no effect, and then the ſurviving parties ſhall ſtand in his place, if they think proper, and ſhall and will jointly and equally advance and pay the ſhare and proportion of the party or parties ſo dying, and in caſe of refuſing or declining ſo to do, then the other or others of the ſaid ſurviving parties, who ſhall be willing ſo to do, ſhall and may advance and make good the deceaſed's ſhare, and be intereſted in and intitled unto the ſaid premiſes in proportion to the money he or they ſhall ſo advance: And for the true performance of this preſent agreement, each of the ſaid parties, doth hereby bind himſelf, his heirs, executors and adminiſtrators, unto the other and others of them, and his and their reſpective executors, adminiſtrators, and aſſigns, in the penal ſum of three thouſand pounds of lawful money of Great-Britain. In witneſs whereof, the ſaid parties firſt abovenamed, have hereunto interchangeably ſet their hands and ſeals, the day and year firſt abovewritten.

Sealed and delivered (being firſt duly ſtamp'd) in the preſence of JA. HUTCHINSON.	T. HARRIS. (L. S.) J. RUTHERFORD. (L. S.) G. COLMAN. (L. S.) WILL. POWELL. (L. S.)

About

About the beginning of May, being wrought upon by your extreme folicitude and grofs defceptions, concerning the neceffity of it, we began to take the management of the theatre into farther confideration.

As we had obferved from our fettling the firft contract, that from a ftrange puerile vanity that poffeffed you, a perpetual attempt at fuperiority ever mixed itfelf in your converfation on bufinefs; though we could not then fufpect any latent defign upon our property, but rather imputed it all to infirmity of temper, yet we thought it prudent to give a particular charge and precaution to Mr. Hutchinfon our attorney to take efpecial care, to guard and fecure our rights, and authority in this new inftrument, relative to the management, in like manner as we had directed and required him to do in the firft contract with you.

Here, Sir, we would infert this fecond inftrument with the remarks that we intend to make upon it, but there being a matter in difpute between us, that fome time or other muft be fettled, we think the adjufting that point fhould be our next ftep; efpecially as it will be a very proper preface to the article, and ferve to introduce the reader to a more intimate acquaintance with your character and accomplifhments.

Mr. Powell has often loudly complained, that he has been impofed upon concerning the article of management; that he is thereby barely defrauded of his juft right, and of his power over his property, by his fellow patentees. This complaint is as notorious, as that he is an equal proprietor.——The hiftory of Mr. Powell's preclufion is as follows.

On your return from Bath, the beginning of May, we called on you: the firft words you faid to us, and the laft at that meeting, were all tending to prove the certain ruin of us all, if Mr. Powell had any right to interfere in the management of the theatre; and this was the firft time

time the idea of excluding Mr. Powell ever occurred to us. But you repeatedly insisted, that Powell was a man of no degree of understanding; that his boundless and excessive vanity, with his insuperable love of expence, must be the destruction of our undertaking.—To Mr. Powell's private character we were then entire strangers, we knew him only as a performer; you, Sir, was his FRIEND, his INTIMATE.—We objected to the measure as unequitable and impracticable; you persisted and assured us it would be for his good in the end, as well as for the general good of us all.—We therefore acquiesced. Now, Sir, where the dishonourable part of this transaction will justly fall, the bare assertion of either party cannot determine, facts and circumstances must.

On the side of Harris and Rutherford it may be urged, that it does not appear in the least probable, that the same men who brought Powell into the partnership, who opposed Colman's intended monopoly of power, and who honestly established an equality among them all, by the *first* instrument, should so suddenly, and for no apparent reason, be for precluding Powell from all power by the second instrument: it is to be observed too, that Harris and Rutherford have never once pretended to more than that moiety of power, which their moiety of property naturally gave them; *that they have never since in any single instance desired, or intended to carry into execution any one measure that was or might be objected to by Mr. Powell.* But it appears evidently from the very first, that Colman used every means to engross the whole power to himself. Is not this one proof, that Colman was the man who suggested, prosecuted, and accomplished the plan of engaging Powell, to give up all right over his property.

But still you say, and have given it under your hand to the public, (for the truth of which the immediate jewel of your soul is pledged) that Rutherford and Harris were the contrivers of Powell's preclusion. —In judging of this point, the public will no doubt be led to consider, that Colman was Powell's avowed friend, that Colman was brought into the partnerſhip by Powell, ſo that it is not reaſonable to think, that after ſuch obligations, Colman could be perfidious enough to contrive and compaſs the excluſion of his friend. In anſwer to this reaſoning, we will make uſe of your own words in your True State: "*Powell* "*however ſhewed great repugnance to giving me the direction; but on my* "*expoſtulating with him* ALONE (do you mark, Sir, ALONE) *on this ſub-* "*ject, and reminding him of his firſt application to me, and my declared* "*reſolutions at that period, he (Powell) frankly confeſſed, that he had been* "*adviſed to the contrary, but that on reflection he returned to his original* "*intention, and was content to put his fame and fortune into my hands.*" Did Mr. Colman ever throw ſo ſevere an imputation upon us, as he has now done upon himſelf? Tickled with the vanity of ſhewing how implicit a confidence Powell had repoſed in him, he has inadvertently diſcovered how unworthily he obtained it, and the uſe he made of it, leaving us at a loſs which moſt to admire, his own ſubtilty or his friend's ſimplicity. We would aſk Mr. Powell, if we ever offered the ſmalleſt attempt, or expreſſed the moſt diſtant hint of our deſire, that he ſhould reſign his power into your hands; indeed his frequent complaints during the tranſaction, and very often ſince to many of his friends, and to one reſpectable gentleman, in particular, of your continually importuning him day by day to give up his voice, ſets this matter clearly enough to view: but if there yet remain any doubt, take the following tranſaction.—Some time in November laſt, Harris, Rutherford, Colman, and Powell, met to adjuſt their differences. Powell complained loudly of the article of management, as an infamous fraud upon his property, and an abuſe upon his good-nature, (for ſo he termed his ignorance and credulity) and in plain Engliſh ſaid, "That the precluding him from a power over his property, was a d——d rog—ſh tranſaction." Harris and Rutherford blamed him much for not diſtinguiſhing who contrived or brought him to conſent to that meaſure, and declared they were ready that inſtant to return him the equal ſhare of power he

4 had

had vested in him by the original article. But to this Mr. Powell's bosom-friend with great warmth absolutely refused to assent, affirming vehemently "*The power I have I will keep, I will not part with a jot of it.*"

It will avail you nothing to deny the truth of this anecdote. We have often since repeated the same offer. We now leave the impartial reader to determine which of us is guilty of suggesting, of accomplishing, and of continuing the exclusion of Mr. Powell.

The infinite pains you have taken from time to time, to misrepresent and elude every clause in the following article, must certainly have imprinted indelibly every syllable of it in your memory. Yet we must beg your patience whilst we give it you once more at full length.

Whereas T. Harris, J. Rutherford, G. Colman, and W. Powell, by certain articles of agreement, dated the 31st day of May last, did agree to purchase of the representatives of John Rich, Esq; deceased, two patents for exhibiting theatrical performances, and the several leases of Covent-Garden theatre, and the rooms, buildings, conveniencies, furniture, cloaths, scenes, decorations, music, entertainments, and all things belonging to the said theatre; and the said T. Harris and J. Rutherford, were thereby authorized to treat for, and purchase the same, at a sum not exceeding sixty thousand pounds, and the purchase money was to be advanced by the said parties equally, and they were to become jointly *and* equally *concerned in the management of the said theatre, and were to execute proper deeds and instruments for that purpose, when the said purchase should be compleated. And whereas the said T. Harris and J. Rutherford, have accordingly contracted and agreed with the representatives of the said John Rich, for the purchasing the said patents, leases, premises and things, at and for a sum of sixty thousand pounds, and which purchase is to be compleated on the first of July next.*—So far is a recital of the first article; now follows what may be called the acting manager's clause.

Now the said several parties having perused, *and fully understanding the* purport *and* contents *of the said contract, do approve of, and confirm the same, and having also, in consequence thereof, taken into their consideration, the management of the said theatre, they have, for the* better, *and more* easy conducting the business thereof, *as well as for their joint and equal benefit and advantage, agree, and do hereby mutually declare and agree, that notwithstanding every thing contained in the said agreement already made between the said parties, the said G. Colman shall be invested with the direction of the said theatre, in the particulars following,* viz. "*That he shall have power of engaging and dismissing performers of all kinds, of receiving or rejecting such new pieces as shall be offered to the said theatre, or the proprietors thereof, of casting the plays, of appointing what plays, farces, entertainments, and and other exhibitions shall be performed, and of conducting all such things as are generally understood to be comprehended in the dramatical and theatrical province.*"

By virtue of this clause, you have assumed to yourself the title of *Acting Manager*,—a technical, undefinable, tyrannical term, by which you have imposed on all the inferior players, and servants belonging to the theatre, and by infinite pains have persuaded them, that under that title you have an unlimited absolute power over every department of the stage.—If you had informed them justly, they would have known that this is but one clause of the articles, which clause has no force in law, reason, or equity, independent of the provisions and restrictions contained and expressed in the fourth.—We now proceed to the third clause.

"*And the said T. Harris and J. Rutherford, shall be desired to attend to the controulment of the accounts and treasury relative to the said theatre.—Provided always, and in as much as the said T. Harris and J. Rutherford, will* have leisure to attend to the affairs of the said theatre, *and the said W. Powell is to be engaged as an actor or performer on the stage, (for which purpose, separate articles are intended to be entered into between him and the other parties) in which his time and attention will be chiefly employed and taken up,—so that he will not be able to apply himself in managing the business of the theatre.*

In the third clause you will observe that Harris and Rutherford have the department of the treasury particularly assigned to them, and are said to have leisure to attend to the affairs of the said theatre, by which it is evident that it was by no means intended you should bear the burthen of the sole management.—But as to your friend Powell, he poor man, appears to be a mere parenthesis, and of the insignificant kind too, of no mark or power, but to interrupt the sense and order of the instrument.

Now, sir, to the fourth, or the controuling clause, which clause you have directly violated in the progress of your conduct throughout the whole of the past season.

It is therefore hereby further agreed, that the said G. Colman shall from time to time, and at all times hereafter, communicate and submit his conduct, and the measures he shall intend to pursue, unto them the said Harris and Rutherford.—So far surely is very full, explicit, and intelligible, nor do we see any room to exercise the arts of quibling and chicanery: but to proceed.—"*And in case they shall at any time signify their disapprobation thereof in writing unto the said G. Colman, then and in that case, the measures so disapproved of, shall not be carried into execution*, any thing before contained to the contrary notwithstanding." Now, if you will do us the favour to read this *fairly* to your friends the box-keepers, treasurer, house-keeper, wardrobe-keeper, under actors, carpenters and candle snuffers, they will explain to you the *power* that is annexed to your boasted title of *Acting Manager*. This, and only this, to *propose* and to *submit*, and if we approve, to *execute*,—*not else*.—They may tell you too that this is all the power any equal partner ought to have.—It is all that law or equity would give, or any honest man demand.—And give *us* leave to tell you

you, it is all the power you ever ſhall have, while we are proprietors of Covent-Garden theatre. The following is the fifth, which we think may with propriety be termed the amicable clauſe.

" *Yet nevertheleſs with reſpect to the ſaid W. Powell, it is intended and agreed, that he ſhall at all times give his advice and aſſiſtance relative to any part of the buſineſs of the ſaid theatre, when thereunto deſired by the other parties.*"

Thus, ſir, have you provided for the man, " *Who was content to put his fame and fortune into your hands.*" Unleſs he is called upon by the other three proprietors for his advice and aſſiſtance, it is an abſolute infringement of the articles for him ever to obtrude his opinion in any matters whatſoever.

No ſooner was the foregoing article executed, than your deſign of diveſting us of our legal, natural, and equitable power over our property, began to appear too plainly to be doubted by us.—Your friends, agents, authors, actors, printers, box-keepers, news-writers, Powell and Colman, all affirm that Colman is inveſted with the abſolute management of the whole theatre: for you well knew, when once the public are impreſſed with a falſhood, it takes ſome time to undeceive them.—Another ſtroke of your policy was, to exert all your talents of ſlander and ridicule againſt us. Our youth, our inexperience, our way of thinking, our courſe of life, and our conduct in every particular, were rendered as contemptible as your labouring invention could paint them.

The ſeaſon at length arrived for opening the theatre, previous to which a rehearſal was appointed, and it being the firſt under the new proprietors, the whole company were ſummoned to attend. We thought it encumbent on us not to omit this opportunity of ſeeing the performers thus convened, and accordingly entered the theatre with all the

chearfulneſs

chearfulneſs of young men, fond of a new, promiſing and agreeable purchaſe.—But how were we received? We expected the performers, (eſpecially the capital ones) would have been introduced to us: but inſtead of ſhewing us any marks of civility, you impetuouſly came up to us with the appearance of offended pride and enraged importance; ſtopped us ſhort, and bade us go off the ſtage, leſt we ſhould interrupt *the buſineſs of the theatre.*

Petulant and ill-mannered as we then thought your treatment in this inſtance, we now perceive it was a part of your original policy, to keep us as much as poſſible, ignorant of all matters relative to the theatre, and of every perſon belonging to it; which plan is obviouſly conſiſtent with your original one, of worming yourſelf by degrees into the ſole and arbitrary direction of the theatre.

On the 14th September the theatre opened; every day giving us freſh reaſons to reſent your inſolence. We will not here re-enter on the propriety or impropriety of your engaging Mr. and Mrs. Yates; but ſhall only tell you, that as it was a meaſure diſapproved of by us all in conference on that head, and a meaſure of great conſequence to us all, it ought not to have been taken without the conſent of Harris and Rutherford, eſpecially not in defiance of our known opinion.—The reaſon you aſſign for this precipitate engagement, will not bear you harmleſs, for you knew you had the ſtrongeſt aſſurances that the managers of Drury-Lane would not engage them.

As to the affair of Cymbeline, the falſhood of your repreſentation in your pamphlet, is capable of proof: if we did not think the time would be miſpent in agitating an obſolete queſtion. You are ſenſible, that by your excellence in the art of ſtirring up a fire, you made it abſolutely neceſſary for us to forbid a repetition of this performance.

Upon

Upon receipt of this prohibition, you and Mr. Powell thus conformed to your articles; *you* threatened to ſhut up the theatre, and *Mr. Powell* to appeal to his friends and the public for redreſs. (See *True State*, p. 36.) About this time we began to perceive, by the deluge of tradeſmens bills, that an immenſe expence for the wardrobe, &c. had been incurred by Mrs. Powell, without our knowledge or conſent.—We therefore could not but think it highly expedient for us to examine minutely what property had been brought into the theatre. On enquiry, we were told by the wardrobe-keepers, that great part of the property was in the poſſeſſion of Mrs. Powell, at her houſe in Ruſſel-ſtreet, Covent-Garden. We then, with as much politeneſs as we were maſters of, deſired that Mrs. Powell would ſend to the theatre what belonged to it; and that ſhe would not give herſelf the trouble to incur any more expence without our knowledge. We immediately received an anſwer from W. Powell, that our requeſts could not be complied with; that Mrs. Powell was inveſted with the care of the wardrobe by Mr. Colman, and that we ſhould find he, Mr. Powell, was not that *cypher* we ſeemed to imagine. (See *True State*, p. 38.) This anſwer might have juſtified our reſentment, though it excited only our riſibility.

We do not find that the managers of Drury-Lane, give any precedent for this conduct of Mr. Powell. All their wardrobe, *appropriated* and *unappropriated*, is in the theatre, under the care of proper officers, equally reſponſible to them both.—But we find in Mr. Powell's anſwer, that *Mr. Colman* inveſted Mr. and Mrs. Powell with the care of the wardrobe. You ſeem here, ſir, to have power far beyond a director; you are a theatrical *deity*, for in this mimic world nothing is to exiſt but by your *fiat*. Your arrogance ſaid, let Powell be a cypher and he was cypher. Your caprice revokes his deſtiny, and this cypher becomes a manager; while Harris and Rutherford, for conſpiring together how to preſerve the ſmall remnant of their liberties, are compelled to bend the knee to their theatrical Moloch, or endure the fiery ordeal of his diſpleaſure.

To

To relieve your attention a little from the confideration of ftubborn facts, I will here attempt a parallel between yourfelf and another *acting manager* of great notoriety in former days. You will find his hiftory in Cibber's Apology: this gentleman was a patentee partner, bred to the law, and like you too appointed *acting manager*; fubject to the conftant infpection and controul of his partners, who like us were then confidered as controuling managers, he promifed to raife the revenue of the theatre greatly, juft as you have done; he began his management by refufing to fubmit the little matters of theatrical bufinefs to his partners; then he refufed to fubmit greater matters, 'till at length he fhook off their infpection and controul in every refpect: (fo far is not the comparifon exact?) He then proceeded to raife a thoufand ftories of the ignorance and tyranny of his partners: endeavouring to incenfe the publick againft them as men and managers. He boafted daily what full houfes his management produced; that he meant all for the good of his partners; that he was going on profperoufly, and fhould continue fo, if they would but be quiet—your conduct exactly!—But, inftead of having raifed the profits of the theatre, he leffened them many thoufands, juft as you have done, Sir—at leaft (by the account given in to his partners;) then, Sir, he engaged whatever fervants and performers he thought proper; obliging them to obey none but him; and laid out whatever fums he pleafed, without the confent or knowledge of the other proprietors--altogether juft as you have done.—But to complete his character of *acting managing*, he at length took exclufive poffeffion of the theatre, patent, wardrobe, &c. &c. and referred his fellow proprietors to the court of Chancery for redrefs. Thus far the comparifon holds:—but we truft here it will break off, for this *acting manager*, proceeding by bills in Chancery, fuits in law, and every pettyfogging trick, fo tired and harraffed his fellow proprietors, that they were in the end heartily glad to give up their property, and to leave him in entire poffeffion, rather than have any more concern with fuch a man.

To return now to our narration:

The ſchemes and arts that you practiſed to creep into an excluſive management, and in conſequence of that into an excluſive poſſeſſion, were various, and inceſſant in their operations. But among them all, your favourite ſcheme to that end, was that of being thought an able and a *ſucceſsful* manager, and to ſupport that character, it is incredible to thoſe who know not your arts, what an enormous burthen it hath been to the partnerſhip, not leſs than thirty, forty, fifty, and ſixty pounds in orders, were generally ſent into the theatre each night; and on one night in particular in ſupport of one of your own pieces upwards of one hundred pounds. Thus Sir, you ſupported your fame, at the expence of our common property.——

About the latter end of February, we were informed you were tampering with the performers, ſervants, &c. &c. and endeavouring to prevail on them to enter into articles with *you only:* which articles, it ſeems, you were prepared to execute upon your own proper authority, without any reference to us, and our privilege of reviſing and diſſenting from or confirming the ſame.

This appeared ſo manifeſt a violation of your engagements, and ſo directly contrary to the expreſs letter of our articles, that we could ſcarce give credit to it: however, in order to guard againſt ſo dangerous a meaſure, we immediately ordered Mr. Garton the treaſurer, to ſerve the following notice, *mutatis mutandis,* upon every perſon belonging to the theatre.

SIR,

I AM directed by Meſſrs. Harris and Rutherford, to give you notice, that you cannot be conſidered as belonging to Covent-Garden theatre

 after

after the expiration of this ſeaſon, unleſs the engagements you may enter into for the next, be confirmed in writing by one or both of us.

Covent-Garden theatre,
Feb. 25, 1768.

J. GARTON.

This notice we thought had nothing offenſive or unreaſonable in it, yet you, Sir, and Mr. Powell, were incenſed to the higheſt degree; and that part of the company who were dependants, and others who wanted to pay their court to you, did, in imitation of you and Mr. Powell, exclaim againſt it in the moſt abuſive and bitter terms.—One gentleman in particular, an intimate and avowed friend of yours, and formerly, as we have been told, a military man; (you know how to chuſe your friends!) when the above notice was given to him in the green-room, (before great part of the company) threw it into the fire with the utmoſt indignation: then ſtamping on it, added this explicit comment to the act: that if he had power, he would ſerve the authors as he ſerved this notice—thruſt them into the middle of the flames.—

This kind of language has been frequently held by this intimate friend of yours in public coffee-houſes, and wherever he reſorted, as we have been informed by many gentlemen, who have heard and been ſhocked at his indecent behaviour. Every ſervant and inferior actor in the theatre, knowing how much ſuch conduct pleaſed and delighted you, imitated in all places this gentleman's behaviour.

Thus you form a contrivance to deprive us of our property, and if we legally endeavour to defend it, by ſending a proper notice to the company, not to enter into engagements without our concurrence, you inſtantly excite them by variety of falſhoods and others arts, to factious abuſe, contempt, public ſcurrility, and falſe reports, againſt our conduct and characters.—By this kind of craft you ſee, Sir, to what a dilemma you reduce us, we muſt patiently ſubmit to the falſe reports and abuſes of the under actors and ſervants in our pay, or we muſt implicitly reſign our property to be diſpoſed of as your arbitrary humour ſhall direct.

But theſe indecences, which to you who are the companion of thoſe who utter them, might be irkſome; to us, who do not hold ourſelves obliged to enter the liſts with our own ſervants, were ever, and ſhall continue to be regarded with the contempt they merit. You poſſeſs the ſaving art of transferring your own quarrel to other men, and we have no more reſentment againſt theſe engines of yours, whom you have enliſted as the factious abettors of your arbitrary and illegal deſigns, than we ſhould have againſt your footman, who brought an impertinent meſſage or letter from you.

We began now to be very deſirous of knowing how the company were to be fixed for the enſuing year, and wrote to you often for that purpoſe. On the 21ſt of March, we obtained a plan of the alteration you propoſed. On the 25th of the ſame month you received our anſwer, in which we aſſigned very minutely our reaſons wherever we differed from you, and requeſted we might have yours in return as ſoon as convenient, to the end, that a plan for the enſuing ſeaſon might be ſpeedily formed for the general good.

About this time, ſir, as you kept boaſting of your ſucceſsful management, Mr. Rutherford and myſelf offered in the preſence of ſeveral gentlemen, to inſure to you for three years, a ſum equal to the produce of that management: whatever more might appear on the books at the cloſe of each year, to be ſhared equally, if you would give yourſelf no more trouble about the management. This you refuſed; but offered us, if we would withdraw ourſelves, a ſum equal to our our ſhare in the profits of the preſent year; but what further ſum your

manage-

management might produce, you and Mr. Powell were to ſhare between you.—At the ſame meeting, you frequently in the moſt agitated manner repeated, "*Will you ſell? Will you ſell?*"—As no reaſon ſuggeſted itſelf to me, why I ſhould be obliged to ſell any more than yourſelf, you know I made you this offer: viz. "To put my ſhare with yours, on the inſtant up to auction, and whoever of the two (Colman and Harris) ſhould bid moſt, ſhould have both;" *this too you refuſed.*

After many letters and interviews having paſſed on the ſubject of ſettling the buſineſs of the theatre, in which you artfully delayed coming to any determination, and endeavoured by all methods to keep us profoundly ignorant of your tranſactions or intentions. We ſerved you on the 15th of April, with a general notice to conform to your articles:—yet notwithſtanding all theſe precautions, we were much ſurprized a week or two after, to hear that you were engaging the company under pretence that our differences were all amicably adjuſted.

Exceedingly alarmed at this intelligence, we the ſame day ſent for ſeveral of the performers; who all aſſured us, Mr. Colman had taken them unawares, that they underſtood it was entirely agreeable to us, or otherwiſe they ſhould not have entered into any engagement with him. One in particular of eminence in his profeſſion aſſured us, he was ſo much concerned at being thus deceived, that he would go immediately to Mr. Colman, and endeavour to get his agreement cancelled: he accordingly went, and afterwards ſent us the following letter.

SIR,

S I R,

I Waited on Mr. Colman this morning, and according to my promiſe, demanded the cancelling of the agreement I had made with him, in the manner you deſired; his anſwer was, *he would not*.

As ſuch, I hope you will conſider I have done every thing you wiſhed me to do, and flatter myſelf you will look on Mr. and Mrs. Mattocks as deſirous of doing their buſineſs, without entering into party.

I am, Sir,

April 28, 1728.

With reſpect, &c.

G. M A T T O C K S.

In this ſituation, in order to prevent as much as poſſible the effects of your promiſes, threats, and miſrepreſentations, in the performers, ſervants, and others, we cauſed the following paper to be printed and delivered to every performer, &c.

TO THE PERFORMERS AND OTHER PERSONS BELONGING TO COVENT-GARDEN THEATRE.

THE many partial, arbitrary and unwarrantable proceedings of George Colman, Eſq; one of the managers of Covent-Garden theatre, being manifeſtly injurious to the intereſt and property of us Thomas Harris and John Rutherford, we thought ourſelves obliged, with the advice of counſel, to give him the following written notice.

T O

TO G. COLMAN, ESQ;

IN purſuance of articles of agreement entered into, between you the ſaid George Colman, and us Thomas Harris and John Rutherford, whoſe names are hereunto ſubſcribed, and alſo William Powell, bearing date the fourteenth day of May, 1767, we do hereby require you to communicate and ſubmit unto us, the ſaid Thomas Harris and John Rutherford, all future meaſures, which you ſhall intend to purſue, reſpecting the direction of Covent-Garden theatre; and more eſpecially, we do hereby conjointly forbid you engaging or contracting with any performers, artificers, or ſervants, of any kind or denomination whatſoever, for the next ſeaſon, or for any other term or time at the ſaid theatre, without firſt communicating and ſubmitting to us your intended contracts or agreements with ſuch performers, artificers or ſervants, and every of them; and we do hereby further in particular conjointly prohibit you from receiving, contracting for, or getting up for performance any new pieces, which may be offered to you for the ſaid theatre, or on behalf of the proprietors thereof, and from reviving any old plays or performances of any kind, and alſo from caſting any plays to be performed at the ſaid theatre, without firſt communicating and ſubmitting to us the ſaid Thomas Harris and John Rutherford, all and every the meaſures you ſhall intend to purſue in theſe reſpects, and alſo all ſuch meaſures as regard your future conduct and management of all things comprehended in the dramatic and theatrical province of the ſaid theatre; ſo that we may, if we ſhall think fit, ſignify our diſapprobation thereof in writing to you; in which caſe, the ſame are not to be carried into execution, purſuant to the ſaid articles: And we do hereby further give you notice, that all contracts or agreements made, or to be made by you with any performers, artificers or ſervants whatſoever, contrary to the tenor of this preſent warning or notice, ſhall be deemed and conſidered by us as null and void; and that we ſhall forbid and prevent the payment of the

ſalaries

falaries, or other allowances or gratuities thereby ftipulated or agreed to be given, made, or paid to fuch performers, artificers or fervants, and every of them ; and fhall alfo prohibit and prevent the payment for getting up, or performing of any new pieces received, contracted for, or ordered to be got up by you, contrary to this notice, and the payment of all expences attending the fame. At the fame time we do affure you, that we do not mean to fignify our difapprobation in writing of any meafure whatfoever, which you fhall intend to purfue, and fhall be duly communicated and fubmitted to us, refpecting the aforefaid particulars, or any of them ; unlefs we fhall be fully fatisfied and convinced in our own judgment that the fame will not be conducive to the entertertainment of the public, and the real interefts of the other proprietors of the faid theatre, and ourfelves: It is, at the fame time, proper for us to apprize you, that thefe being terms and conditions which you are bound by the faid articles of agreement with us to comply with, we fhall, in cafe of your breach of them, purfue all fuch legal remedies to procure fatisfaction and redrefs, as we fhall be advifed. Dated this 18th Day of April, 1768.

THOMAS HARRIS,

JOHN RURTHERFORD.

And whereas we have received information that the faid George Colman has fecretly and clandeftinely entered into articles with certain perfons, now belonging to this theatre, in defiance of the above notice or warning, in open violation of the articles fubfifting between us, and in contempt of our legal proteft in writing to him delivered ; it is therefore judged expedient, in regard to the fecurity of the company, to give this general notice, That fuch agreements are, in the opinion of counfel illegal, and therefore will not be affented to, or deemed obligatory, by us ; and that all perfons who have, or fhall at any time enter into any agreement with the faid George Colman, without having the affent in writing of one or both of us, will be confidered as entering into a combination with the faid George Colman, to diveft us of that natural and equitable right over our property in the faid theatre, which we are determined by every legal method to maintain.

Many falfe and malicious afperfions alfo having been openly as well as covertly propagated, that we mean to difcharge feveral of the performers, &c. to lower the falaries of others, and to weaken and throw the whole company into diforder and confufion, than which nothing can be more contrary to our intentions. All perfons, therefore, who are defirous of being fatisfied of our defigns refpecting themfelves in particular, or the theatre in general, are requefted to apply to us, at the faid theatre, or at either of our houfes refpectively.

Covent-Garden Theatre,
April 27, 1768.

THOMAS HARRIS,

JOHN RUTHERFORD.

We were now informed, that Mr. Colman was negociating with every perfon belonging to the theatre, and devifing every means to engage them. In order as much as in us lay to prevent this, we fent for many of the principal performers, cautioned them not to enter into an engagement with Mr. Colman alone:—again and again explained to them, that no engagement with Mr. Colman alone could be binding on us or them, contrary to notices given to both parties. We even went farther, and, that it might not be urged, againft us, as it had been, that our protefts were frivolous and capricious, and had no other object than to prevent the public exhibitions of the theatre we offered to engage any of them in a manner conformable to our articles with Meffrs. Colman and Powell, which we were advifed we legally might do. But we found your artifices had taken too much hold of many amongſt them; and upon this diſcovery we entirely declined any further engagements with them.—At the ſame time we cauſed the following paper to be exhibited in both the green-rooms.

OBSERVATIONS OFFERED TO THE CONSIDERATION OF THE PERFORMERS AND OTHER PERSONS BELONGING TO COVENT-GARDEN THEATRE.

WHereas ſeveral falſe and deceptive inſinuations have been thrown out, reſpecting the preſent circumſtances of Covent-Garden theatre, it is judged expedient to offer the following obſervations to the parties concerned.

I. That as George Colman, Eſq; is inveſted with the management of the ſaid theatre by an article, in which he is expreſly bound to ſubmit all the meaſures, he may intend to purſue in ſuch management, to T. Harris and J. Rutherford, and to put no deſign in execution which they may diſapprove: he the ſaid George Colman has no right or authority to act as ſole manager, without making ſuch ſubmiſſion of his meaſures to the ſaid Harris and Rutherford, who are by virtue of the ſaid article, ultimately to determine what ſhall or ſhall not be carried into execution by the ſaid Colman, reſpecting the management of the ſaid theatre.

II. That all contracts with performers, or others, made by the ſaid George Colman, for himſelf and fellow proprietors, againſt the conſent, or even without the knowledge of Harris and Rutherford, are and muſt be null and void, ſo far as they regard the ſaid Harris and Rutherford, on whom they cannot be obligatory: the ſaid George Colman not being authorized, but publickly and expreſly forbidden by them to enter into any ſuch contract.

III. That as the ſaid George Colman, notwithſtanding the repeated remonſtrances made to him by Harris and Rutherford, ſtill perſiſts in neglecting to ſubmit to them the meaſures he intends to purſue, in the management of the theatre, and alſo in purſuing ſuch meaſures as they diſapprove, they Harris and Rutherford, are juſtifiable in preventing the farther proceedings of the ſaid Colman, to the injury of their property, and in oppoſition to the tenor of the articles ſubſiſting between them.

IV. That notwithſtanding the undoubted right of Harris and Rutherford to prevent the farther miſmanagement of the ſaid theatre, there is reaſon to believe from the apparent diſpoſition of Mr. Colman, that if the ſaid Harris and Rutherford do ſo exert themſelves in oppoſition to the illegal and unjuſtifiable conduct of the ſaid Colman, an interruption will enſue to the buſineſs of the ſaid theatre.

V. That an interruption to the buſineſs of the theatre muſt be attended with very diſagreeable conſequences, both to the company and the proprietors.

VI. That if, in order to prevent ſuch an interruption, Harris and Rutherford do aſſume the management of the theatre, in default of the ſaid Colman, they are juſtifiable both in law and equity, for the ſubſequent

REASONS.

I. That the negative power given them by article as comptrolling managers, does not supercede their positive power, as two equal and joint proprietors of the theatre; for that they do not, on any consideration, either expressed or understood, thereby resign or give up, that natural and equitable right, which every man has to the disposal and management of his own property: so that they are still at liberty to act positively with regard to such property, as if no such article existed; in which last case, they would undoubtedly have as much right to manage the joint property of the theatre, to contract for and discharge performers, &c. as either or both the two other proprietors.

II. That on the other hand both Colman and Powell do, by the said article resign and give up their right as simple proprietors; Mr. Powell expresly, for a valuable consideration allowed him as a performer, resigning all pretensions to manage; and Mr. Colman intelligibly for the emoluments accruing to him as a dramatic writer, consenting to act as manager subject to the controul of Harris and Rutherford; who expecting no other profits from the theatre, than what must arise from the good management and common interest of the whole, think it extremely unjust they should be deprived of the privilege of providing for its security; especially as for the reasons assigned, they and they only are legally impowered to determine what measures are to be pursued in the conduct of the said theatre.

III. That notwithstanding Colman and Powell are by the said article legally incapacitated, the latter to interfere in the management

at

at all, and the former to manage otherwife than is approved by Harris and Rutherford; while the faid Harris and Rutherford lie under no legal reftraint from acting in default of Colman as mafters of their own property, and joint patentees of the theatre; it is yet by no means the defire of Harris and Rutherford, to infringe the faid articles, or fuperfede the faid Colman as acting manager, they requiring only that he act in conformity to the article by which he was conftituted fuch: in which cafe he actually admitting their negative right as comptrolling managers, they would not willingly exert their pofitive right as patentees and proprietors.

It is hoped, that on this fair and impartial reprefentation of the cafe, none will be fo mifled as to adopt fuch abfurdities, as that any perfon can be invefted with an *exclufive* right of managing at his own pleafure, by an article that authorifes him only to manage under the controul of others; or that Harris and Rutherford can have no other right over their property, than to complain ineffectually of Colman's mifmanagement of it, while he himfelf is authorized to proceed in open breach of the very article, by which he claims the privilege of managing at all. They hereby, therefore, confirm the notices already given to Mr. Colman, and the performers, that they are not nor will deem themfelves bound by any contract or engagement entered into by Mr. Colman, without their confent firft obtained.

T. Harris.
J. Rutherford.

Such was our fituation, when on the fourth of May Mr. Rutherford by accident was preffed by the crowd at Ranelagh clofe to you. He could not avoid expoftulating with you on your conduct, he told you, and *he told you truly*, how extremely defirous we were of ending a

contention

contention which ferved only to weary the patience of the public, and facrifice our joint interefts. In confequence of this accidental rencontre you appointed the fucceeding evening, for the four parties to meet. Mr. Rutherford and myfelf met you, with a fixed determination to ufe every poffible method of finally clofing a difpute, which had for fo many months harreffed and diftreffed us; we were determined to give you up all your *points*, as you call them, though we were too fenfible many of them were very injurious to our property. Indeed we never did mean litigioufly to contend with you about matters of inferior moment. This, from firft to laft, has been the *only point* we had in view, viz. to have an equitable controul over our *property*, *and the mangement of it*. In this difpofition we met you, when it was foon underftood that all arrangements relative to this theatre might very eafily be adjufted to the fatisfaction of all parties. The following point was the only one in which we differed from *you*; and in juftice to Mr. Powell, we muft declare he likewife differed from you throughout the whole of the arguments, equally with ourfelves. You infifted that you fingly had a right to form the mode of engaging performers, and that no one but yourfelf *fhould* fign an article with any performer. We urged that the making agreements with performers was a meafure of the greateft expence and importance in our undertaking, and that by our articles you were obliged from time to time, and at all times, to fubmit your conduct, and the meafures you intended to purfue; and that upon our difapprobation the meafure was not to be carried into execution. We farther urged, that from the nature of our circumftances, having an undivided moiety of the property, from the common ufage and nature of partnerfhip, from the exprefs letter of our article, from common fenfe and common equity, as we were liable to pay the half the expences or damages that might occur in our undertaking, we thought it but reafonable that bonds, penalties, and expences, amounting to fo many thoufands a year, fhould *not* be entered into in our names without our knowledge and confent; which could be no otherwife affured to us, than by our

figning

figning the agreement; and that if you intended to article none but fuch as we approved, there could not poffibly arife an objection to every article being figned by the four proprietors.

This reafoning having no kind of weight with *you*, we made you this propofal.—That our articles refpecting the management fhould be laid before fome one or two of the moft eminent counfel, *to be nominated by yourfelf*, who fhould have power given to prefcribe a form for engaging performers in future, and who fhould determine who of us *were*, and who were *not* to fign the faid article.

Mr. Powell received this propofal as became him; he declared it to be his opinion that we ought all to fign the articles with performers, but obferved that the offer of referring it to counfel was fair and candid in the higheft degree. You yourfelf, fir, even *you*,—allowed it to be fair, but faid *you muft take two or three days to confider of it*. We then parted in appearance moft amicably difpofed to each other.—Mr. Powell now openly avowed the equity of our proceeding, and publicly declared to all his friends, that if our difputes were not entirely ended, it muft be altogether Colman's fault; and indeed was fanguine enough to fay, that it was impoffible Colman fhould not confent to our unexceptionable propofal. But how were his and our expectations defeated, when, after impatiently waiting the expiration of two days, we received the following note.

SIR,

SInce I had the pleafure of feeing you and Mr. Rutherford, I have advifed with my friends and counfel concerning your joint propofal. They are all unanimoufly of opinion, that my right to contract with performers in the manner I propofe, is fo clear and obvious on the face

of

of our article, that there is not the leaſt occaſion or foundation for a reference. A reference implies a doubt which they do not admit, nor can it reaſonably be expected that I ſhould appeal to other counſel to decide a queſtion between us, when my own have ſatisfied me that the point is indiſputable.

I am, Sir,

Your moſt obedient humble ſervant,

G. COLMAN.

I forbear making any remarks upon this evaſive epiſtle: You are not to be told what were the motives which induced you to reject this equitable propoſal; and the reader, I am perſuaded, will anticipate me in the concluſion to be drawn from it.

During theſe tranſactions we heard nothing from you relative to the adjuſtment of affairs for the enſuing ſeaſon; we therefore ſent you the following letter.

SIR,

WE wrote to you the 19th of April laſt, and again on the 10th of May, reſpecting the ſtate of our affairs; to both which letters we have had no other anſwer than yours of the 11th inſtant, importing only that you would with all convenient ſpeed give us an anſwer, and that it was wholly owing to ourſelves we had not received one ſooner. This we are entirely at a loſs to underſtand: but we plainly perceive you can make any evaſion to avoid acquainting us with your meaſures and intentions; but, Sir, being ſenſible how very much you have hurt the property, and injured our fortunes by your management this year, you cannot but imagine we are extremely anxious about the next ſeaſon; therefore, to keep us ſo perfectly ignorant of your tranſactions reſpecting the company, and of your intentions in regard to the plan of buſineſs for the next year, cannot be deemed conſiſtent with honour, equity, or honeſty.—We requeſt of you, Sir, a plain, preciſe anſwer; and not ſuch as we have hitherto received from you——evaſive, ambiguous, or indirect.

We are, Sir,

May 17. Your humble ſervants,

T. HARRIS.
J. RUTHERFORD.

To George Colman, Eſq;

A few days before this the following letter was ſent to Mr. Powell.

SIR,

BY an article entered into on the 28th of May laſt, we each of us covenant not to act, write, or have any ſhare, intereſt or concern in any theatre whatſoever: yet notwithſtanding this expreſs and clear clauſe, in a converſation the latter end of November laſt, we proved to you that we were then diſpoſed to ſerve you by agreeing to your going to Briſtol, though that was a ſtep diſagreeable to us all—agreed by all to be prejudicial to our common intereſt, and Mr. Colman refuſed his aſſent thereto;—ſince that time the whole tenor of your conduct has been ſuch as to make it impoſſib'e for you to pretend to our friendſhip or favour: you have in oppoſition to our common requeſt and legal prohibition, been aſſiſting in the performing of Cymbeline; you have neglected to deliver up that part of our property in your poſſeſſion, viz. cloaths, ſilks, &c. &c. though formally required ſo to do, on the 31ſt of December laſt; you have continued to load us with great expences without our knowledge, and contrary to the notice given you; you have twice refused, viz. on the 29th of December, and on March 1st, to attend or consult with us on the affairs of the theatre; you have from the beginning to this time been in the most perfect combination with Mr. Colman; you have aided him, and given him colour of pretence for breaking his articles, co-operated with him in sowing dissentions among the company, and in injuring the property by his bad management through the whole of this season; you have suffered your name to be affixed to Mr. Colman's pamphlet, which contains much scandalous abuse, and many falsehoods respecting us, without your having seen it, or knowing the contents of it before published; so prompt were you to wrong those who had ever before shewn themselves eager to serve you; and you have yesterday for the first time play'd Hamlet for a benefit, contrary to the common interest, and our earnest desire; you have schemed and assisted Mr. Colman to divest us of our rights, and to lessen our property in the theatre; of this the whole of your conduct, and your repeated declarations at different times (of which witnesses can be produced) are sufficient evidence.

Now, sir, on a review of our past behaviour, we persuade ourselves you are not *mean* enough to ask an indulgence, nor *weak* enough to expect one; and as we never will be justly accused of acting ambiguously or covertly, we give you this notice, that you are in all matters to conform to the letter of all the articles entered into between us; particularly that wherein you are not to have any share in, or perform at Bristol or any other theatre whatsoever; and you are hereby again required without delay to deliver into the theatre, all cloaths, silks, and other effects, which are the joint property of the proprietors, and which may be now in your possession.

We are, Sir,

Your humble servants,

T. HARRIS.

J. RUTHERFORD.

April 26, 1768.

To William Powell.

The article referred to in the above letter, in which all parties covenant to have no concern in any other theatre, you remember, ſir, was warmly inſiſted on by you, in order to prevent Mr. Powell from going to Briſtol. (See *True State*, p. 42 and 43.) Mr. Powell at firſt objected very ſtrongly againſt it, but at laſt your threatning, perſuading *art* convinced him that *this* clauſe was alſo for his intereſt, as well as *that* wherein he excluded, himſelf from having any ſhare in the management of his own property. Here, Mr. Colman, you moſt generouſly reſolved that your boſom friend Powell's fame and fortune (which he had intruſted you with) was in no account to ſtand in the way of your aſſuming dignity. (See *True State*, p. 42.)

To the above letter we received no anſwer. Indeed, all we intended by it, was to exhibit the man to himſelf; and though we had no deſign to revoke the conſent we had paſſed for his going to Briſtol this ſeaſon, yet we held it expedient to recall his articles to his memory, in particular, that wherein he is put under diſabilities from acting at any other theatre whatever; fairly intimating to him at the ſame time, that we did not find ourſelves inclined to grant him any ſuch indulgencies for the future.

But alas! to our ſorrow we muſt acknowledge the force of that doctrine, you ſo often, and ſo triumphantly repeat.—" *What the d——l ſignifies articles, when there is no penalty?*" Very little truly, ſir: how can we expect you will do juſtice without compulſion? for want of which, to refer you to your articles, is juſt as fruitleſs as to appeal to your conſcience.

Notwithſtanding the letters of Mr. Harris to Mr. Powell of the 26th April, ever ſince the night we propoſed to refer to counſel the mode of engaging the performers, Mr. Powell appeared to be conſentaneous with us. On the 19th of May we received from you a very long letter, filled as uſual, with falſe facts, falſe reaſoning, and falſe ſuggeſtions; all which we were not ſurpriſed at. But we were very *much ſo* at obſerving the uſe you made of Mr. Powell's name; expressing yourself frequently in the plural number, and making Powell in some measure responsible for your actions and assertions. We thought proper therefore to send a note to Powell, desiring to know how far he would be responsible for the contents of your letter. Upon the receipt of which, Mr. Powell came immediately to my house, where he found Mr. Rutherford. He then assured us he had no concern in the letter, that Mr. Colman had frequently drawn him in to concur in acts which he afterwards repented*.

Notwithstanding this apparently candid and implicit declaration, we received from Mr. Powell the next day the following letter.

SIR,

May 21st, Saturday noon.

I Have received your letter, respecting one you say you have received from Mr. Colman, and desiring to know if I look upon myself equally with him responsible for its contents. Whatever my opinion might be, in regard to Mr. Colman's conduct respecting our affairs, or of the contents of the letter in question (wherein, I presume, he has not made mention of my name, but where 'twas necessary to relate his business for the purpose of his letter) I cannot suffer myself to be responsible for the contents of any thing whereto I do not subscribe my name.—I have the greatest faith in Mr. Colman's intentions for the general good, and I hope and rely, that his conduct will tend to reconcile you to his measures, and produce peace and unanimity to us all.

I am, with compliments to Mr. Rutherford,

Your very humble servant,

W. POWELL.

* At the same time, among other things, he informed us, Mr. Colman had entered into engagements with the house-keeper, carpenters, and wardrobe-keeper. A new species of intrenchment, which we believe was never practised by any *acting manager* in the world before.

It

It appearing by the ſtile and tenour of this letter, that Mr. Powell had been conſulting with Mr. Colman, it was thought proper to return the following anſwer.

TO WILLIAM POWELL, ESQ.

May 24th, Tuday.

SIR,

I Yeſterday received yours dated Saturday noon: I muſt tell you I think the writer of it cannot be the ſame perſon, who was with me on Saturday morning; your converſation to Mr. Rutherford and myſelf, was then ſo very different from the ſtile of your letter, in which there is ſo much evaſion, and ſo much duplicity, that I think I may venture to aſſert nobody but Mr. Colman could be the author of it. It gives me much concern to obſerve, that notwithſtanding your repeated declaration, " *that you wiſhed we never had had any concern with Mr. Colman,* " *and that we three had originally undertaken the theatre without him, in* " *which caſe you was abſolutely certain we never could have diſagreed*; *that* " *you entirely diſagreed with Mr. Colman in his attempts to engage the per-* " *formers by himſelf*; *that you diſapproved of his arbitrary diſpoſition, and* " *of his having frequently made uſe of your name, without having been* " *authorized by you.*"—I ſay, Sir, it is matter of concern and aſtoniſhment, that you ſhould perſiſt (diveſting yourſelf of all pretenſions to judgment in your own affairs) to place ſo implicitly your whole dependence on the man who originally deprived you of your right of interfering in your own affairs, who continues to do it, notwithſtanding we have offered to reſtore you to your right, who has either wickedly or weakly ſo miſmanaged the theatre, as to leſſen the cuſtomary profits of it nearly one half; and who is now endeavouring to fix himſelf ſo firmly and excluſively in the theatre, as in future to have

us

us and our fortunes entirely at the difpofal of his capricious or infidious inclination.——Whatever regard you may think proper to pay to thefe hints now, be affured there will come a time, when you will acknowledge them to have been as deferving of gratitude from you, as has been all our preceding conduct towards you.

I am, Sir,

Your very humble fervant,

T. HARRIS.

To this letter Mr. Harris received no reply.

Nothing worth your notice occurred between this and your clofing the feafon, which you triumphantly did with the play of *Cymbeline*, in order to prove to the company how *glorioufly*, how *compleatly* you had carried *your point*; to prove too the folly of Harris and Rutherford, in prohibiting fuch an *attractive* play, the houfe was to be *made* full :—all your partizans, exult what a houfe! what an amazing houfe for the time of year! but you know, Mr. Colman, the real receipt of the houfe fell far fhort of the nightly expences of the theatre, and *that* notwithftanding your new occafional prologue; indeed there were fixty pounds worth of *orders* in the houfe;—fo it muft be confeffed the houfe was *tolerably* full, and this aufpicious night at once crowned your fuccefs as a manager, and immortalized your name as a poet.

The feafon now being over, we appointed Mr. Garton the treafurer to meet us at the theatre on the of 10th June, in order that we might examine his accounts. After we had gone through them, we informed Mr. Garton they appeared to be all very correct and right, but we perceived he had paid feveral bills, notwithftanding our exprefs orders to the contrary. To this he pleaded only your order, fir; and indeed gave

gave us to underſtand he ſhould pay all bills in future, which you directed, notwithſtanding our prohibition. You will readily allow, we ſuppoſe, that we might reaſonably object to a ſervant who profeſſed he would pay away our money without our permiſſion.—We therefore told him for the future we ſhould be our own treaſurers, and that the balance of the caſh-book being ſo exceedingly ſmall, it was incumbent on us to examine very carefully into the diſburſements; not that we had the leaſt ſuſpicion of him, for that we were ready, if he requeſted it, to give him a full and legal diſcharge that moment: *but*, that as Mr. Colman had moſt arbitrarily conducted our property through the whole ſeaſon, it was highly neceſſary for us minutely to look into the accounts; for which purpoſe we ſhould ſend the two books down to Mr. Harris's dwelling-houſe. To this Mr. Garton making no reſiſtance, the books were given a ſervant of Mr. Harris, to carry home.—We then immediately waited on Mr. Durant of Portman-Square, (who had given a bond of ſecurity for Mr. Garton) with an intention to aſſure this gentleman, who patronized Mr. Garton, that we had no other objection to Mr. Garton's conduct, than his abſolute devotion to the orders of Mr. Colman, and that in defiance of our proteſt and diſſent.

While we were with that gentleman, Mr. Garton came in.—We then, in preſence of Mr. Durant, aſſured Mr. Garton that we had not the leaſt thought of doing him any injury, that we were ready at that moment to ſign any paper he or Mr. Durant ſhould think neceſſary for his ſafety, either a receipt for the books, or a general releaſe; that we were ready at any time to ſettle his account, and give him a proper diſcharge, though we ſhould have no objection to continuing him as treaſurer, if our property was *ſafe*; but that as the treaſury was the only department in which there remained for us the leaſt ſhadow of reſtraint over Mr. Colman's miſconduct, we could not ſuffer Mr. Garton to deprive us of it. Mr. Durant then allowed he could not ſee the leaſt reaſon for Mr. Garton to give himſelf any concern about the books.

Notwithſtanding this Mr. Garton a day or two afterwards called on me and demanded his books, ſaying, if he had known as much *then* as he did *now*, we ſhould have had his life as ſoon as his books,—and that he had ſerved his king and his country,—and that it was unheard-of cruelty to deprive him of his bread. To all which I obſerved, that I had as much reſpect for thoſe gentlemen who had ſerved their king and country as any body could have, but could not ſee why on that account we was compelled to provide for Garton; and after remonſtrating againſt his *unprovoked* inſolence, diſmiſſed him. Since which we find, ſir, your litigious diſpoſition has prevailed on the man to lodge an indictment againſt us in the crown-office; ſetting forth, that with clubs, ſticks, ſtaves, and fiſts, we aſſaulted, beat, bruiſed, and wounded the ſaid Jonathan Garton: and this very probable account you and your emiſſaries have circulated all over the town. You likewiſe took care to have it inſerted in the news papers, that "*for ſome outrageous proceedings in Covent-Garden theatre, one of the proprietors was taken up by a* judge's warrant, *and that another fled from it to France.* How ſcandalouſly contemptible the propogation of ſuch falſehoods, for the ſake of a momentary triumph, when you muſt know, or will ſoon to your coſt be taught, that it was *your* proceedings, not *ours* were illegal.

On the 10th of June we ſent you the following letter.

S I R,

YEſterday upon examining our accounts kept by Mr. Garton, we diſcovered that he had paid ſeveral bills, againſt the payment of which we had proteſted, and he was ſo candid as to inform us, that he ſhould purſue the ſame mode of conduct in future; that is, to pay all bills which he ſhould judge proper for payment, notwithſtanding we might ſignify our diſſent thereto.—From theſe circumſtances we found it neceſſary to diſpoſſeſs him of the power of acting as our treaſurer; which we have accordingly done, and have now in our poſſeſſion (as comptrollers of the treaſury) the journal and ledger belonging to the theatre, and ſhall continue to act for ourſelves, until we may judge it convenient to appoint a treaſurer on our behalf. The India bonds that are in the banker's hands cannot be ſold without an order ſigned by all four; if you and Mr. Powell will authorize either of us to diſpoſe of as many of theſe bonds as may be neceſſary, we will either of us diſcharge all ſuch bills as we think proper; at the ſame time we ſhall carefully obſerve to pay none againſt which either you or Mr. Powell ſhall proteſt.

We are, Sir,

Saturday, June 11, 1768.

Your humble ſervants,

T. Harris.

J. Rutherford.

After reading this letter, we leave the tradeſmen, &c. &c. who have any demand on Covent-Garden theatre, to determine who it is that with-holds the payment of their ſeveral bills. To ſatisfy them ſtill farther, I am ready with your conſent to take on myſelf the care of diſcharging their reſpective demands, and at the ſame time to enter into any bond or penalty you pleaſe, not to pay any demand whatſoever, without having previouſly the written conſent of Mr. Powell and yourſelf.

Our next care was to ſee how the wardrobe was circumſtanced, for we had been informed that Mr. Powell had, with your permiſſion, carried ſome of our moſt valuable cloaths to Briſtol. In order to examine into that matter, as well as the general ſtate of the wardrobe, we appointed Whitfield, the mens wardrobe keeper to attend us on the 10th of June.

'But instead of the wardrobe-keeper, you, sir, attended with Mr. Garton, and another gentlemen, an attorney, (whose name we will not mention, as his general character bespeaks him to be a man of honour and integrity in his profession; as a proof of which, we are informed you now employ him no longer.) You may remember you immediately attacked me in terms the most scandalous and provoking; seeming at one and the the same time, under two very different influences—your fears impressing you with a sense of danger, and your witnesses presenting you with an idea of security: but you then experienced I was not compounded of those very irascible materials you ascribe to me; *anger* is not the passion which your insults at present excite.

You informed us, that *you* had ordered the wardrobe-keeper to attend us;—but that *now* you had ordered him away again, and that you had taken the keys of the wardrobe from him, and that *there* we should not enter.—Upon which, sir, you know that I, in your presence, and in the presence of Mr. —— the attorney and Mr. Garton, put my foot against the wardrobe-door, and burst it open in order to come at the truth of your sending, or permitting the cloaths to be sent, to Bristol; but when we got into the wardrobe, not being able to find the inventory books, and having no wardrobe-keeper to direct us, we suspended our enquiry, until we could procure them. To which end I clapped a padlock on the door, put the key in my pocket, and left you, Mr.——and Mr. Garton together in the theatre.—At the same time we left orders for the wardrobe keeper to come to us for the keys of the padlocks.

Soon after we discovered that many things were taken away by Mr. Powell. What in the whole might be wanting it was impossible for us to ascertain.—Some of the cloaths were of the richest in the wardrobe, and others made new on purpose for Mr. Powell last season.—— Now, in our judgement, this act, whereby you either sent or consented to the sending, the cloaths of Covent-Garden theatre, &c. to be made ufe of at Briftol theatre, without our knowledge, is a licentious abufe of our common property, and indeed (harfh as the expreffion may feem) a pofitive breach of truft in you:—we fay, it is a breach of truft, and our authority for it is the following claufe in our articles.

" *It is therefore hereby further agreed, That the faid George Colman fhall* " *from time to time, and all times hereafter, communicate and fubmit his* " *conduct and the meafures he fhall intend to purfue, unto the faid T. Harris* " *and J. Rutherford, and in cafe they fhall at any time fignify their dif-* " *approbation thereof in writing unto the faid George Colman, then and in* " *that cafe, the meafure fo difapproved of, fhall not be carried into execution;* " *any thing before contained to the contrary notwithftanding.*"—But your injuftice in thus abufing our property, you endeavour to explain away by an affidavit argument. Swearing before a magiftrate, Mr. Colman, is the moft folemn awful act of fociety, and though a man may fo con-ftruct an affidavit as to elude the queftion in difpute, it will never pafs upon the *world*, and the man who practices that kind of *dexterity*, will ever wear a brand in his reputation odious and deep, as public con-tempt can imprefs upon it.

The two points your affidavit attempts to prove, are firft, that it is ufual to indulge performers with cloaths; and fecondly, that the value of the cloaths Mr. Powell took, did not amount to more than 150*l.* or 160*l.* at moft, a fact which we do not believe. But be this as it may, we muft obferve to you, fir, that if a partner embezzles or perverts the property of a partnerfhip which he has in truft, to his own private emolument, either openly or clandeftinely, the turpitude of the crime does not arife out of the *quantity* or *quality*, but out of the *perfidy* of the act.——But your affidavit-man fwears, " *it is* ufual *to lend performers, and fometimes* " *very* inferior ones, *dreffes from the wardrobe of the theatre royal, and* " *that at the clofe of the very laft feafon, Meffrs.* Shuter, Davis, Fifher, " *and Signora* Manefiere, *were* indulged *with the ufe of dreffes and other*

" *properties from the wardrobe of the ſaid theatre, for their own particular* " *uſe, at the theatre wherein they performed in the* COUNTRY."——We believe, ſir, upon recollection you will find that Meſſrs. Shuter and Davis have been for this laſt two or three ſeaſons engaged at Mr. Foote's theatre in the Haymarket, and have not been in the *country*. But ſuch little ſlips as theſe, we allow, are of no kind of importance in a *theatrical affidavit*, eſpecially if they contribute to the better carrying on the plot.—We will allow, that it *may* be *uſual* for a Fiſher or Manaſiere and others, to be *indulged* with a dancing dreſs or two, to be uſed in the country, which is too dirty to be worn by them in town, or that from their ordinary nature they cannot much be damaged.—We are ſenſible, ſir, that your affidavit-men are gentlemen of moſt extenſive conſcience; but we aſk you, whether you can aſſert that it is cuſtomary to indulge any performer with rich and *periſhable* cloaths, to be exhibited, worn and dirtied in country companies? Aſk Meſſrs. Garrick and Lacy that queſtion, ſir;—they muſt tell you that ſuch indulgences would ſoon make the wardrobes of the theatre royal as contemptible as that of a ſtrolling company.—But ſuppoſe we were to grant you, ſir, that it is uſual to lend rich cloaths to performers to be uſed in ſtrolling companies, what would that avail you? — It is uſual to lend money, yet if your ſervant was to lend your money *without your conſent*, we doubt if you would fail to diſcharge him.

But this deponent farther ſwears, " *That he has received the cloaths* " *from Briſtol, ſafe* uninjured *and* unimpaired *in* any degree." Here, ſir, embroidered velvets, ſilks, &c. are ſworn to have been conveyed 240 miles, have been probably worn at Briſtol theatre, and yet are received back ſafe, *uninjured and unimpaired in any degree.* Really, ſir, when you make a man ſwear, the leaſt you can do for him is to take ſome little care of his reputation, whatever may become of his conſcience.

But he farther perſiſts in ſwearing, " *That ſeveral things and proper-* " *ties belonging to Briſtol theatre were uſed and employed in many plays*

" *acted last season at Covent-Garden theatre.*"—Do, sir, be so obliging as to make one more affidavit, and let us know what these things and properties were. We never heard of any before, nor do we *believe* there were any of any value or consideration.—At the same time we beg the favour of you to make the *womens* wardrobe-keeper swear, that Mr. Powell has taken no cloaths from the *womens* wardrobe: it would be a great satisfaction to us, as at present, we are a good deal in doubt about that matter.—But to return to our narrative.

On the 11th June we called again at the theatre; and, observing a tall ferocious figure keeping the door; we asked by whose authority he was planted there? He answered by Mr. Colman, and immediately drew forth the following paper.

I George Colman, one of the proprietors and manager of the theatre royal, Covent-Garden, do hereby appoint W. Flight, of the parish of St. Pancrass in the county of Middlesex, to be assistant house-keeper to Charles Sarjant the house-keeper of the said theatre, and jointly with him, for me, *and in my name*, as manager of the said theatre, to keep possession thereof, and of the house adjoining thereto, occupied by the said Charles Sarjant; and hereby order and direct the said W. Flight, not to suffer *any peeson whatsoever* to stay or abide in the said house or theatre, but as the said Charles Sarjant shall direct. Witness my hand this 11th of June 1768.

Witness G. COLMAN.

Joseph Younger, prompter to the theatre.
Charles Sarjant, jun. box-office-keeper.

By the terms of this commission, Mr. Flight of the parish of St. Pancrass, was authorized and empowered by Mr. Colman of Great Queen-Street, to exclude us, the joint and lawful proprietors of Covent-Garden theatre, from

from entering in or abiding upon our own premiſes, unleſs Mr. Sarjant, one of our hired ſervants, ſhould pleaſe otherwiſe to direct in our favour; and all this ordered and enjoined to be done for you, and in your name, without any mention made of your joint tenants and proprietors.

The next day by accident we both of us ſeverally met Mr. Sarjant's ſon, one of our box-keepers, who informed us, that Mr. Colman had taken away the keys of all the doors in the theatre, and that the doors were all barred and bolted, but that if we applied we alone might be admitted through Mr. Powell's houſe in the Piazza, in which there was a door which communicated with the theatre.

Being well adviſed that we could not juſtify entering our own premiſes through another man's houſe, and being well aware of your litigious diſpoſition, we determined not to go into the theatre through the houſe of Mr. Powell, who was then at Briſtol.—We therefore, on Monday the 13th of June, ſent a ſervant with a written order for admittance, he was refuſed by Mr. Sarjant, who urged your expreſs order for that purpoſe. We then deſired two gentlemen to accompany us to the theatre, and in their hearing demanded entrance of Mr. Sarjant, who anſwered us, thruſting his head out of a barred window, that Mr. Colman had got all the keys of the doors, and he could not let us in. We immediately diſpatched Mr. Sarjant junior, whom we met under the piazza, to you, ſir, with our compliments, deſiring you to ſend the keys of the theatre, informing you that we were then waiting with two friends, and wiſhed to take a walk in the theatre. He very ſoon returned with anſwer this (delivered in the hearing of the above mentioned two gentlemen) "*That you would not ſend the keys: that you had ordered all ingreſs to the theatre to be denied us, except through Mr. Powell's houſe, and even that way, we, and we* only *muſt enter.*" With this very extraordinary rebuff we returned to our reſpectative homes. The time between this event and Friday morning, we paſſed in reflection upon your unaccountable treatment of us; and

in

in consulting and advising with several gentlemen of great eminence in all departments of the law; who all concurred in assuring us that no damage could arise to us from entering our own premises, and turning our own servants out, who refused us admittance. Accordingly, on 17th June, after six o'clock, Mr. Harris, attended by two witnesses, again demanded admittance for himself and Mr. Rutherford, at Mr. Sarjant's door; he answered from within, in the hearing of the witnesses, that by Mr. Colman's order they would not admit us. Harris then came to the door in Hart-street, where Mr. Rutherford was waiting for him, attended by some servants, and told him the result of his demand at Mr. Sarjant's door; whereupon Harris and Rutherford ordered their servants to open a window on the north side of the said-door, where they entered with their servants. One of your servants, who kept possession of the theatre for you, having struck one of ours, it was with the greatest difficulty we could prevent ours from doing mischief to their opponents, we were therefore obliged to turn them all out of the theatre. Being thus in possession, we began immediately to take a survey of the place; and never were men so much astonished as we were, to find ourselves in so compleat a fortification. Emery, the master-carpenter to the theatre coming at that instant, we ordered him to be let in; and taking him about the theatre with us, we observed to him how *advantageously* he and his men had been employed for the last week or two in cutting our boards and timber to pieces in order to bar and fortify every avenue and window in the house, even those which were thirty or forty feet from the ground. The fellow, with a good deal of awkward embarrassment, scratching his head, replied, "*Why, gentlemen, I told* "*Mr. Colman, all I could do would signify nothing against a sledge-hammer.*" I thought, says he, it was a strange undertaking. We then asked him if he too was engaged by Mr. Colman, he said he was. On our telling him, that it was unaccountable to us how house-keeper, wardrobe-keeper, and carpenters, should think of entering into articles; he confessed he never heard of any such thing before in his life, but that Mr. Colman

had

had taken him one day entirely unguarded, and in a manner compeled him immediately to ſign an article. The more we examined the theatre, the more we were aſtoniſhed at your exceſſive precaution to prevent our getting into it. On the ſame day we ſent you a letter from the theatre, importing "*that we did not mean to retaliate your behaviour; on the contrary, we had given orders to our ſervants, at all times to admit your and Mr. Powell.*"

Reflecting now very conſiderately on our ſituation, and on your paſt conduct; *That you had from the beginning laid a plan of driving us out of the theatre; that in the execution of that plan, you had perſevered through the whole ſeaſon, paying no more regard to us than if we were entirely unconcerned in the property; that you had very eſſentially hurt the whole property, and the profits of the paſt ſeaſon in particular; that, in fine, you had engaged to act under your direction ſolely, every perſon belonging to the theatre, upon pain of large penalties; and had at laſt abſolutely forbid our entrance into our own houſe.*" For theſe reaſons we determined to remove from the theatre, to one of our dwelling-houſes, ſuch part of the property as might the moſt effectually prevent your proceedings, until a plan ſhould be formed, which would as effectually confirm to us thoſe legal and equitable rights in the theatre, of which you had ſo unwarrantably diveſted us.

With this view only we ſent down to my houſe in Surry-Street, ſo much of the wardrobe as we imagined would make the remaining part uſeleſs, together with the muſic, prompt-books, &c. &c. belonging to the theatre; of all which we have an exact inventory, and they will be immediately and ſafely returned to the theatre, whenever a fair equitable plan for the future government of it ſhall be fixed upon. It has been urged by ſome, that it would have been much better for us at once to have applied to the court of Chancery for redreſs, and that there we muſt have found a certain relief, and reparation for all

paſt

paſt damages, this too, ſir, has been always your language."— "*If I injure you, why don't you apply to the court of Chancery for redreſs?*"

There is no doubt, ſir, the court of chancery would redreſs us. But delays are dangerous. Of this the hiſtory of the *acting manager*, recorded by Cibber, is a memento. A long Chancery ſuit would be but a very poor remedy for the injuries you are *daily* doing us.

About a month ſince we were again amuſed by you with the hopes of a fair reference.—By our reſpective counſel a meeting was appointed for all parties in Weſtminſter-Hall. We there met, in order, if poſſible, to fix on a mode of arbitrating all differences, both parties brought preliminary articles to be agreed to, before the general concerns ſhould be referred.—On our part were produced theſe two.

1ſt. That the contracts which you might have made without our knowledge and conſent, for the enſuing ſeaſon, ſhould be reſcinded, unleſs agreed to by us.

2d. That no ſervants who were employed in ſhutting us out of our own houſe ſhould be employed in future.

Surely theſe can never be deemed unreaſonable by any perſon, when at the ſame time he is aſſured, that we never wiſh, nor ever did wiſh to engage any performer, ſervant, &c, &c. who ſhould be objected to by Mr. Colman and Mr. Powell.

You, ſir, on your part, inſiſted on the following eight preliminaries.

1ſt. Colman and Powell ſhould not be obliged to ſell.

Meaning, we conceive, that if the referrees ſhould think it neceſſary to oblige either of the parties to ſell, it muſt be Harris and Rutherford.

2d. All contracts to be made by Mr. Colman to be confirmed.

Can this be a reaſonable preliminary, to be obliged to confirm all contracts made by you, without having the leaſt knowledge how many, with whom, or upon what condition they were entered into? For we are at this time entire and abſolute ſtrangers to all your late proceedings, except what we gather from uncertain report, and ſome few of the parties who have engaged with you.

3d. No legal proceedings to be ſtopped.

The meaning of this preliminary we did not enter into, as no legal proceedings were begun, nor had we any gueſs at your litigious intention of making Garton put us in the crown-offiee; or of your inquiſition, &c, &c.

4th. Powell's article to be cancelled, and another made, allowing him more explicitly the largeſt ſalary in the houſe.

That you ſhould think it proper to give Mr. Powell this douceur, we were not at all ſurpriſed; but it did not occurr to us why we ſhould give any further indulgence to a man, who, after having attached himſelf to you, had ſeparated himſelf from you, diſapproved of your conduct, and then without the leaſt reaſon implicitly and blindly ſuffered himſelf yourſelf to be duped by you again.

5th. The books to be reſtored to Garton.

The books were never intended to be kept from Mr. Garton, ſo as to prevent his making up his accounts. We mean, whenever he is diſpoſed to take hisdiſcharge.

6th. The wardrobe to be reſtored, and all damages to be made good by Harris and Rutherford.

4 To

To that we ſhould have no objection, provided we are not obliged to make good the damages Mr. Powell has done.

7th. Colman ſtill to be the *acting* manager. If any alteration in the controuling power, it muſt be lodged in the other three proprietors.

Here the cloven foot indeed appears plainly: ſo the article muſt not be meddled with, or it muſt be altered in your favour!

8th. That all bills and all claims upon the theatre, ſhould be diſcharged.

Whoever will attentively conſider the above preliminaries muſt obſerve, that there is not a ſingle point on which an arbitration could turn, which is not moſt artfully and ſubtilly provided for by Mr. Colman, that is to ſay, on every point they muſt determine abſolutely for Mr. Colman, or otherwiſe ſome one of the preliminary articles will prevent their conſidering it at all. And theſe, Mr. Colman, you called fair, candid, and honeſt propoſals, and have thrown the groſſeſt abuſe on us for not conſenting to what you call a fair reference.

Mr. Harris and another gentleman calling in at the theatre one afternoon, found therein Mr. Powell and yourſelf, with each a candle in your hands; lighting and ſhewing the theatre to two of your counſel, your attorney, and another gentleman. Mr. Harris was at a loſs to know whether they came as *witneſſes*, or for what other purpoſes. The ſervants of the theatre, however were ordered to ſhew you, and your friends, all poſſible reſpect. Beſides this fact, we defy you to prove at any one time, that either yourſelf or Mr. Powell, or any one that came by your order, was refuſed entrance into the theatre: indeed it is notorious, that Mr. Powell, the week he was in town, frequently amuſed himſelf by running in and out of the theatre, abuſing our ſervants, ſwearing they were in a *wrong cauſe*, laying his hand on his ſword, and even threatening their lives.

After these exploits, the valiant Powell returned quietly again to Bristol: but you, sir, still wretched and restless, ran about the town to counsel and to magistrates; at sometimes raving and storming, at others affecting to be perfectly easy, and declaring to two persons in particular, that for your part you had given every thing up; that you did not suppose the theatre would open next year; but that you did not fear that you, by your annuities, could support the loss much better than any of us; so that by your perseverance, you must carry your point, and we be ruined.— While your mind was in this agitated state, several magistrates of the first eminence for knowledge and integrity refusing to be concerned in the affair, you most fortunately found out one ——Wright, Esq; of Great Pulteney-Street, justice of the peace for Westminster; him you prevailed on, by what means you know best, to proceed by an inquisition. Whenwithout giving us the least notice of his intentions, he issued his precept to the sheriff of the county, to reinstate Mr. Charles Sarjant, in the possession of the theatre, and to turn the *two* men, (for we had no more) which *we* had placed in the theatre, *out* of it.

No sooner had ——Wright, Esq; of Great Pulteney-Street, put Mr. Sarjant in possession, but you immediately triumph'd; and by paragraph after paragraph attempted to impose upon the public, that we were turned out of an illegal possession.

You, Mr. Colman, was bred to the law, and knew better; if you do not, ask your new friend Mr. Wright. He by this time, I dare say knows law enough to tell you, that where four people are tenants in common, if one of them is in possession, the four are legally in possession, and that exclusive possession in such a case is nonsense; that therefore our going into our own premises on the 17th June last, could *not* be called a *forcible entry*;— and that finding a servant who had barred our own doors against us, and opposed our entrance, there could be nothing illegal in turning him out of doors, or even gently putting him out of the window.

As to your charge of our depriving your friends of their bread; is it just, that we should be compelled to feed the mouths that

are

are ever open in the moſt indecent abuſe of us ?—If Mr. Benſley will ſuffer himſelf to be wrought upon by you, to go into coffee-houſes, and there harrangue the company with vociferating abuſe of us, and this perpetually without ever having received the *leaſt* injury from us; muſt we retain ſuch a performer ? and muſt his ſalary be therefore increaſed, though one upon whoſe ſervices in the theatre the pleaſures of the public do not eſſentially depend.

If Mr. Garton pays away our money without our conſent, and afterwards commences an expenſive proſecution againſt us, without having the leaſt injury done to him on our parts, muſt we be *compelled* ſtill to retain him, to diſpoſe of our money as he thinks proper ?—If Mr. Sarjant thinks proper to bar our own doors againſt us, muſt we be compelled to retain him as our *houſe-keeper ?*

If Mr. Whitfield will not attend when ordered by us, but oblige us to break open the door to get into our wardrobe; if he will lend a part of it without our conſent, and afterwards make ſuch affidavit as you ſhall dictate; is it (think you) proper we ſhould truſt ſo valuable a part of our property in the hands of *ſuch* a man ?—Theſe are your friends, and theſe are the people whom we are depriving of their bread.—No, Mr. Colman, the *officers* belonging to the theatre ought to be equally reſponſible to all the proprietors. We deſire to appoint none who ſhall be objected to by you, at the ſame time we are determined to ſuffer none to remain in the theatre to whom we think we have ſuch ample reaſon to object.

We have now attended you ſir, from our firſt interview to the date of this letter, in which we have ſhewn the riſe and progreſs of our ſeveral actions reſpecting our partnerſhip in Covent-Garden theatre, we hope we have fairly and fully explained the nature of our compact, and pointed out the deſigns of each contracting party, ſo as to ſet them fully and fairly forth to your, andthe public view.

We

We have suffered your usurpation throughout the whole season, to our great and manifest loss and detriment.—You have one argument, and only one, which is for ever in your mouth, and on which upon all occasions you rest your defence.

If you think there is either wit or decency, good breeding, humanity, or *argument* in the imputations you have thrown upon *me* on the score of Mrs. Lessingham, be it so: not to deprive you of your only defence, on that consideration, and on that *alone*, I shall submit to it. Yet reflect!—think a moment on your own situation!—how daring must it appear in *you* of all men living, to publish such aspersions? But you knew you were safe.—You knew I should scorn to retort, and that I should never measure weapons with you on the ground of scurrility. And yet, the world, Mr. Colman, on whom you have so impertinently, and so perpetually obtruded these imputations, will shew you no favour. You who have thus vainly endeavoured to divert the public eye from taking a steady view of your conduct and your *motives* for it, and have employed the name of a woman, like the shield of Ajax, to screen you on every occasion, must by every man of sense and spirit be abandoned to *general derision*.

But what has contributed most to raise your self-importance in the eyes of others, is your constant declaration that every step you take is by the advice of your old friend and learned counsel Mr. Dunning. This respectable name, is by your example, echoed through every channel of the theatre: while box-keepers, wardrobe-men and carpenters, imitating the familiarity of their principal, bandy about one of the best opinions in the kingdom, as their warrant upon all occasions.—To this gentlemen's great abilities, and to his use of them as an advocate, we pay the highest respect, therefore you will pardon us if we thus publicly declare, we believe you have made a false and an un becoming use of his name on the present occasion: for we think it impossible that the know-

ledge

ledge and integrity of a Dunning, could advife you to the treachery you practifed in betraying your friend Powell to refign his fame and fortune into your hands.—Impoffible he could interpret the fecond claufe of our article, fo as to give you an independant and uncontroulable power over our property, or that the fourth claufe does not give us an abfolute power to fuperfede by our written difapprobation, whatever meafure *we* may judge to be contrary to the common intereft of our partnerfhip.—Impoffible he fhould fay you had a power to incur what expences you pleafe refpecting the theatre, without our knowledge or confent.—Impoffible he fhould abett you in making a factious ufe of the actors and fervants of the theatre, by clandeftinely feducing them into bonds and penalties in our names, for many thoufands of pounds; obliging them to obey none but yourfelf, and without our confent or knowledge, making all fuch engagements as might conduce to your defigns, in open defiance of public notices ferved upon *you* and *them* to the contrary.—Impoffible he fhould advice you to take an exclufive poffeffion of our theatre, and to bar, bolt and barricade us out of it, and by warrant under your own hand given to our common fervant, entitle him to tell us that we fhould not enter into the theatre. Impoffible Mr. Dunning could diffuade you from putting that queftion to arbitration, concerning the proper form of engaging performers. Impoffible he could recommend —— Wright, Efq; of Great Pulteney-Street, to fummon an inqueft upon a fuppofed forcible entry or detainer of our own property, and to difpoffefs our fervants placed by ourfelves in our own premifes, without giving us the leaft notice of his proceedings.— None of thefe acts we fay, fir, were advifed by Mr. Dunning, nor by any other able advocate whatfoever: it is impoffible.—They are meafures of defperation, and were prefcribed by one who means to carry his point at the expence of principles, infinitely more valuable than the ftake for which we are contending.

We have already informed you, that while your defigns upon our property are fo dangerous and fo notorious, we cannot truft ourfelves again

again to treat with you in private; but in conformity to our profeſſion in the prefixed addreſs, we ſhall now proceed to lay before you, and the publick, the following propoſals, (for which I have proper authority from Mr. Rutherford) and to which we expect *your public anſwer.* We truſt they are plain and intelligible, and we ſeriouſly mean they ſhould be fair and equitable.

I. Will you ſubmit all paſt tranſactions to arbitration?

II. Will you conſent that proper ſecurity be given by each party for a ſpecific performance of the preſent articles?

III. Or, as the preſent article reſpecting the management was entered into upon no valuable conſideration on our part, and therefore was legally revocable, ſhould we find it neceſſary, will you revert to our original inſtrument of the 31ſt of March; by which all parties were to be equally concerned in the profits and management of the theatre.

IV. Laſtly, Will you in caſe you have any objection to private arbitration, join with us in inſtituting an amicable ſuit in Chancery, and take the ſenſe of that court on our preſent articles and paſt tranſactions.

If theſe propoſals ſhould be found ſuch as it becomes men of honeſt principles to offer we hope you will give the world a proof that you have ſome title to that character, by accepting them, or publickly propoſing others equally equitable.

T. HARRIS.

F I N I S.